RULES OF PLAY

A Sins and Secrets Standalone Novel

H. N. DeFore

ISBN Print Copy: 979-8-9873852-4-1

Cover design by: H. N. DeFore
Printed in the United States of America

To my husband Dean, for always putting up with the endless plot bunnies.

TRIGGER WARNING

This is a dark romance that can be read as a standalone novel. This novel does depict some instances of sexual assault not in great detail. There are also mentions of violence, torture, and vivid BDSM scenes including choking and some bondage. Please read with discretion.

1 MYLA

His fingers worked their way down the curve of her torso, tongue still battling for dominance with hers. With each breathy intake he'd flutter his fingertips back up to a taut breast, before dipping again to barely miss her exposed, aching clit. She had a hand shoved into his trousers, fingertips teasing and toying with the head of his cock. There was a hefty outline as her opposite hand pumped his length over the material. Both her nipples were already straining against the clamps, her legs spread wide by the silky straps he'd tied around her ankles. The opposite ends rested in his hand, and he'd tug her wider with each teasing flick of her fingers against his head.

Releasing his cock from his pants, he dragged her back by her hair and shoved her down the length. Her eyes bulged as he pulled at the straps, tugging her legs until she couldn't possibly open further, and only then did he drag a digit across her dripping center. She cried out in surprise and bucked, his hand flying up to flick one of her trapped nipples. He kept his other hand firmly in her hair, pumping her head over his throbbing -

Just as I'm starting to get in the mood for this, it comes crashing down as someone knocks on my window. I squeal and throw my phone across the car, cheeks burning.

Okay, I know the car isn't the best option, but I don't have any others. I'm not getting it the way I need at home, and I know better than to ask again. This is the last alternative.

Trying to finger myself in the parking garage at work is the closest to a cry for help as I'm gonna get. Liam isn't going to bother me here, but no one else is supposed to either.

Snapping my head to the window, my humiliation drops a hair. *Laci*. Well at least it's my best friend and not some chump hoping to help out.

She's laughing hysterically at my plight, and I resist the urge to bury my head beneath my sweater as she taps the glass again.

This is not how I like to start my Mondays, but the weekend was brutal and I need something to make me feel better. My neck is sore, my thighs hurt, and I didn't even get off.

Liam says it's for the greater good that he's training me. But all he's accomplished so far is teaching me to not enjoy sex with *him*.

Jerking open the door I nearly smack Laci in the head. She's too busy snickering to care, stepping towards my trunk so I can get out. "Have you ever heard of privacy?"

"Don't finger yourself in the parking garage and you won't have this problem," Laci replies with a shrug, snorting as she tries and fails to regain some composure. Her long blonde hair is falling out of a messy bun, her makeup perfectly in place. "Or at least learn to ignore peepers."

"So you were peeping?" I ask, flushing. Attempting to smooth down my skirt, I grab the discarded heels in my passenger seat and slip them on. Instinctively my fingers tug at the neckline of my dress, remembering the collar I wanted to take off before shuffling to work.

Guess I'll be wearing it today. The skin beneath hurts but I'm not interested in giving Laci more of a reason to dislike my boyfriend. We're in a rough patch, a misunderstanding of sorts, and I'm determined to fix it tonight. I've got a breakdown of where I think things went astray and I plan on talking to him, if I see him before bed.

Liam will be thrilled if I wear it all day like he wanted. I wouldn't mind if it didn't hurt, but the cheap leather is cutting at the rings around my neck. I play with my scarf as I lock my car, ignoring the way Laci's humor dies.

She hates him. I know she does. She has no idea what's going on, but I know I asked for this. *Literally*. I brought the lifestyle up and Liam ran with it.

In the wrong direction.

"I was going to be a good friend and check in on your latest attempt," Laci continues, schooling a grin on her face. She bounces on the balls of her feet as we head for the elevator, and I'm sure it's for my benefit. I asked her two days ago to back off a little on my dating life. There are two cups of coffee balanced in her hands, and I know from experience they are both hers. "I didn't think I'd catch you... in the moment."

"Shut it," I growl, shooting my bubbly strawberry-blonde bestie an irritated look. Her hair looks even girlier than usual next to my messy brunette locks as I walk beside her. "If you must know it didn't go... well."

"I assumed operation Get-Myla-Off failed on all fronts if you're having a play at it in the car."

It would be almost comical, except it's not. She knows Liam is heavy handed. Anita, my other BFF, is a trauma doctor in training at one of the level-one trauma centers here in Denver. I veered away from her the second he started acting out and my friends noticed my change in attitude. It's been this way for months.

I'm probably delusional, but I want things to work out for us. Laci is trying to make a joke out of it because she knows Liam's left me high and dry for weeks. I told him I wanted a more adventurous sex life, full of toys and dirty talk and risk, the works.

I didn't expect him to flay my skin open for it. I can't get off when I'm bleeding.

"Pity," Laci sighs, drawing me from my thoughts as we slip into the elevator with a few other patrons. She doesn't know he's ripped my skin open or she'd already be up his ass. "Liam really is nice to stare at. How long does a relationship really last if he can't get your rocks off?"

Liam is easy on the eyes. Sandy hair, light eyes, lean frame. We look amazing together, his light looks contrasting my chocolate locks and gray eyes. He's over a head taller than I am, shy of six feet by an inch or two. I'm only five foot five, so he doesn't completely tower over me. Still, he's handsome if he isn't pissed off.

"Shh!" I hiss, watching three sets of curious eyes angle our way in the lift. Thankfully the parking garage is used by a number of businesses in the area, and none of these people work with us, so I'm saved from that embarrassment. The moment the doors open up to our floor I grasp Laci's wrist and drag her out of there. "Do you have to talk about it so loudly?"

"Hey, you're the one touching yourself in a car. Doesn't that border on indecency?"

"I don't know," I grit out, letting go of her. "Desperate times call for desperate measures." Pinching the bridge of my nose I take a deep breath. "Could we just not discuss this anymore? You're always late; I didn't think it would be a problem this morning."

I don't want to talk about sex. It makes me think about the weekend and I don't want to go there.

"I was trying to be supportive and bring you a coffee after what could only be a rough, unsatisfying anniversary," Laci replies, handing over a cup that feels half full. She shrugs when I give her a knowing look. "I needed twice the caffeine as usual to keep me up this early."

"You're a saint," I giggle, shaking my head. "I told you I'd dish at lunch. I have a depo I've got to help Phil prep for this morning."

"Ah, Phil. There's someone begging to grant you an orgasm. If you're resorting to mindless car masturbation maybe you should give him a go."

"He's our boss!"

I know it's all in jest. Phil drops as much work as he can in my lap, and he's not shy about dirty old man glances, but he isn't gonna bend me over anything. He's too sexist for it. He once lectured me after a meeting about how sleeping with coworkers only results in pointless HR problems.

Charming.

"He'd bend you over a desk and remind you why he's the boss." I guess Laci hasn't had this chat with Phil yet.

"He's old."

"Maybe age garners experience."

I shake my head, wandering off towards my section in the office. I step into my office, empty at this hour because the file clerk isn't in yet and David is never around.

Well, *desk*. As an entry-level first-year attorney in one of Denver's most prestigious law firms I haven't earned a comfortable, private office yet. Mainly I do grunt work, overflow from the paralegals, and excess work from whichever attorney in the building feels like overworking me that day. A lot of the cases I've handled since being hired two months ago are overseen and managed primarily by Phil, with other associate attorneys helping out. I don't currently manage any cases of my own and likely wouldn't for my first year here, not in this top-level firm.

There's already a pile of work growing on my desk, and I give Laci an exasperated look. "Won't your boss wonder where you are?"

"Girl I'm here earlier than usual," Laci laughs, sitting on the only clear corner of my desk. There's still so much to be done from last weekend. "Marcy might have a stroke if I'm on time."

"Or maybe she'll quit complaining," I suggest, sitting down on my chair. There's notes everywhere, and as I power on my computer I notice several messages from Phil about the deposition at nine. "Or be grateful that her employee is on time for the first time since being hired."

"Oh she'll be fine," Laci replies, swinging her legs. Two weeks of inconsistent arrivals won't keep her employed much longer, and I stuck my neck out to get her the job. "I plan to dip back out for a few. I haven't even gotten my morning buzz." The file clerk Kathy glances our way as she sets down her bag, eyeing us with disdain. She's not my favorite employee around here. Usually I don't see her until closer to ten, but Phil probably called her in to help with prep.

"But of course you announce it to the room," I mutter. "You've barely had this job for two weeks Laci. Please don't make me regret helping you land it."

"I'd never." She blows a kiss towards me before hopping off the desk. "But you're swamped and this looks miserable. I bid you ado."

Breathing a sigh of relief once she's gone, I drop my head into my hands. If I ever live down the embarrassment of Laci catching me with my skirt pushed up I'll be lucky.

I'm not even satisfied with my attempt. I thought watching something closer to what I had in mind would help. But I couldn't distract myself from the ache of my legs and the pain around my neck.

Liam promised he'd make this enjoyable for me. So far it's been worse than before.

Subconsciously I finger the collar around my neck, his failed attempt to get into more of a dominant mindset. He just keeps missing the mark. I chose the high neckline on purpose, and his cheap choice of jewelry has me feeling dirty and not at all sexual.

I showed him ideas of what would make me feel beautiful. He complained they weren't functional enough for what he envisioned, or that they're too expensive. This reminds me of something he bought at a pet store.

Flying through deposition prep helps me ignore the dull ache in my core begging for release. Phil buzzes me a half dozen times before the deposition starts, interrupting my progress every time. When I'm finally able to assemble the binders just how Phil likes them I head towards his office, and someone has the nerve to bump into me and send the stack flying.

After not getting a proper orgasm for way too long, I'm ready for a fight. My eyes zip to the person standing in my way, and I'm ready for the challenge.

"Maybe learn to stack those better," David says smugly, sipping a steaming mug of coffee. My half-drank and now cold beverage taunts me from the corner of my desk. "You're making a mess."

David, despite being a thorn in my side, is a savory treat to look at. Smoky black hair he keeps buzzed on the sides and a little longer on the top, devilish blue eyes, and sun-kissed skin has every girl in the office swooning. He's fit, though the dapper business suits hide just how refined his muscles are. I've caught sight of his arms and chest multiple times since being hired; when working long days he sometimes loses the suit jacket and unbuttons the top of his shirts, rolling up his sleeves. Way too many of my colleagues find a way to come visit him when that happens. Today he has all his clothes in order, at least for the time being.

"Maybe you should learn to watch where you're going!" I seethe, ignoring the mockery in his gaze as his brows shoot high on his head. Hot or not, he is distracting me from my all important meeting, and he's just making my life harder for the fun of it. With a scowl I bend down to shuffle the papers quickly back together while he stands by watching. "And please, don't bother helping with your mess!"

"*I'm* on my way to take an important call on the Schrieber file," he replies, lazily shrugging his shoulders. "Marcy told me on my way in that she's on hold. Wouldn't want to keep her waiting."

"That really would be the worst thing to happen for you today, since the rest of us have been here since we opened." Just because he convinced the Schrieber family to hire the firm for the colossal PI case, David thinks he's some sort of insta-star.

He steps past me before clicking his tongue, spiking my annoyance up another notch. "I could've sworn I heard Phil bitching about you in his office on my way in here. Maybe I was wrong."

I curse under my breath as he saunters away, wondering how many typos I can sneak into the next pile of crap he drops on me. Standing briskly, I carry the binders as carefully as I can to Phil's office. As one of the partners for the firm, Phil hand-picked who he wants working on his immediate team.

It is both a blessing and curse to have him leering at me. Phil works top-dollar cases so I get to work on and handle a lot of complicated files. Unfortunately David works on his team often as well, and as an associate attorney and not just a first year, he has one-on-one client interaction and sometimes he is even the first chair attorney.

Eight months ago, before I even finished school, he did the intake on the Schrieber case and sweet-talked the wife into hiring the firm for her daughter's collision case. It's an extremely high profile case, with damages rising into the seven digit area, and already it's preparing for trial. Phil was so impressed he let David take the lead to see how he handles the pressure.

He's excelling. I might be petty, but watching someone who got ahead of the curve, excelling so far ahead of me, leaves a bitter taste in my mouth. David's parents are loaded, so he didn't have to work during school and finished ahead of the game plan with what I've heard are top marks. I just finished this past May, and I got hired the moment I was licensed. Even then, seeing David jump the corporate ladder makes me want to slam my head into the wall.

We went to the same high school and fate kept us together through college and law school. I don't have my parents blessing pushing me to get ahead, and my mom could care less what I'm doing with my life.

A sharp knock has Phil opening the door, shooing me inside and stalling my runaway thoughts. The deposition is by phone, the client appearing from home, so it's just the two of us in the office. He glares as I hand over his copy of the file, setting out all necessary paperwork as he continues talking, his gaze already elsewhere.

He might think I'm hot, but I messed up by being late to the call. Even if it was David's fault I got derailed, I doubt Phil cares. He waves a hand for me to sit, and doesn't look at me again throughout the call.

Blast it. All this silence just gives me time to think about my aching core and the drop in sexual enjoyment with Liam. I did research, he claims to have done some too, but our results aren't lining up. I see our newfound D/s dynamic drastically different than he does.

The collar burns beneath my blouse, another reminder of the stall in our relationship. My skin hurts and I want to rip it off, but if I take it off I know I'll throw it away and then who knows what Liam will say.

Or do.

By the time Phil disconnects the call I'm already way behind the schedule I planned out for the day, and my mind can't settle back down. I missed a call, a total teachable moment, to fantasize about my failed sexual fantasies. Phil glares as he clicks off the headset and the phone drops back into place, catching my attention.

"I told you I wanted this fifteen minutes before the call."

"There were a lot of revisions," I replied smoothly, crossing my arms. Phil is always so upright. "And apparently the printer was acting up. I got everything together as quickly as I could. I did email the contents sheet to you for reference. I apologize that I was late getting in here."

Phil huffs, running his fingers through peppered hair. He is without a suit jacket today, and for some reason he's wearing a god awful orange tie. "You know my expectations, Myla. You have to get everything prepped. I don't want excuses. This depo was on the books for months."

"But changes came in late Friday night and this morning. I worked as quickly as I could."

"I still expect you to adhere to the deadline," he replied with a shrug. Phil has deep set brown eyes, nothing special to look at, but they seem to burn a hole through me whenever he finds my work less than satisfactory. He told me within a day of hiring me that he was the primary pull for the firm to take me on, and if he saw my potential slipping I could be terminated.

Staying in Phil's good graces is important for my career, even if it has me grinding my teeth together.

"Tomorrow we have the Luxs in the office to prep for trial," Phil continues, shuffling the binder back into a messy pile and returning it to me, even though he barely looked at it. "Refile this. You'll be helping with prep for tomorrow as well. David is second on the case and will sit in too. Perhaps you should take some notes from him about meeting your deadlines."

My nails dig so hard into my palm I'm certain I'll draw blood. "I'll ask him."

Damn fucking David. He's worked here a little over a year and somehow has all the partners wrapped around his finger. If the Schrieber case progresses well there is even a chance of making him partner once the year is up.

Partner. Before thirty. It's my life goal to be set by thirty, and I'm nowhere near.

David is though. Handsome, snarky David. I could scream.

He's my age, which makes everything worse. I never really crossed paths with him during any of our schooling, just knew he was one of the hot rich guys that didn't have anything to worry about. Now he's dangling his success in front of my envious eyes and laughing every time he gets to rub it in.

There's always a group like that at school, full of charm and sex appeal. And David certainly knows he's got most of the female population ready to come at the crook of his finger.

Just thinking about him gives me a headache. If I didn't need some stress relief before I sure as hell do now.

"He knows how I like my files," Phil continues, dragging me out of my thoughts. "Have him give you the breakdown again. And Schulte? I like your outfit choice today."

Gritting my teeth together, I force a smile and ignore what a dentist would say to me for ruining my teeth. The hemline of my suit is shorter than usual on purpose, even if it makes me feel uneasy. I needed easy access in the car, and I wanted to be able to butter Phil up if something dumb like this happened today. My self-loathing shoots up another notch. "Thank you Phil."

~~~

By day's end I'm straight tired of everyone's shit. Liam blew up my phone just after lunch, annoyed that I placed some suggestive toys on the bed this morning. I wanted to set the mood for this evening and avoid flaying my skin open again like last week. I'm not ready to trust him again with anything that could slice through me. The silk ties aren't even that bad compared to some of the videos I've watched. But Liam is piss poor with knots and I don't feel like giving him a lesson plan.

Laci is already gone for the day, along with most of the staff. I'm burning the midnight oil, ignoring my friend's suggestion to go home and relax. Liam doesn't relax me anymore and his annoying texts make me want to stay at work all night.

There goes my chances of getting properly plowed, but at this rate I'm not in the mood to play with Liam tonight. My throat burns, and I just want to slip out of here and deal with my unsatisfied sex drive before I have to deal with him. Instead I'm ignoring everything around me, working to push off the problems at home.

Besides, I have plenty of things to catch up on. Phil is demanding a tight knit ship tomorrow, and David was less than helpful with suggestions before he left. He's likely to swoop in with all the answers ten minutes before the meeting starts and claim he gave me the same list today.

He could at least play fair. The constant urge to strangle him grows with every passing day.

Thankfully, I'm certain I am the only one left on this side of the office. People rarely stay late on a Monday night, and now that I've satisfied my need to catch up
~~~

there is something else that needs attending to.

I desperately need to cum. Liam hasn't gotten me there in weeks, which just infuriates him. If I go home with this much pent up frustration, we're definitely going to fight and those never end well.

And besides, there aren't any cameras in this room.

Kicking off my heels, I prop up my feet against the edge of the desk and let my skirt fall open. Opening the tab from this morning I brush aside my thong, immediately caressing and pinching on my clit to get my blood going. I need this, I know I do. And the office has to be safer than the damn parking garage.

Selecting a different video I give it another go. I start to tease myself ever so slowly as the video kicks on.

The woman in the video is suspended, her body held in the air by ropes tight around her. She's gagging, choking on a sizable dildo as the guy walks around her, a flared whip in hand, trailing it along her exposed skin.

Drawing his arm back he lets it slap against her nipple, emitting a shriek. Her body shakes with pleasure but there's nowhere to go as he flips the toy in his hand around, a sharper end snaking out to strike -

"You could've just asked."

Shrieking, my feet slam off the desk back to the floor, ripping my still dry fingers away as my phone tumbles to the floor.

David stands just inside the space, adjusting the sleeves of his shirt. I could've sworn he left already, briefcase in hand, and I know I didn't hear him come back in. My cheeks are on fire as he stares down at me, hypnotic blue eyes cutting through my skin.

I'm almost ashamed to admit how turned on I am under his gaze. The video didn't do a lick of good, but

David's penetrating eyes have my body responding in ways it hasn't in months.

Damn, traitorous body. Liam would go feral if he saw me sitting here drinking in another man's gaze.

I should feel embarrassed, but the heat pooling low in my body says otherwise. He doesn't say anything else as he walks towards me with the same intense look.

My throat is dry as he stares me down, the collar on my neck an afterthought. I swallow, sitting a little bit straighter the closer he gets.

My body and my brain are not on the same page. Reason tells me to stand up and run home, desire tells me to sit right here and see what he does.

He stops right in front of my desk, leaning in closer. Desperation has me leaning in as his lips pull to a smirk. "I didn't take you for an exhibitionist."

Okay, that's not what I thought he would say. Leaning back a little, my brows pinch together. David chuckles, nodding to the hallway. Dread settles over me as I glance the same way, registration kicking in.

The hall camera. Even if our section doesn't face it directly, it can see in here.

I gasp, leaning back fully. Not only have I embarrassed myself with video evidence, but if Liam ever digs around he could potentially find it and see me in here with David.

Jumping up from my seat, I nearly bash my head into his. He leans back a little, eyes sweeping over me.

My voice stutters when I speak. I need to be able to get off and feel better, and I honestly forgot about the hall camera. Now I'm in this awkward situation with my hottest (and most annoying) coworker in the office, and he's giving me a look that makes me want to sit back down and take off my panties. "I, I was just-"

"Watching porn at the office?" He asks with a smirk, bending down to speak in my ear. I almost melt against him, my inner feminist revolting. "I could hear that video in the hall. I'm sure the camera caught it."

His words do nothing to allay my fears. I'm biting my lip in response, fighting back against the smooth timbre of his voice. Does he always sound like this? I find David to be sarcastic, but right now his voice rains over my skin and has every nerve on fire.

And not in the same way Liam does.

God, I need to get out of here before I do something I regret all because of a rejected libido.

His fingers trail up my arm, playing at the high neck of my shirt. My eyes find his, and good lord I'm panting without him doing a damn thing. He's got a permanent smirk on his lips as he glides his fingers over shirt. "If you're that desperate to cum all you need to do is ask, Myla."

Lord, my name on his lips is sin. I can't bite back the moan that escapes me.

David chuckles, one hand sliding down to rest low on my back, the other flicking at the hemline of my skirt. "Well, aren't you acting like a good girl."

I'm gonna regret it later, but his words have me arching into him now.

I've asked Liam to speak to me like this before, and it doesn't come naturally. I almost hate David for making it seem like a given.

He's sliding his hand up my skirt, and I'm coiled so tight I don't even care. My legs kick open wider on instinct, and the smirk is back on his lips. "You're eager."

I bite back the whimper that threatens to rise in my

throat. I need to keep some of my damn self control.

Running his hand back up my spine sets my skin on fire, his other hand skimming as high on my thigh as it can without touching my center. I'm scrambling against the chair, wishing I had something to push against to get his fingers in the right spot.

His other hand snakes back to my front, barely brushing over the tops of my breasts before sliding up, gripping gently at the curve of my neck.

My eyes shoot wide, meeting his. He flexes his fingers along my neck, his opposite hand trailing over my lace covered clit. He's watching me, testing his fingers along my throat.

It makes me catch my breath. Liam's never managed to do that, not in a good way, but I don't want to think about him right now.

David's fingers trail down my throat, and l stop breathing altogether when he touches the top of the collar on my neck, quirking an eyebrow.

God, what am I doing?

His hand leaves my throat, trailing down to touch the cheap leather. I still, the horiness slipping away.

David is suddenly interested in my neck, his hand sliding back up to my thigh. He runs a finger over the hidden collar, brushing over it more than once. "Is that a collar, Schulte?"

If I wasn't already frozen, I am now.

He tugs at the neckline, and I'm too terrified to pull away. What the hell am I doing? One fickle chance to get my rocks off and I'm throwing caution to the wind. He eyes the leather as it comes into view, and I'm taking shallow breaths now.

Dear God, I need to pull away. I don't know why I'm

so self-conscious about something I could try and brush off. He isn't trapping me in place, but his bright eyes drink in everything in front of him. I should move, but I'm rooted in place. I don't let anyone see this, least of all someone I consider my enemy.

Shame tugs at my belly. I don't wear this cheap thing proudly like a badge of honor. It's ripping my neck apart, and I feel ashamed as he studies the collar, moving the top aside to stare at the damn thing.

If David mocked me before, I can only imagine what I'm in for now.

What will Liam say if he finds out?

I gasp when he grips the ring at the base of the collar, tugging me closer. The edge in his eyes is harder than before, like he's edging on anger. "Whose is this?"

2 DAVID

I swear, she's going to cream herself as I grip the ring at the base of her throat. Her gray eyes stare up at me, pleading.

I don't think she even realizes what she's doing. There's a mix of lust and fear in her gaze that I can't quite unravel.

It's not a great collar. Cheap as fuck, actually. You can spend thousands on gold and diamonds to decorate someone's neck and stake your claim. Wherever the hell this came from, nobody cared to make her feel good wearing it.

She's frozen in front of me, the uncertain lust still swirling in her eyes. I'm not sure why she hasn't pulled back yet; I can see the edges of fear creeping into her body language.

That won't do.

I slide my finger through the ring, dragging her closer. She cringes, but it's so quickly replaced by lust I don't linger on it. "Boyfriend?" Myla blinks at me several times, hesitating. She's treating this like an act of fear, so it's not a funky outfit choice. I cock my head. "Master?"

She jolts, grinding herself into my leg. More contradictions flicker across her face, like there's an internal war going on. "What?"

I lean closer, leaving a wet kiss high on her neck. She is way too tense for someone who was just fingering herself at the desk. I tug on the collar, and she hisses out a breath again. I need answers before I jump into something I want no part of. "Whose collar are you wearing?"

I slide my finger along her drenched pussy again, and I swear she's going to come undone before I even get my fingers in her.

Her voice is nothing but a breathy moan. "Boyfriend."

"Is your boyfriend going to approve of me touching you like this?"

She stiffens in my hold, and I don't need her to answer. That little tremor is back in her voice. "No."

I smirk. Exactly what I wanted to hear. I knew the answer without asking, and Myla looks too good to pass up right now. "Good."

I slap her clit, and she bucks hard against me. Moving to grip her thigh, I meet her gaze. "Up."

She's eager to please, wrapping her legs around my hips despite the hesitation in her gaze. I shoot her a smirk, planting my hand high on her thigh to lift her up.

Her grip is vicious on my shirt, and I don't give a damn that it'll wrinkle. I just don't need Phil having video evidence of me getting her off.

I'm not giving him the satisfaction of watching her either.

Myla is lost someplace between lust and fear, and I don't get the combination. She seems cautious of *something,* but her willingness towards everything I've done so far doesn't make me want to stop. She admitted to the boyfriend but it's not slowing her down.

I set her on my desk with a gentle thud, out of the line of the camera. Phil can't say shit over what he can't see. My fingers are back at her pussy again, soaked through the thin lace there. Her gasp is loud and strangled when I brush it aside.

My finger is still locked in the loop of that collar, keeping her eyes turned to me. I plan to watch her when she comes undone, and I won’t allow her to look away from me.

She's eating it up, desperately rocking against me on the desk. I smirk as her fingers drag down my shirt.

Myla is always controlled. Watching her come undone is a pleasure all its own.

I slap her clit again, earning another strangled cry. She fists her hands into the fabric of my shirt, trying to toss back her head. My grip on the collar doesn't lessen, keeping her eyes on me. "You like it when I slap that pretty little pussy, don't you?"

It's been a while since I had a casual, quick fuck. This should be fun.

Her eyes are frantic, fingers dragging up and down my torso with her nails. She touches my belt but doesn't undo it, a note of uncertainty flashing in her gaze as I drag my thumb over the sensitive bundle of nerves.

She screams, physically *screams*, and I let go of her collar to clamp a hand over her mouth, eyes flashing. "None of that now. We don't want security coming up here."

I can't believe how quickly she came. I've barely touched her and she's rocking against my hand. She’s clearly been neglected.

I don't care how sexually charged you are. You don't get off that quickly unless you've been denied.

Myla’s nodding, rocking her hips along my thumb. I give her a moment before pulling my hand off her mouth so she can take a strangled breath. "Doesn't seem like much of a boyfriend. How long has it been since you came?"

She's coming back down to earth, gray eyes meeting mine again. My finger shifts back to the collar, watching her. She looks up through her lashes at me.

Damnit. She's so good at submitting. I'm not sure how the so-called boyfriend can be denying her. I almost don't think she's going to respond when the words slip out. "A while."

Clicking my tongue, I drag my finger lower, watching her eyes bulge. She's responsive, easy to tease. She'll feel like sin when I sink my cock inside her.

Her boyfriend isn't my problem, and it's not like she's telling me to stop. She's too lost in the feeling. I wrap my finger through the loop again, pulling hard to test her bounds. She liked my hand and she's wearing the collar, so she can't be that against it.

Her voice is a whimper, and it's different from the lust-infused cry a moment ago. She's tensing, her hips stilling against me as I continue to circle her pussy with a finger, refusing to press into her.

I pull harder on the ring, earning another cry dipped in pain, pulling the collar away from her skin. She's closing herself off for some reason, despite loving the orgasm I just gave her greedy little cunt.

I pause, distracted by something along her neck. There's redness under the edge of the collar, by her collarbone. She whimpers as I study, her hand locking around my wrist.

Meeting her eyes, I can see the fear has returned. It kills the mood for me, and I lean back from her, sliding my hand out of her skirt.

Her eyes are bright, guarded, staring up at mine. I hold her gaze, my other hand tugging on the blouse.

"David-"

I pull at the neckline, letting go of the loop in the collar. There's an angry red circle around her throat where the skin has been rubbed raw. In a few spots I think it may have bled and dug in. I swipe my finger over the mark, listening to her barely controlled gasp, eyeing the red stain on the tip of my middle finger. It's not much, but she doesn't seem pleased that it's there.

My eyes meet hers, and there's shame in her gaze. I have no idea if she likes the collar but I have no doubt she doesn't like the effects.

Placing a hand on either side of her, I lean in. Ideas of fucking her over my desk until she screams vanish. I can't get off with her throat bleeding, and the fearful look she gives me seals the decision. "This is what your boyfriend picked?"

Squirming on the desk, she tries to look away. "It's not like that-"

"He doesn't know it cuts into your skin, or he doesn't care?" I snap, aware my voice is angrier than it should be.

She pushes in my chest, and I take a step back. I'm still half hard, but I won't fuck her like this. It's ruining the pleasant illusion I had going on, and I'm not fucking anyone that looks at me fearfully.

Really kills the boner.

She pulls at her blouse until the black leather is hidden again. I've seen plenty of inexpensive collars in leather, but they don't rub the skin raw. This thing could be made for a dog, and it's disrespectful as fuck to put that on anyone.

Myla fidgets, clamping her legs together. Her fingers don't still until she's checked three times that the collar is hidden. When she's satisfied she looks up to meet my gaze, dropping her eyes again.

I don't need to care. I don't. I can simply let her hop off the desk, walk out the door, and it's not my problem.

But those gray eyes look up at me through heavy lashes, the scent of her orgasm still hanging in the air. If not for that damn bloody ring around her neck, she'd be on her knees right now.

Huffing, I try to not show my irritation. "If you don't like it, take it off. Is it locked on?"

Those expressive little eyes widen, something I've always liked about riling her up. You can get so much expression out of her with little effort. "No! No, it, uh, it fastens."

"Then take it off. Your skin needs a break."

Myla wrinkles her nose, ready to argue with me about it. I pull at my tie, watching her gaze fall to the movement. Even now she's affected by me, subtly rubbing those lush thighs together.

How is the boyfriend not keeping her under wraps? She acts like he doesn't get her off, ever. If she's wearing it for the reasons I think, he should be doing a significantly better job. Or I'm just that much better.

And it shouldn't be cutting her skin, not like it has.

Her hands are at her neck, wincing when she touches the black band. I can't see the bottom of it, but I'm sure the leather is shredded if it's ruining her skin. "It doesn't need to come off."

Moving to hop off the table, I shove my knee back between her legs, and her eyes damn near roll back in her head. She stays in place, gripping the hard edge of the desk, as she looks up at me. "Yes, it does. I don't think you have a pain kink Myla. Give yourself a break. Afraid he'll be mad?"

I'm digging my own grave. Fuck, I don't need to be this interested. But button-up Myla has a kinky side, and I'm drunk on it.

The damn collar needs to come off. Whoever the boyfriend is, he's being needlessly mean to her.

"No," she snaps, but it's too forceful to be real. "I like wearing it."

I scoff. Yeah, *right*. Reaching out, I flick over the band, listening to her hiss. If she refuses to take it off I'll let it be, but she's putting herself through extra pain for no reason.

"I have another one coming," she continues, and I'm used to this. Myla rambles when she's nervous. "It won't cut. I picked it out."

Interesting. She's more forthcoming than I would expect. "Did you pay for it?"

She frowns, confused. "Well, yes, I ordered it."

"Then he isn't really *giving* it to you, is he?"

I step back from her, pinching the bridge of my nose before I snap again. There are rules to these things for a reason, expectations.

Clearly the boyfriend blew right past those.

A vibration catches our attention, and Myla tenses at the noise. It's gotta be her phone.

She's off the desk in an instant, shoving me out of the way. "I'm late. I've gotta go."

She isn't even past me when my arm snakes out, grabbing her around the waist as I spin her back into my chest. There's a soft gasp as she plants her hands on my chest, and it makes me want to lift her up again.

Grabbing her chin, I hold her gaze. "You'll tell him to buy you one. Not one you ordered. He needs to buy it."

"What does it matter?"

I shake my head, teeth digging into my cheek. All the signs are there even if she's avoiding it. "That's one of the rules. He's giving you a collar for submission. Make him earn the right."

Myla is putty in my hands, listening. I could probably have her hands down my pants in an instant, but the redness on her neck sticks out in my head. The lusty haze in her eyes lasts only a moment before she joins me back in reality. "I don't think that's going to work, David-"

"Try," I growl, suppressing the urge to tell her my honorific. It's on the tip of my tongue but I bite it down for now. I don't want to freak her out and send her running now that I've discovered her sinful hidden side.

There it is again, that heavy lidded look that makes me want to shove my cock deep inside her. She wets her lips, not helping the picture. "Why?"

"Because it's one of the basics of submission," I growl, stroking her chin. I lift it a hair higher, forcing her to arch up and look at me. "When we talk about this, you should know the game you're playing." My lip twitches and I can't help myself. I want to test my bounds. "If you decide to quit putting up with the rings around your neck, you can come find me. And you'll call me Sir."

Her whole body shakes at the command, and I dig my fingers lightly into her hip. If she doesn't stop we'll be here all night. I shouldn't push my luck, but she's got my mind all fucked up right now. Her eyes flutter, drinking in my words, but she doesn't say anything back.

I wait a beat, and when she doesn't speak I lean in

closer. My own internal rules are screaming, but I need to hear these words from her. "Say it."

"What?"

Grinning, I breathe into her ear. "Don't ruin your streak now. You were being such a good girl for me. Now you're going to go home and tell that boyfriend of yours that you want a new collar that doesn't hurt, and he's going to pick it out. And if he fails, there will be a punishment."

Her nails dig into my shirt when she speaks, her body wound tight once more. I don't know if I just tipped her over the edge. "Yes Sir."

3 MYLA

What am I doing?

I didn't have the balls to tell Liam about the collar. He was irate when he got home and found it off my neck last night. We argued for ages, but ultimately he put it back around my throat before bed. My skin aches this morning, but I wait until I'm leaving for work the next day before throwing it in the trash.

I'll say I lost it. That's the sensible answer. Then I'll show him the one I ordered and all will be good.

It doesn't matter that he didn't buy it. I'll still wear it as his. It's what we talked about, and what I agreed to.

David stays on my mind all night, and the fact that he never actually touched my pussy is a crime in itself. I didn't realize it until I was back in my car, and the sheer embarrassment of the situation settles over me.

You'll call me Sir.

His words bounce in my head as I step back into work. It's so wrong, but listening to him speak, thinking of him catching me like a dirty little secret and slapping my clit is the only thing that got me to orgasm when Liam fucked me last night.

How fucked up am I?

Afterwards Liam called me a good girl, despite the fact that I almost forgot it was him. It didn't send the same pang of longing through me, and I'm ashamed to admit it. I can't tell Liam that, but what am I supposed to do about David? I'm pretty sure everything he does is calculated and finessed to work in his favor.

If I have to envision my enemy to get off to my boyfriend calling me a good girl, something is crooked in my head.

I've no doubt he fucks different than Liam. The idea excites me. Liam isn't doing it for me, and feeling what David has to offer down the hard lines of his body and the dick I felt pressing into my stomach makes my head spin.

How am I supposed to face him today? Do I casually pretend I took his words to heart and that things are chipper at home? Does he expect repayment for making me see stars?

Maybe this is a game of his, one specifically to make me squirm.

Phil is in extra early this morning, talking to Bridgett, another partner attorney. There are technically four, though the original owner rarely practices anymore and is basically a placeholder. It's his law firm, but Phil pilots the ship. Bridget and Melissa have a say, but Phil likes to think he's the most important person here.

My heart almost stops when I see David in office earlier than ever. His desk is halfway covered by the wall, but I spot him with his feet kicked up working on something, probably for the Lux case. I've heard Melissa pulling him in on high-stakes criminal cases, but that's not my area of interest. He's welcome to take on every criminal case he wants and leave the personal injury lawsuits for me.

My traitorous body heats at the mere sight of him. I'm fucking hopeless.

Probably best to pretend that last night didn't happen. I don't need him getting the impression that I'm okay with cheating.

But dear God, he needs to stay away from me or I'm gonna slip and call him *Sir*. Anything to get those hands back on me.

I've never humored the idea of a Sir. Liam is playing at being a Dom. I don't have a daddy kink and I won't call him Master. And something classic like Sir feels... unrelated to Liam. I don't think I've ever heard anyone refer to him as Sir, even in everyday life.

With that self-assured confidence, David makes it really hard to maintain my high level of hatred for him.

Unfortunately, he seems to have no problem getting in my space. Boundaries aren't a thing with him now that he's had his hand up my skirt. I've barely been in ten minutes before I see him wandering out of his office with a stack of papers in hand.

He smirks when our eyes meet, handing me the pile. I try to reign in the inner demon in my head demanding I say "yes, Sir" to see what he'll do. "Add these to the binders. Make some copies. It's just Andrew Lux coming in. His wife won't be in prior to trial."

With a scowl, I snatch them out of his hand. Just wonderful, he's already lost the suit jacket this morning, his sleeves are rolled up, the top buttons undone before eight in the goddamn morning. Our fingers brush as I take the stack from him and I can't stop my mind from going to dirty places. Why does he look so yummy first thing in the morning? What happened to the bedhead?

The only thing he has is bedroom eyes, and I don't need them on me at this hour.

David laughs at my blush. "Don't look so embarrassed, Schulte; we can play again after work."

Slamming the stack down, I look around to see if

anyone heard. My body betrays me with longing, but I've got to stand firm. "No! We won't. That was a one-time deal."

"Didn't look like you wanted it to be a one-time deal yesterday when you were screaming."

"It was an error in judgment."

"Really?" He laughs, shaking his head. His hands are in his pockets now, but I can see them flexing like he's working to keep from touching me. "I thought the collar was a nice touch. Wearing it again today, or did the boyfriend listen and order you something better?"

The boyfriend. He never says "your". I get the feeling he doesn't give a single damn about Liam, not that I made him sound all that important yesterday. His fingers trace the neckline of my blouse as my mind tries to focus. I glare up at him, swatting his hand away before anyone sees. The skin was still tender, and the humiliating red lines aren't something I want to revisit.

I saw his eyes yesterday when he noticed the marks. Even if David doesn't like me, he was pissed when he saw those. I know it's unorthodox, but I read so long as both parties agree to them it's not abusive behavior in a D/s relationship. I prefer to think of it as a kink. And I agreed to them. I want to wear a collar and feel naughty no matter where I am.

The marks don't matter. It's all a learning curve. I clear my throat before answering him. "It's not any of your business, but no. I threw it away."

I'm almost positive it came from a pet store now. I want to be used as a submissive, not treated like a pet. The one I ordered online is infinitely better.

David clicks his tongue, eyeing the room. "Pity. You were so good at listening last night."

I almost snarl, getting in his face. "I'm not calling you *Sir* at work!"

He chuckles, and I'm on edge as he gently squeezes my hip before releasing. "You just did." He leans in a little closer, and my body internally screams for more. "I was talking about making him buy you a proper one. Didn't work out?"

I freeze, his tone low and seductive. I'd almost risk the dirty talk if it means I get to orgasm again like yesterday, and I don't even care if Liam isn't here. We've been together a year and I've never felt as overwhelmingly satisfied as I did last night. It's addictive.

"Throw it away out of fear, or did you decide letting him torture your neck wasn't a punishment fit for the crime?" David hisses, snapping the illusion. The seductive tone is overshadowed by anger, and I'm surprised at his sudden change.

"It hurt," I admit, feeling my skin heating up. He's speaking way too candidly for this early in the morning. I'm not going to lie, there's no point when he already saw the marks. "I didn't like it chafing my skin."

He licks his lips as he eyes me, and dear lord I need that tongue elsewhere. Leaning in closer, I almost arch into him before catching myself. "Personally, I think a collar belongs on your throat. So I can tug on you when I want you. Or a chain to drape over your skin, and clip onto your clit."

God, I'm panting. I should pull back, but I've thrown caution to the wind and my curiosity is sky high. David isn't prowling the internet for answers as we talk; he already has them. "Not leather?"

"I hate leather," he growls, and I'm going to come undone if he keeps up. "Gold, silver, something classy for the daytime." He leans closer and it's all I can do to keep from gripping those firm biceps. "With a plug for your ass so I can tease you whenever I want."

I pull back my hair to stare into his eyes. I didn't realize they made a set like that. I thought it was a collar or nothing. Where the hell did he learn these things?

"He needs to buy you a collar that doesn't look like it came from PetCo," he continues mirroring my own thoughts. We're being careless at this hour of morning but I'm too distracted to care. "It won't chafe if it's a quality product, which is what the boyfriend should be picking."

I gasp as he reaches forward, tugging the neckline of my blouse to the side. The little sores around my neck cry out in protest as he drags a finger lightly over the marks.

Letting go he leans back, eyeing me. "Buy better quality shit and this won't happen. Letting your skin get torn up isn't respectful." He lifts my chin up, and I glare up into his ocean blue eyes. He sure is bossy. Maybe I should expect it if he wants to be called Sir. "You're going to tell him tonight. If he refuses, you won't wear his collar again."

Who the *fuck* does he think he is? I push his hand away, glaring. "And where do you get off thinking you can have an opinion?"

David smirks, and I'm already regretting my word choice. "I think I can get *you* off, better than whatever excuse you have for a boyfriend. And you like it too." He's in my space again, and I'm trying to silence my inner slut who wants me back on the desk. "You want me to give you what that boyfriend isn't. So he either shapes up and gets a better collar, or the next collar going around your neck is mine."

He pulls away, stealing my breath with him. If I wasn't worked up before I sure as hell am now.

Shooting me a wink, he turns and leaves. *A wink!*

Spinning to yell at him, I notice the file clerk arriving early to help prep. She gives me an odd look as she sets down her bag, and I make myself busy with the paperwork David left behind. My skin is afire, and I need to get my head out of the gutter before I mess something up.

He's not my boss, and he sure as hell isn't my boyfriend. So why is he so interested in what I'm wearing, and if Liam buys the proper shit?

This isn't me. I'm not a cheater. I don't have flirty, sinful conversations with my enemy who wants me to call him *Sir* in the middle of the office. I've got to pull myself together.

I just can't get him out of my mind all day long. Is he into me or just enjoying the game? David is gorgeous, and he's the kind of guy that knows it too. He could just be fucking with my head because he found me exposed in the office.

At least he's trying to be discreet around the rest of the staff. I don't need the gossip mill making its way back to my BFF, or worse, Liam. He could hold it over my head for all I'm worth, but so far nothing. I don't know if I should be thankful or not.

Yesterday was a one off, and I can't let it repeat no matter how the idea sends sparks down my body. I don't need distractions while I try cementing my place here at the firm. Liam is an outlier, and hopefully he won't blow up too much when he realizes the collar is gone. I'll just replace it with the one I bought, tell David he was good and got a proper one, and we're home free.

Somehow, that makes it sound like I'm more worried about David's opinion than Liam. That can't be right.

I need to stop thinking about David. And Liam. And anything that doesn't have to do with the Lux case. Dropping myself back into the desk chair my fingers fly across the stacks of work, getting into the details we're supposed to fine tune before trial.

David's new stack annoys me until I finally look at it, and it's a good thing too. This is what Phil will have a cow over if I miss it.

At least I get to sit in and listen to prep this time, a rarity. I grab the binders when it's time to head in, ignoring David's smug smirk as I sit on his side, opposite Lux, with Phil at the head of the table. I take notes as they talk, trying to bite down my annoyance at Phil's praise for David.

David is a superstar at prepwork, and the client relaxes the longer he talks. No wonder he's convinced so many clients to sign on. Phil will still lead the case and direct conversation, but for the most part he seems content to let David guide. It is both impressive and infuriating. If he does well enough he could potentially lead at trial too.

I want to bang my head into the desk. He has everything I want, including the next orgasm I'm chasing.

We break for lunch, and Phil offers to buy David's food. They step into his office to chat, effectively excluding me. Of course Phil is excluding me! Even if I am doing all the work, it will never matter so long as I'm shackled with Phil as the lead attorney. If this wasn't one of the best law firms to learn from, I'd be out of here. Fuming, I storm back to my desk, silently cursing the pair. David really is a devil in disguise.

Maybe I should try harder to like criminal cases, or hop over to Bridgett's side and handle workers compensation claims.

Laci finds me sulking, coffee in hand. She looks about as moody as I feel, soft blonde locks tucked into a loose braid. Her hourglass body fills out the tight dress too nicely, drawing the attention of every dickhead in the office. She's got on sky high stilettos, a clutch gripped beneath her arm. The dress is fairly low in the front, giving anyone who wants it a great look down her dress. Laci eats up the attention, and she isn't shy about it. Handing off a cup, she smirks at me. "How's the meeting going?"

"Well I've been iced out from lunch," I grumble, shooting her a look. Laci scoffs, shaking her head. This isn't the first time Phil's used his sexism openly at work. I take a sip of the drink, make a face at the cold, thick blend sliding down my throat, and hand it back. "That's awful."

"It's my cup from this morning," she replies, shrugging. "Do you have enough time to run to Ben's?"

Smirking, I hop up from my desk. I'll always find time for my favorite coffee shop. "If we hurry."

~~~

"That twat," Laci breathes as we reenter the building. I have a scant few minutes before the meeting picks up again and my feet ache after the jog from Ben's Coffee Shop. Damn these heels, I should've gone with flats. But these shoes make my legs look sexy, and I hate myself for wanting David to notice. "How dare he touch
~~~

you?"

"I hate to say it but I enjoyed it. Although I can never admit that to David." He already knows, but at least I haven't told Laci about his "Yes *Sir*" requirement. She'll die of laughter, or go and flirt with David herself. She's always ready for a good time, but I don't want her interfering.

I sound crazy, acting like this is something more than a happy accident. David is playing a game, and I'm falling into it.

I can't help myself. He's in control, demanding, and everything I imagined Liam being. I wasn't trying to seduce him, but his hands and that bedroom voice linger in my head everywhere I go. It's only been a day. What am I supposed to do now?

Laci bursts out laughing, snapping me out of my mental spiral as we hop into the elevator. "No, his ego doesn't need the inflation." Wiggling her brows, she bumps her hip into mine. I'm tender from Liam's grip, but I'm not going to let her know that. "Maybe he'll be down to play again if Liam can't get the hint."

"Liam's doing fine."

She's glaring at me now, and my eyes dance away. Laci is suspicious of my relationship, asking too many questions. David looks at the marks around my neck with disdain, but Laci would call and report domestic abuse before she humors the idea that I like it.

I do like it. I want him to be rough. He's just not found the right rhythm yet. I stop my thoughts before I start comparing months of trying a D/s relationship with Liam to the thirty minute adventure with David.

"He's not fine," she hisses with a shake of her head. "He's a bore to talk to, and those boyish good looks will only last so long. Plus he's too damn heavy handed in the bedroom."

I start, eyeing the elevator. A few people glance over but no one wants to comment. Good. "Laci-"

"I'm just saying, you sure seem sore a lot for someone who never gets to cum."

Staring at the ceiling, I wonder if there's a way to censor her. Grasping her arm I drag her off the elevator to our floor, glaring. "It's getting better."

Yesterday was better because David left me riled up, but that's beside the point.

I should talk to Liam tonight. Messing around behind his back isn't sitting right with me, even if it gave me my first release during sex in months. Hopefully he doesn't hit the roof. Things are rocky, and he’s taken his new role too far one too many times. Avoiding it won’t help things, and I need to be open with him. I don't want to ruin the dynamics of our Dominant and Submissive relationship. I'm supposed to respect him and be ready at all times. I can't do that if I'm hoping some guy at work will rail me against the desk.

Waving goodbye to Laci, I down the coffee and refocus. This is an after work type of problem.

Phil catches me as I reach the conference room, somewhat pulling the door closed before I can walk in. David is in there chatting with Andrew, but Phil holds up a hand to stop me. "We're going to go over disclosures. Can you grab the binders for his file?"

"Of course," I replied, moving to head over to the shelves. His hand on my arm stops me, rubbing his palm up to my elbow. I frown, tensing beneath his grip. This spot is at the back of the room, a wall separating us from prying eyes, but his unexpected touch is nothing like

David's. "Sir?"

Another thing that makes me think of David, and I'm ready to bash my head into the wall to cease my horny brain.

Phil stares for a moment, fingertips brushing along my arm. "I believe I have some availability tomorrow afternoon. Book an appointment for us for about an hour."

"Which case do I relate it to?" I ask, eyeing his hand. He's no longer stroking his fingers up my arm, but his hand is a lot closer to my breasts than I'd prefer. Laci's words from yesterday echoed in my head but I shrug them off.

"None. It's related to your position here, Myla. All good things. Bridgett is in court all afternoon tomorrow but if she gets in early she'll visit for a few as well. Melissa is doing trial prep all day, but she'll stop in to chat as well, if there's time."

Mentioning Bridgett and Melissa is a good sign. Maybe they want to offer me a tentative position prior to my year probation or even just more opportunities to hone my skills. It's only been two months, so a promotion is a little early, but I'll take what I can get. Maybe I'll be able to start doing casework with one of them and get out from under this sexist pig. I work my ass off for this law firm. "Absolutely. I'll get it on the calendar right now."

"Perfect. Drop off the files before you schedule." He gives my arm a squeeze before slipping into the conference room and, spirits lifted, I bounce off to grab the binder. By the time I'm blocking out time to speak with Phil, I'm starting to think nothing can dampen my spirits.

I should've known better. Having a boring, happy

day isn't in the books. I signed myself up for complications when I asked Liam to try a kinkier bedroom life, and all it's done so far is come back to bite me in the ass. The day is over in a blink of an eye, and before I know it I'm back at my desk client free, organizing for tomorrow.

It's getting late, and I'll have just enough time to go through and clean up before I'm off.

Someone clears their throat by the door, and instead of glee I feel dread pooling in my stomach. Snapping my head up, I stare into unforgiving green eyes.

The emptiness around my throat cries out to me, and I'm suddenly questioning my choice to throw the collar instead of just stuffing it in my bag. It was an act of defiance, and even the cream I put on the marks hasn't lessened the ache there. But he's not going to care about that, not if he made the effort to come here twenty minutes before close.

"Liam," I say, surprise heavy in my voice. He's never visited me at work before. Some days I'm not even certain he knows the name of my office. "What are you doing here?"

He smiles, but it's forced. "It's my day off."

"I know," I reply, the knot in my stomach tightening. "I'll be off in less than a half hour. What made you stop in?"

Smirking, he leans forward and brushes my hair back. I tense, glaring at him. My hips are still sore from his grip yesterday, and he knows it. The line around my neck is a touchy subject between us, one he will only discuss if I admit that I wanted it. "What, I can't visit my girlfriend at work?"

I shrug, standing to hug him on instinct. I don't

want him standing over me, or giving him any reason to be mad at me. This is work, and I'm just now starting to make progress here. I bite back the sarcasm when I respond. "How sweet of you."

His hands rest low on my waist, and I can feel the sting where his fingernails dig in over the tender spots from last night. He isn't smiling at me anymore. "You forgot something this morning."

I stiffen, silently yelling at myself as he tugs the collar out of his pocket. I should've thrown that damn thing out in the parking garage, but I was feeling bitter and wanted to be rid of it. My blood stains the underside where it's rubbed me raw.

Thank God the file clerk left an hour earlier than anyone else. David's door is open, and Liam either didn't notice him or doesn't care. He's dragging his finger up my shirt, and when his hand reaches my throat he snaps out to squeeze over the inflamed flesh. I startle, jumping back as he lets go. It burns, and I reach up to touch the skin, eyes widening at him.

What an ass. I know I'm disobeying, but I don't remember claiming a pain kink. He needs to back up. "What the hell Liam?"

He reaches out to stroke my cheek, and on instinct I slap his hand away. I may have cum last night, but he's still punishing with his hands and that doesn't get me off. His eyes narrow to a glare, and I take a step back. "You wanted the damn thing Myla. You need to at least wear it."

David's reminder plays in my head, and the words slip from my lips before I've thought them through. "Buy a better one, then. This one hurts."

Liam sneers, the shadow of a man I rarely see slipping away. Since I made the suggestion, he's been acting more and more like he thinks bruising me will earn obedience. He steps closer and I shift back, ignoring the rage behind his eyes. "I don't think that's how this works, is it babe? I'm supposed to be in charge, right? So wear the damn thing. Quit making a fool out of me."

"I'm not," I hiss, stuffing the collar under a file. I can't have something like this sitting out at work. "I don't know where you're getting off but this is totally inappropriate! This is my job."

"And you're supposed to be listening," he seethes. He's eyeing me like I've committed a capitol offense. "You wanted to try the Dom/sub bullshit. This is me trying it."

"Liam-"

"But don't make an ass out of me just because you decided you don't wanna play along," he continues, stepping closer. "I'm playing your stupid game."

"This isn't what I meant and you know it," I breathe out, looking around. I'm certain David is getting an earful. I never saw him leave the office, and he hasn't yet made his presence known. I don't want to mention it to Liam; he's gotten annoyed in the past when I interrupt him. At this rate David will know more than I ever wanted him to about my personal life. "You've let your friends confuse you about what this is supposed to be."

He leans forward, placing his hands on either side of me. My back stiffens, and without meaning to my eyes dart towards David's office. He's still not paying attention, and he either doesn't care or he's waiting to see how things play out. He had me just like this yesterday, except my legs were open for him and I wanted his touch. My breath hitches, but it's not because Liam turns me on. I don't think I've ever been drier, not that he would know the difference.

Liam is in my face, hot breath hitting me square in the nose. He smells like he forgot to brush his teeth all day. "Wear it."

"I'm working." It's absolutely an excuse, but I don't want that thing back around my neck. "We can talk at home. Or at least wait until I'm off."

No drama, that's what I need to stick to. If Phil catches wind that I'm causing problems in the office he might withhold whatever possible promotion he had in mind. I want the advancement, so I need to get Liam to chill out and leave.

"Wear it and I'll go," he snaps, his hands scratching at the cheap wood of my desk. "I'm meeting with Chad anyway after this. You'll be home when I get there and we can talk more tonight."

"Right, talk." Pushing on his chest, I hope he takes the hint and leans back. I need room to breathe. "After work. At home."

He moves to wrap the collar around my neck again, and I'm ready to jump off the desk. My skin hurts too much to have it back just yet. "Wear it."

“Liam-”

He grabs the hair at the back of my head, gripping until my scalp screams. I press my lips together and keep from making a sound. He gets more aggressive when I complain. His other hand is fumbling with the collar, unable to latch it without both hands. “Wear it you little bitch.”

“Problem?”

The air escapes my lungs, and I'm not certain if I'm ecstatic he finally decided to do something or horrified. Liam snaps around to glare, the hand in my hair tightening until I want to whimper.

This isn't what we talked about. I don't want him to pull my hair out, I just wanted to spice up our sex life. None of that matters now though, not as I meet David's eyes across the room.

He's pissed, something dark I've not seen before slipping behind his gaze. Liam doesn't let up, and I feel the tension in his hand. This is why I didn't want him causing a scene.

4 DAVID

If looks could kill, I'd be dead twice over. My eyes dance between Myla, pressed against the desk by this cuck, and the guy I can only presume to be the boyfriend.

No wonder she's unsatisfied.

Snapping his arm back, he drops the collar on the desk like I haven't already noticed it and straightens up. He shoots Myla a look as he does so, bumping his hip roughly against hers. I don't miss the cringe she tries hiding, or the disapproval of her visitor.

I don't know where this guy gets off, but that's not how you treat anyone. I've seen how she reacts when she's horny, and the mistreatment is obvious enough around her neck. I'm certain I know what Myla is looking for, and he's way off mark.

Her eyes confuse me, a gray mixture of relief and fear. She's mortified I caught them, but the gratefulness in her look makes me glad I ended my call.

I should've done it as soon as I heard this guy come in. He only spoke in hushed tones, but I could catch snippets of the conversation from Myla.

Boy wonder turns to me with a grin, brushing off her unease. "No problem. We're just making plans for tonight."

Of course you are.

I eye him critically. *Liam*, that's what she kept saying. He's nothing impressive, an above average height guy with light hair and decent muscles. He's dressed like he's in high school in a band t-shirt and cutoff jeans. I know it's August, but if he's even close to Myla's age he's on his way to thirty like me. That's not the look that gets women to drop their panties.

Smirking, I glance towards Myla. She rubs at her hip, stopping when she notices my gaze.

So many secrets with that one.

I heard the *little bitch* comment, and she's busy not so discreetly rubbing at her head. I decide to let it be for now. If he's this bad at covering himself he'll slip up soon enough. They always do. "Before you go, Schulte, we need to finish the binders for trial tomorrow. Phil needs them before eight and I'm not coming in that early." I smirk at the boyfriend, watching their reactions. His face is a poorly veiled mask of annoyance, and Myla is trying to silently tell me to shut up. I nod at Liam, wondering if he knows how to take a hint. "You don't mind do you? She is still on the clock for another fifteen."

His hands clench, and it's another red flag. I thought Myla was smart, getting hired at this law firm and all, but right now I don't see it. He's doing nothing to hide his behavior, and if he's this open in front of me I wonder what he's like behind closed doors.

Another poser. They're everywhere, giving the lifestyle a bad name.

He doesn't take her hints, but for now he'll listen to mine. "Of course. I'll see you at home tonight, baby. Walk me to the door?"

Myla hesitates, and Liam leans back over her to grab the collar. It's gone when he tugs on her wrist to head to the elevator, and I'm less inclined to think he'll do something dumb in front of the few lingering staff members.

Still, I find myself grabbing a random file off Myla's desk and following them a few steps behind. The copier has an excellent view of the elevators.

I don't hide my intentions. Liam eyes me as he kisses her by the elevators. His hands are up high, right where mine belong. I don't like it, but he won't get the chance to lock that crappy collar around her throat again.

She's beyond tense, I can see it from here. The old broad Marcy isn't paying any attention, sucked into something on her smartphone. I open the file but don't do anything, watching their body language.

There's no response from her. I haven't even felt her sweet little pussy, but she arched into every touch I gave her. Now she tries to lean away from him, forcing a smile that doesn't touch her eyes. Boyfriend is oblivious, or maybe he doesn't care. When he finally leaves, after four or five unnecessary kisses, I'm debating how long I can keep her in office.

He's marking his territory like a dog. She rolls her shoulders when he's finally gone, nervously playing with her fingers.

This is why I hate fakes. Whatever he's trying to teach her makes her insecure and scared. It's all there, plainly on her face. One hand remains closed, eyeing me as she slowly walks back and I realize that damn collar is clenched in her grip.

Give me a break.

I collect the file I've done nothing with, following her back to our desks. She doesn't turn back to watch me, keeping her back unnaturally straight.

At least I wait until we're back in our section before I dig in. "How does that bruise feel?"

She spins on me like I've discovered a secret, fingers dancing between her neck and her hips. Interesting. "Uh - the, *my* neck is fine. Tender. That's it."

I scoff. It was a hell of a lot more bruised than *tender* this morning. Studying her as she shifts back towards her desk, I notice her hesitate then deposit the collar on her desk. It's not like I haven't seen it already. Without asking I grab it off the desk, studying the frayed leather.

"Give that back!"

Ignoring her, I eyeball the broken collar. It's no surprise her skin is trashed, the edges on one side are worn through. There's dark stains where her blood stuck, and I'm seeing red as I look it over.

It's gotta be a dog collar. Even cheap ass ones are nicer than this. I move my arm when she goes to grab it and grip onto her wrist. She hisses, dropping to her knees.

I let go, eyes widening at her. It has to be a reflex; I didn't grip that hard. Myla stays on her knees, open the perfect amount, wide eyes looking up at me. My dick twitches at the sight, and I need to settle down.

Horrified eyes blink up at me, digging into her skirt. I need her up, *now.*

My eyes flicker over my shoulder to that damn security camera in the hall. Phil will jack off to this *and* give me hell for it.

She gives me a disconcerting cry when I jerk her up, hands balled tight into fists. I don't have the patience for this right now. I drag her back towards my office, needing us to be out of line of that camera, and slam the door.

Myla rips her arm away from me, which is both annoying and reassuring. She doesn't get a chance to speak before I'm leaning over her with a glare. "*That's* your boyfriend?"

Nervous fingers fiddle with the fabric of her blouse, and she goes back to ignoring my gaze. "Yes... that was Liam."

Gripping her chin, I make her look up at me. She's avoiding my eyes and I don't like it. Half the time, Myla's busy trying to bite my head off for one-upping her. I can't stand her uncertain, nearly fearful reaction to me.

It's all wrong, every little reaction. His poor conduct and her willingness to deal with it, even in public. I hold her gaze before showing her the collar. "Why do you wear this for him?"

Almost immediately, she's on the defensive. "I'm not wearing it-"

"Why *did* you?"

She bites her cheek, like this is a hard question. "It's nothing. We were just playing around and I - I wanted a spicier sex life." She shakes her head like it's just now occurring to her what she's said. "We don't need to talk about my personal life."

"Right, it just keeps being a problem here." She blushes, and I know without question her mind is on yesterday. I've been thinking about her against my better judgment, and having her luscious body a few inches from mine has my thoughts traveling south. I release her chin, running my fingers down her jugular.

Her moan is seductive, entranced. My hand is over her lips in an instant, leaning in close. "It's still during office hours."

That sobers her up, even if there's only a few minutes left in the day. She's shaking her head, trying to step past me to the door. "I should be heading out-"

"So you can go play house with the guy abusing you?"

Myla stills, staring at me with horrified eyes. "Liam isn't-"

My hand is back at the neckline of her blouse, and she stills. "Really? Because I've never left cuts and bruises due to a collar." My hands drag down the curve of her body, her hands gripping tight to keep from touching me. But her body responds no matter what, arching under my touch. She's lovely like this.

I grip her hips, earning a strangled gasp. I assumed there was something wrong there with the way she's been acting. Myla's hands are at my chest, pressing back. I lighten my touch, sliding my hands to the small of her back. "Even if you think he's a Dominant, Master, whatever, unless you consent to being marked he shouldn't leave anything on you."

I've stolen her voice, the air settling around us. Her eyes stare into mine, and a lifetime passes before she manages a response. "How-"

Letting go of her, I dig out my wallet. She's thrown now, watching me pull out a card that I hand to her. "I belong to a club. You show all of the signs of a Submissive." I let my eyes trail over her slowly, smirking as a blush burns against her cheeks. "You don't hide it well. I knew what you were going for when I saw the collar. And a moment ago when you fell to your knees like you've been trained to-" I cut myself off, letting the words hang in the air.

Her mouth hangs open, hands lifeless against my chest. When she doesn't give a response, I press against her back. It's enough to at least snap her from the trance. Her eyes look up at me, putting things together. "The collars."

That's not what I'm waiting for her to say. "What

about them?"

"You mentioned chains that-" she cuts off, clearing her throat before she tries again. "Chains that clip to your clit or have built in toys for pleasure. You hate leather. You know all these things." She gestures around wildly. "The Sir kink-"

"You're catching on," I reply, praising her. Her eyes flutter, and I slip that detail away for later. Leaning in, I sense her breath picking up. "Now we're back on track. I told you to only call me Sir when we talk like this."

"Not in front of my boyfriend."

Especially in front of him. She's not refuting me, and I'm pretty sure she's trapped someplace between lust and confusion. I grasp her chin again, listening to her contented sigh. "I told you to get him to buy another collar or I'll be picking one for you. He didn't pass the test."

She tenses. "That's not going to work with Liam."

I chuckle, and if anything she's shifting closer not away. "He had a chance. He's taking liberties with you. I'll be keeping that sad excuse for a collar."

Pulling back from me, she's already shaking her head. "No, that's not going to happen. Liam-"

"Is a little bitch," I reply, quoting him from earlier. "He thinks he's entitled to more than he is. Submission is earned, not taken."

I swear, she nearly melts at my words. "This is a fun game here, but my home life is a different story. I can't just disobey him and show up wearing something else on my neck."

There's about four things wrong with that, but I don't have time to correct her here. "You're not going home wearing it tonight." I pocket the collar, catching her hand when she goes to dig it out. "And the only reason you should be shoving your hand in my pants is if you plan on sucking me off."

Her fingers retract, but I can see the heavy lust in her eyes. There's a temptress in there, begging to be let out. Obedience is nice, but I like when my partner has fire. If she stays with Liam much longer he'll beat it out of her.

I refuse to watch it happen. The boyfriend is a sheep in wolf's clothing, and he's trying to exert control he doesn't have. "No collar tonight. Tell you boyfriend I noticed the nice built-in one he's left on your neck."

"I can't-"

"You don't have to say it in so many words, but you do need to be clear you're not wearing it." I stare down at her hips, dragging my gaze up her body again. I've always acknowledged Myla had a curvy figure, but now I'm invested in the full picture. Her legs are fit, and so far as I've seen there's no marks where her clothing won't cover. "Tell him people at work are suspicious." My jaw clicks as I bite back the budding anger again seeing the telltale signs of abuse. "If there's one new mark on you tomorrow, I'm matching it on his skin."

Myla is lost, I can see it in her doe-like eyes. Be it my conviction that Liam needs to stop leaving marks, or the fact that I've decided to fucking care, I have no idea. "Why does it matter to you?"

It's a loaded question. I'm sure she's realized I'd love to bend her ass over my desk, but telling her that seems insincere after demanding her boyfriend be more respectful. Brushing it off, I tap the card I handed her. "Look this up. The internet is full of fakes. You won't get all your answers on a web page, but read the rules of conduct. Maybe you'll notice what your boyfriend lacks."

She grips the card, that uncertainty back in her eyes. She's chewing on her full bottom lip, and I want to take it between my own teeth and sample her. "If a website can lie, why should I believe this?"

I smirk, wondering when this will come back to bite me in the ass. "If you're interested in what a real D/s relationship is, I'll take you to see for yourself. You believe Liam's treatment is normal when it's not. It's time for a reality check."

Her eyebrows scrunch together in the cutest little crease. "At a club? You see these things at a club?"

"It's a kink club," I reply, working the card out of her hand. It's against my better judgment, but I want her to be able to reach me after the stint with the boyfriend. I don't trust that look in his eyes. Scribbling my number on the back, I hope she doesn't fucking drop it. I don't need people calling me all night. "You'll message me if little Liam gets out of hand."

It's not a request, and after a flicker of hesitation she nods, slipping the card into her hand again. I don't like it, I'd rather toss her up on the desk and fuck reason into her. Liam's convinced her this is okay when it's far from it.

"David-"

"Sir," I groan, stuffing my hands into my pockets. I need her to work with me. There are rules to follow, and although I'm not a stickler for rules, there are some I have to abide by.

Truly, asking her to use my honorific might be a step in the wrong direction, but the sound is too sweet to give up. If I had any idea how sultry she would sound saying it, I'd have demanded she start addressing me as Sir the moment she started working here.

Liam's already given her a fucked version of what this is, for whatever reason. I'm not going to do something else out of line. Submission is earned and respected, exactly like I told her. Rushing forward to get my dick wet destroys the values of it, and Myla is looking more and more appealing.

I haven't participated in the club in months. I like my partners to be long-term without commitment. A kinky newbie yearning to learn is the perfect candidate.

But taking a partner isn't something I do lightly, and I won't have her thinking this is something it's not. She needs to see what a D/s relationship should be, sans abuse.

She wets her lips. "Sir. Liam won't like it."

"He's not supposed to. Do the research yourself. You'll see where he's lacking."

Myla opens her mouth to respond before shutting it again, and I don't push. The last two days are strange enough. If I push too much she might run off, and I want to keep testing her.

I nod to the door, eyeing the clock. It's well past five, and I do have something to do this evening. I didn't need to before, but it's time I revisit an old haunt. "We better get going."

It snaps her out of this lustful haze, and with a jerky nod she slips past me to the door. I don't stop her from leaving, studying her figure as she leaves.

She's barely gone a moment when peels of laughter catch my attention, and I'm pinching the bridge of my nose. *Goddammit.*

"So you *finally* upgraded," Laci chirps. Myla's bubbly friend is one of the most gossip-fueled people I know. "I have to tell you hon, I approve."

5 MYLA

A sex club.

He gave me a card to a sex club.

He gave me a card to a sex club with his number scribbled on it.

I'm walking back into work the next morning in a near daze. This is out of the ordinary for sure. The only thing grounding me to reality is the dull sting on my ass from yesterday.

Liam was irate about David. He kept going on about me fucking my boss, and it took nearly a dozen tries to explain that David isn't my boss, Phil is.

I mean, he still didn't give a fuck, but at least I set the record straight.

He got home late from being out with his friends, and we had to have sex. It's become a given whenever he gets home. I usually just lay there and wait for it to be over. It's unpleasant and unsatisfying, but Liam thinks he's the best damn thing to happen to me.

But last night I was worked up. I spent hours before he got home researching that card and David was right; the internet is one giant black hole. There wasn't too much information online, but you had the option to fill out an application and receive a terms of service packet that is required for entry to even dig up information on the club.

Shamefully, I filled it all out. They don't just let

anyone in. It's very strict, and the list of behavioral expectations was a mile long.

You get lanyards when you enter. It's all color-coded. If you're in a D/s relationship (or they even have participants who follow a Master and Slave lifestyle) there's a certain color for that. Colors for people searching for partners, newbie's. The works.

You have to dress nice. It's not black tie, but like date-level dressing. I read everything available twice over but didn't submit my application, fear pricking the back of my neck.

There's an option for two visits before a membership is required. The starting price is a grand for monthly access, including shows. I didn't look past that. The amount alone made my eyes widen.

I'm still technically an apprentice here. I can't toss that much money out.

But a trial period couldn't hurt. Nothing more than that. The gears in my mind spin wildly at the possibilities. One of the required questions is relationship status, which stills my hand as I consider.

I could get inside information from people who are more than experienced, and tell Liam all about what I learned! He probably won't let me go, but if I learn and perform well, and then tell him the little detail about where the information came from, then I'll be fine. Maybe he'll want to try it out too.

Liam must've realized I was distracted during sex last night. I forgot to keep my fake moans going, and when I didn't pretend to orgasm he lost it. The slash on my butt hurts, but I should've known to pay more attention. He doesn't like it when I *pretend* I don't like it.

But that's not the problem right now. To get into

the club you need an invitation or to go as someone's guest the first time, membership aside. You can't just find a card and call. I guess that protects everyone involved.

So the only way I'm going is if David takes me. I wonder if he knew that little detail before handing me the card.

And how the hell did he find out about it?

I'm distracted through the first half of the day. David is off working with Bridgett, so there's really no catching him. I guess I could text him, but I'm not that desperate yet and once I send a message out, he'll have my number. He's already shared the problems he sees with my boyfriend. I don't want to give him the option to dig further.

Laci plops down on my desk just before lunch, two coffees in hand like usual. There are bags beneath her eyes like she hasn't slept, and her hair is tossed back in a messy bun.

She's wearing flowy pants, another sign she's not feeling herself. This girl lives for skirts. I reach to grab one of the cups and she tugs her arm away. "They are both mine."

Oh, it's that kind of day. "Bad night?"

She sets down one of the cups, rubbing her eyes. "Restless. Couldn't sleep."

Laci sleeps like the dead unless something is bothering her. Before I can dig she's hopping back up, heels clicking on the floor. "Now you've avoided me all day. We're going to lunch, and you're going to dish on David."

Oh, this again. Looking towards his office once more, I give up and follow Laci's clicking steps out of the room. Talking to David has to be done privately, and as much as I love my best friend, I'm not ballsy enough to do this in front of her.

~~~

I catch David after Bridgett's teleconference ends, between calls for Phil. He glances up from his desk, hypnotic eyes watching me closely. The cut on my butt burns under his gaze, but I try to not let on. "We can talk before you leave?"

It comes out as a question. That's not even close to standing my ground. A bemused smirk pulls at his lips and he nods. I don't even get a verbal confirmation before Phil's voice is yelling from my desk, and I'm off again.

It's almost closing time when I manage to step into his office, watching as he glances up from the Schrieber file. It's been chaotic for a Wednesday, but if I don't do this today I'll chicken out. Wordlessly I tug the card out of my pocket, and David gestures for me to close the door.

His smirk is in place before it even clicks closed. "I assume you looked it up."

Nodding, I try to not seem eager. This is exactly the hands-on type of experience I'm needing. Things have fallen to the wayside with Liam and I need to be able to get back on track.

I can't be as disappointed as I was last night. The sting on my ass is a constant reminder. "Yes, it's exactly what I've been looking for."

David isn't like Liam. Liam would jump on something like that and demand to know what I mean. He'd take this as a personal slight that I'm so interested in learning more about sex, specifically the BDSM world. David on the other hand folds his hands beneath his chin and stares at me, raising an eyebrow. "Tell me more."
~~~

I'm surprised. I didn't think this was an analysis type of thing. There's one cushy chair not covered in paperwork on this side of his desk, and I sink down into it, his eyes following me all the way. I have this man's undivided attention, and I'm unsure if it makes me excited or nervous.

Maybe a little bit of both. It's empowering, watching how interested he is in what I've got to say. Liam is on his phone half the time, or stuck in a game, or twirling his finger to get me to hurry up with whatever is on my mind.

David is invested. I sit a little straighter, and I think he notices. "I want to go to the club."

"Why?"

At least he's direct. There's no game here between us. I purse my lips, tapping my fingers nervously against my knees. He glances down at the action, but just as quickly focuses on my face again. "I want to learn more."

He cock his head to the side. "Why?"

Okay, so we can't just dodge around the question. "I want to learn. I went online and read the rules and regulations for the club but it's not enough. I want to understand."

David eyes me, raking his gaze from my forehead to my toes. "Is this so you can impress the boyfriend?"

I sit even straighter, surprised. What else would it be for? "Yes. We need-"

"No." He stops watching me, picking up the file he abandoned like the matter is closed.

I scoff, waiting for a beat to see if he'll elaborate. But his eyes don't even rise from his work. My eyebrow twitches as I lean forward. "What do you mean *no*?"

"I mean *no*," he replies, flipping to a new page. I

don't even think he's reading it.

"You wanted me to look it up!" I burst out, standing. "Is this some stupid joke to you? I want to learn more."

"You want to learn more so you can turn around and submit to your cruel boyfriend." His eyes flicker up to mine, and I recoil at the anger there. "And I'm not taking someone else's girlfriend to a sex club. That's asking for a fight."

I press my lips together. Just because I'm attracted to David doesn't mean I plan on dumping Liam. We're in a rough patch, that's all. I just need to work on my abilities and everything will be better. But I can't do that without more insight. "No one has to know-"

"Do you hear yourself?" He asks, cutting me off. His fingers make condescending little air quotations when he speaks again. "*No one has to know.*" Standing as well, he glares down his nose at me. "Are you afraid of people there knowing you have a boyfriend, or are you just afraid he'll raise his hand to you if he finds out?"

Stiffening, my feet step back. It doesn't matter what he says. David doesn't understand us. "That's not your problem. I'll keep it quiet if you'll take me."

David just shakes his head, looking past me. "No. When you're finished dating him I will. I'm not taking you there while you're in any relationship, and sure as fuck not as long as you're dating him."

"I just need to know," I press, feeling the edges of my control slipping. David has to agree or I'm back at square one with no idea how to be better at this. Why must he be so stubborn? "And my relationship isn't any of your business. So unless you're going to teach me, I'm out of ideas."

His eyes narrow, and I straighten as he takes the

few steps around his desk to sit before me. Even though I'm above him now, I still feel like he's in control. "You're not ready for me to teach you."

A spike of lust catches me off guard, and I grip my arms to keep from touching him. Everything about David is alluring, from his charming good looks to that smooth as sin voice, even down to the woodsy scent of his cologne. This man breathes sex appeal, and I need to keep my distance.

Everything was simpler when I hated him. He has no idea what I'm ready for. If I can take on Liam, I'm certain I can take him. There's no emotional attachment getting in the way.

I've already let David touch me once. Doing it again is more than a mistake. I square my shoulders, meeting his gaze. "Yes, I am. We've covered that I'm eager to learn. I read the club's expectations. I just need to know where I'm failing so I do a better job."

David rolls his eyes at me. "What makes you think you're failing?"

I scoff. "I'm not telling you that!"

"But going to a sex club with me is fine," he says, his voice ringing with laughter. "You realize a *sex* club is exactly that, sex. People go there to find a Sub to their Dom, a Master to their Slave kink, to experiment and play in various rooms throughout the club and sip their drinks. They have shows, training classes. My guests don't have boyfriends." He smirks up at me. "If you can't even tell me what's wrong with your relationship how do you expect us to sit around while people play and fuck each other a few feet away?"

My eyes widen, even as my skin heats. David doesn't hold back, telling me exactly what the club is like.

I like that he's candid, but listening to him explain is getting to me. I need to be focused, not horny.

This is a business transaction. The goal is to be a better partner for Liam. Squaring my shoulders, I hold his gaze. "I can handle it."

David's lip twitches, and I'm almost certain he's keeping back a smirk. "The answer is still no so long as you have a boyfriend."

"I'm doing this for him!" I snap, leaning closer. "I can't just dump him."

Clicking his tongue, David stands. He crowds me without warning, and all I do is tilt my chin up to glare. We're almost pressed together, his chest brushing against mine, and if I moved my hips forward, I'm certain I'd feel something against my stomach. Even soft, he's packing under there. As though he senses my dirty thoughts, he chuckles, brushing back a bit of my hair. I jolt, and he drops his hand again, something flashing through his blue eyes before speaking again. "No, it doesn't seem like you can."

He moves away faster than I want, and my body reacts to the loss of contact. My shoulders droop a little as he moves back around the desk and starts organizing files. "You need to look at your relationship, Myla. You have all the makings to be great and feel everything you desire, but I won't teach you a damn thing if you're planning to run back to the bastard turning you black and blue."

The burn of my blush stings more than my hands slapping against his desk. He doesn't glance up from organizing and my irritation spikes another notch. I don't care now about the mark on my ass. He's just trying to say he's better than Liam.

I'm being stubborn, I know I am. Laci doesn't like Liam either, but David doesn't even know him. They met for half a second and now he thinks he's entitled to an opinion. No one gets to pick apart my life like they are that much better than I am.

"You don't know anything about us," I snap, and he finally glances up again. There's a hard edge to his eyes, like he's trying to keep his emotions out of them. "You've only seen a few things and now you think you know everything."

"I've seen enough," he replies, shaking his head. His hair is unkempt this late in the day, the raven black locks a mess atop his head. He must've run his fingers through it all damn day. "The club is an option for you to see firsthand what a relationship like this *should* be like. It's not a hands on test so you can show your boyfriend easier ways to manipulate you. I will take you as a guest if you break up. That's it."

"Then why did you even bother giving me the card?"

Shaking his head sadly, I feel like he's dismissing me. "You should know the answer to that, Myla. I don't like Liam. And from what I've seen you shouldn't either."

I'm finished listening to his crap. If the only purpose was to talk down to me about my relationship, he could've kept the damn card. And I don't want his number either. Biting back a snarl I whirl around and storm out of his office without a word.

We can go back to snapping at each other over work. That's all there is between us. I rip the closest file off my desk, determined to focus until the clock hits five. David can glare at me from his door for all I care.

My eyes still as I catch the security camera that

monitors this section. Damnit, I have no idea what happened to the tape of us together, and I'd rather no one have video evidence of my chat with Liam either. One way or another I have to figure out how to get my hands on the camera footage and erase it. That won't be complicated to do in a busy office at all.

Is that against company policy? Probably. Am I going to try tomorrow anyway? Absolutely.

~~~

When I open my eyes, my head still hurts.

I'm trying to replay the last few hours in my head since I got home. Liam is off Tuesdays and Wednesdays. He works at a pizza place as a manager and closes down the building. It's better than when he was unemployed for sure, but he always told me to be up when he gets home. It's not a problem on Wednesdays since he's usually here.

He was home when I got here. He wanted me to wear something new and had drinks poured for us. It's hazy but I remember that. The sun is gone now, and the clock tells me it's nearly nine in the evening.

There's a pulsing in my head, like it hurts. I don't remember why.

I'm yammering mentally. Why is that? Grabbing at my head I gasp at the pain, pulling back my hand to stare at red, sticky fingers.

Why am I bleeding? Using the back of my hand I rub at my eyes, a dull ringing echoing around me.

Where the hell is Liam? This is our room, but he's absent.

Getting up from the bed I sway on my feet, catching myself on the side table. Looking down, I remember
~~~

changing into this. It's an outfit Liam picked. He wanted me to wear it. Turning to stare at the table, I notice light fingerprints there where my hand was. Right. My fingers are red.

My stomach is screaming, and the ringing in my head still hurts. I wander to our bathroom, running into the bed frame along the way, staring at myself in the mirror.

A gash. There's a gash in my forehead.

I stare at it for way too long before poking at the spot. It's sensitive and stings, my fingers gripping onto the porcelain of the sink. I hiss and pull my fingers away, glaring at my reflection. The blood clotted some time ago, so there's little dried spots on my skin but it's not dripping down my face at the moment

There aren't any other marks that stick out. Just the gash in my head. I should go see someone. I'm bleeding.

Do heads bleed a lot normally? I can't remember.

I'm still wearing the lingerie set he picked out. The straps and panties are torn and it hangs on by shreds. I've read books where the male character does this and it's a huge turn on. Now it just feels... wrong.

I need to clean up. He gets so irritated if I don't take care of things afterwards. If he takes care of me during, I'm supposed to take care of him after.

Did he take care of me? I don't remember if I got to orgasm. I don't remember much of any of it. I'm pretty sure this is the epitome of someone describing being in a daze, and I need to go through the motions here and figure my shit out.

Cleaning my head first, I know this will be a problem tomorrow. A big bandage on my forehead won't do for work, and even a hat or headband won't cover it.

I'll need to get creative. I don't think it's too deep, but I still don't recall anything happening that would result in a gash. I'm positive we had sex, there are all of the signs, but I don't remember any of it. Did I get that drunk?

I toss the outfit, change the sheets that are stained, and clean and put away the toys. My head is screaming and I want to take some medicine, but I don't remember how much I had to drink and I don't want to mix. After changing into something more comfortable, I wander out into the living room, my balance better than before. Liam is on a game, oblivious to me.

He waves me off when I try to talk to him, so I go to the kitchen instead. My phone is on the island and I grab it, looking at the bottle we apparently drank. It's Wednesday. Why the hell did I let him get me so drunk? I've got work in the morning.

Eyeing my phone, I notice Laci called. *Sixteen times.*

Huh. That can't be right. She prefers to text, almost exclusively. I dial out, grab something to eat and go back to the room. Liam doesn't even look up.

"Oh thank god," Laci cries when I pick up. "You've had me worried."

I frown, taking a bite of the chicken salad I brought with me. There's a copper taste in my mouth, and the world wants to tip sideways while I'm sitting here. Maybe I need to lie down. "What's wrong?"

"You called complaining Liam is drunk," she snaps. I cringe, knowing this happened a few times before. She pauses, and I focus on chewing the chicken salad. It's taking a lot of focus. "Did he do something?"

I always say no. Liam is never mean, just heavy handed. He needs me to submit and I haven't.

But the gash. Sometimes I wake up later forgetting

bits and pieces of the night, usually whenever Liam wants to get me drunk. But a gash in my forehead is an entirely different matter. Fingering my makeshift bandage, I think of Anita. She's my other best friend, finishing up her residency at a hospital up north. I almost want to call her and ask if I should go to the ER, but that'll raise questions I don't want to answer.

Like why I don't remember anything, and where the hell the gash came from.

"No, of course not. I have a headache is all. Why did you call so many times?"

"Because you sounded weird," Laci continues, concern lacing her voice. "Like, slurred. And you just told me bye in the middle of our conversation."

"I called you?"

It's quiet for a beat, her hissed breath the only sound I hear. "You don't remember calling me?"

Oh, *that's* not good. A chill shoots down my spine and I sit a little straighter, fighting down the nausea from moving so quickly. I shouldn't feel so sick, even with the head wound. Maybe I do need to ask Liam some questions

Still, if I tell Laci I've got a gash in my head, she'll think the worst. She'll show up here and demand I leave. She'll call the cops.

My heart picks up, blue eyes flickering through my head. David claimed Liam is an abusive ass.

Is he? Anything brutal is always in the name of learning submission. That can't be abusive if it's a lesson. But this feels different. There's nothing kinky about my head. Did I run into something or did that lame ring on his hand cut me?

"Myla?"

Right, I'm on the phone. I need to focus, which is a

lot harder than normal. "Sorry, I've got a lot on my mind."

Laci scoffs, and I hear the disbelief in her voice. There's a jingling sound in the background, and I realize she's grabbing her keys. She has to be. "I'm coming over."

"You don't need to do that," I rush out, panic snapping me out of the daze. The last thing I need is a Laci vs Liam confrontation. She's only a few minutes from me. I don't want her showing up randomly. It'll set Liam off.

Especially when I've been bleeding. And Liam is in a mood. And Laci absolutely hates him.

Getting them in the same house is a horrible idea.

"Yes I do," Laci reasons, and I hear her door slamming. "You're acting weird."

"Liam-"

"*Liam* can suck my ass," she snarls. "Make an excuse if you have to, which you *shouldn't* have to. I'll bring that sweater you let me borrow as an excuse, k?"

She's not going to let up. She did this three weeks ago and it caused an argument with Liam. He doesn't want my friends showing up whenever they like. Yet his friends are welcome to come over or go out with him whenever. It's a double standard I don't care for.

I don't have the energy to argue. If Laci is hellbent on coming over I need to grab some sort of beanie to hide my forehead. I don't wear beanies, but I'm sure I have one for winter somewhere. I could wear one before bed for all she knows, right?

"Fine, I'll tell Liam-"

"You don't have to tell Liam anything girl. If nothings wrong I'll be in and out in a few minutes. No problem."

"And if there is something you see as a problem?"

Laci huffs, and I hear her car turning over. "Myla,

we've done this enough times. Stop trying to cover for him."

I'm surprised. It almost sounds like what David's been saying. They can't think the same thing about Liam. That's ridiculous. My fingers subconsciously touch the mark on my head. I'm confused, but I know I don't want Laci up here giving me more to think about.

"I'll meet you downstairs," I say, grabbing a jacket. I don't let her respond, hanging up the call to search for a hat. Moving around too quickly makes my head hurt, but I ignore it as I locate what I'm looking for and dash back to the living room.

Now Liam cares what I'm doing, tugging his headset off to glare at me. "Where do you think you're going?"

I bristle at his tone, narrowing my eyes. I've been up a little while now, and although the haziness is lessening the headache is worse. I don't have the patience to deal with him right now. He's eyeing the beanie, tapping the controller against his leg. "Laci is stopping by."

He scowls. "I didn't say Laci could come over."

"Oh, she's returning a sweater," I reply, walking to the door. His eyes don't leave my hat. Does he remember what happened to make the gash? Does he even care?

He runs a finger over his lips, chapped and dry. His eyes are unfocused and I can tell he's annoyed that I'm going to go out. He's been like this more and more the past few weeks. "I didn't say-"

"She's probably already outside," I explain, hoping he lets it go. I don't want to wait around for Laci to pop upstairs instead.

He's either drunk or too involved with the game to push it. Shrugging, he sits back down, shooting me one more disapproving glare. I can just make out someone shouting through the headset. "Just be quick."

The game is all-consuming as his gaze shifts away from me, and it's like I'm not even there as he goes back to combat. I shake my head, ignoring the throb that follows, and slip out the door.

We live on the second floor of the complex, and getting downstairs in mid August is easy enough. I spot Laci's car pulling into the lot as she flips me off, pulling in beside the curb. "I planned on coming up!"

"That would be silly," I say, trying to laugh it off. She rolls up her window and shakes a finger at me, pointing to the passenger door.

She's going to be difficult to get rid of. I almost ignore her, but my head is killing me, so I give in and slide into her car. "Laci-"

I stop when she starts driving, completely ignoring me. My hand is still on the door that I've barely gotten closed. "Buckle in."

"Excuse me?"

She points to my hat as she circles the lot. "You're bleeding."

My fingers freeze, letting go of the door handle. I have half a mind to get out, my thoughts flying to Liam. Stilling, I wait a beat before flipping her visor down to find the mirror.

She's right. There's a line of blood from the hidden gash. My bandage must be soaked through, or I opened it up again with all the movement. I brush the streak away, noticing it isn't an excessive amount compared to the gash itself and slowly turn back to her.

Laci's eyes are on fire as she turns out of the lot. "I'm reporting him."

"No, you're not!"

She gives me a look, hands tightening on the steering wheel. "Are you fucking kidding me, Myla? It's obvious something happened. You don't remember calling me, you've been acting weird all evening, you won't let me go upstairs, and you're bleeding."

"You're reaching," I say. It's all quite speculatory, considering I was fine at work. I knew Liam was upset from the last few days, but I try to keep it hidden. The only coworker who's specifically caught on is David, and he's getting too close to home. Laci has her own suspicions, but for the most part we don't discuss it.

Mainly because I refuse to.

"You need to turn around," I snap when she heads for the highway. We live a few minutes apart, but the highway is a straight shot instead of winding streets. I pick at the door, starting to get nervous. "I didn't talk to Liam about leaving."

"So you discussed whatever mark he left on your head?"

I press my lips together. Of course we didn't. I just need to get back before he gets upset. "Not exactly-"

"You're coming to my apartment," she claims, merging as the passenger seat belt light starts beeping. I hate it, but my hands find the buckle to silence the alarm. "We're reporting this. And we're calling Anita and-"

"No," I cut in, feeling my fear spike. Liam would go feral if I reported something. The mark on my ass is a dim memory compared to the throb in my skull. I don't want to explain any of this to anyone. "I'm not reporting anything, Laci. Pull over or I'll jump."

I just want to go home and sleep. Not annoy Liam and not do anything else to make this headache worse.

At least if I jumped I could blame the gash on hitting the concrete, but getting killed isn't on the agenda. I need to get back so I can talk to Liam when he's in a better mood. I have to know why everything is hazy and I'm missing hours of time.

"You're not going to jump. If you won't stay you can at least come back and let me clean the cut. Make sure it isn't anything serious." It's fairly dark now, but I can see the sadness and anger across her face in the lights of her dashboard. "I don't like this."

Once more, my mind flickers to David. I can't help but think he'd disagree with everything Liam might have to say, but maybe they are just different people. Different types of Doms.

Liam sees the need for more correction. More reinforcement. David thinks he's too heavy handed. They aren't the same.

I must have hit my head hard. I can't focus. David should be far away in my mind.

But I do want to clean my head better. Laci has a bunch of stuff at her place. I can let her clean the cut and be back before Liam is off his game. I can do this.

Nodding, we drive in silence, Laci's judgment suffocating the car. I try not to think of what she'd say about the truth, much less what she would do if she knew about my sex life.

David is there in my head once more, and I shove him far away. This is something I'll never share with him.

6 DAVID

Myla isn't here today. Called in sick I guess. Laci is gone too, so I'm starting to think they took a girls day.

Whatever. I have a buttload of work, and within the first twenty minutes of my day (after being an hour late) I've already stopped two major disasters before trial. Myla would distract me all day, and I need focus.

I did manage to wipe the security tape that watches our section. Phil showed me once when we were here late one night on a case, telling me this is how he gets away with sleeping with his assistant. I wrinkled my nose and stuck it out, but now I know how to do this. I don't need evidence floating around the office that somethings going on between me and Myla.

The building itself has some security cameras, but these were installed by the partners. I sneak in and out of the security space without suspicion, and hopefully no one questions it.

I don't even make it through the first half of the day before things go up in flames. Dad keeps blowing up my phone since last night about his stocks. They are worth double right now and he wants to share pointers on the market. I silence his messages for now, hoping to get some uninterrupted work done.

That goes out the window when Laci appears from nowhere, in sweats and a messy bun. I've never seen her so out of sorts. She storms into my office like she owns the damn place, *still* wearing those tall heels she likes, and jabs a finger my way. "Are you dicking my best friend? Cause you ain't in her phone but I know I heard her moaning here the other day and I'm not putting up with another jackass."

"For fuck's sake Laci," I snap, getting up to slam the door closed. The file girl Kathy and one of the associate attorneys both stare at me, and now I've got a new problem to deal with later. "Ever heard of being discreet?"

"Are you?" She presses, arms crossed as she ignores me. Laci is nothing like her best friend. Myla dodges the problem, Laci cuts straight to the point. "Because I only came in here to pick something up. But I decided to come talk to you. I've been trying to pry things out of her all morning." She hesitates, strumming her fingers along a bare arm. "She mentioned you would have the same opinions I do. And I can't watch her go through this again."

"Opinions about what?" I scrunch my brow, staring at her. She's definitely not sick, and she's betting a lot on not getting in trouble for blowing off work. Maybe Myla is off doing the same. I don't like her hinting at things instead of just saying whatever is on her mind.

Laci presses her lips together, and I'm ready to toss her out of my office if she keeps this up. "You don't like Liam."

Scoffing, I cross my arms too, mirroring her stance. "Ballsy statement Laci. No, I don't like him. He can choke and die for all I care. I don't know why it matters."

Laci runs her hands over her face, shaking her head. She glares up at me, the height difference between us not quite as severe as me and Myla, and those heels of hers puts her close to my face. "I can't... God, Myla will have a fit when she hears I talked to you."

"Why?" I snap, the beginnings of unease creeping in.

She sighs, shaking her head. I'm getting more annoyed the longer she stands here dodging questions. "She... mentioned you. When I was questioning her."

Liam. He's about the only damn thing we've talked about mutually. I know they are close, but I doubt Myla jumped into a sex club chat when she's still unsure about it. I'm sure Laci isn't asking my opinion of him by chance. "About her boyfriend?"

"Ex," Laci snarls, and I'm surprised by the venom. "They aren't dating anymore. Or they won't be soon." She huffs out a breath, hands sliding to her hips. Her hair is damp, the remains of her body wash lingering in the air. She's more floral than Myla, the girly scent settling in the room.

I want to ask her what happened to cause a breakup, but that seems eager. I'd rather hear whatever this is from Myla. It has to be dire for her to finally think reasonably. "What do you really want, Laci?"

She lets out a breath, shaking her head. "I don't know. I wanted... I need to know you're halfway decent. Myla won't be at work for the rest of the week because of him."

Rage, blinding and overwhelming, sweeps through me. Something *had* to have happened with Liam. I've never seen her even come in late since starting. Missing days of work might just kill her. Shifting my weight, I glare at the blonde before me. "He did something, didn't he?"

Laci twiddles her thumbs, glancing down. "It's not my place to say."

I bite back a snarl. I don't need to be this damn angry. I knew her boyfriend was an idiot. It was a matter of time before things went too far, and at least it sounds like she's smart enough to finally end it. But the damage is done, and damn it all if I don't want to know what's happened. "So barging in here to ask if I'm banging Myla was a good idea?"

She scowls. "It's been a long night. I'm just on edge." She tilts her head to the side, staring. "Wait, how do you know he's hurt her?"

I'm doing a piss-poor job hiding my reactions. All I can picture is Myla panicking after her ex left, her neck angry and red, her eyes looking up at me like I'm some unknown outlier. I didn't force her, I never have, and she seemed genuinely surprised.

I don't like it. Unreasonably, I'm angry at Laci's statement, like it's a wonder that anyone could ever notice that something's wrong. She's surprised but not contradicting the question, and my skin burns at her silence. He did something bad enough that she's going to miss work. There's no way she stopped in if Myla's in good spirits just to piss me off. I dodge the question. "Why isn't Myla in today?"

"You should ask her yourself," she chirps, glancing around. She grabs a sticky pad and holds it out to me. "Give me your number. I'll give it to her. She was complaining about how she couldn't find yours." A coy smile dances across her lips. "I think she *wanted* to talk to you last night."

It's music to my ears, but I can hardly focus as my mind jumps around, thinking the worst. She's avoiding work, and she thinks calling *me* is a good idea.

I wouldn't do a damn thing right with her. I offered

to take her to the club so I could determine how far her kinks go, and if she agreed to submission I absolutely planned on fucking her for hours afterwards. What she could want to speak with me about can't be good. She likely wants to discuss whatever the hell Liam did and try to reason away the abuse. I can't humor her, not when I've been against him the whole time.

He didn't take care of her. He sure as hell wasn't pleasing her. And he didn't seem to notice at all when I sent her home in dripping wet panties.

A copy of the card I gave her is in my pocket. I brought it to taunt Myla with if she came to work today, reminding her that dumping the now-ex boyfriend is all I required to bring her to the club. Emotionally I don't know if she can handle it, but it's time to take off the kiddy gloves. Myla wants to submit, and the longer she lives in a delusional fantasy that she had a Dominant/Submissive relationship with Liam, the worse it'll affect her psyche.

I pull the card out of my pocket, watching Laci's eyes widen at the description. Scribbling out my number a second time, I close my hand over hers when she reaches to grab it, meeting her eyes. "It's for Myla. The club is invitation only. You're convinced she is no longer dating. If she's interested, she can text me."

Laci is stumped, and it's one of the few times I've seen her utterly speechless. Her eyes widen comically as she stares at the card, giving me an unrestrained once over as she looks between the card and my body. There's a hint of lust there, but nothing like when Myla eyes me. If anything, she's stunned, not turned-on.

Blinking, she gestures to the card. "You gave this to Myla? *Myla.*"

"Yes, I gave it to her. She was mad that I wouldn't take her while she dated someone else. Things have changed." I slip my hands into my pockets, enjoying the speechless look on her face. I want to pry about Myla some more, but it's time to show restraint. She could be adamantly against this, and I don't want to get my hopes up.

I need to see what he's done, the rules he's broken and ignored. Myla was in a fragile place before, and who knows where she's at now.

This is what happens when posers pretend to be a Dominant or Master. Without training and a good understanding of restraint and cues all you end up doing is hurting your Submissive or Slave. He's proven in the past that his hand is too heavy, and his control is nonexistent. Myla needs to understand the difference.

Laci hesitates, and it's on the tip of my tongue to ask if Myla mentioned what she wanted. The gaping expression she's wearing as she slowly slides the card into her pocket is answer enough. "You won't... you aren't going to hurt her?"

The question offends me. I don't know Laci that well, I hardly remember her in high school and the past two weeks I've tried to ignore her, but she should have a better vibe from me than that. "Of course I'm not going to fucking hurt her."

She lets out a breath like my answer is a godsend. "Good. I'm glad you're mad at me. Liam only ever told Myla to stop talking to me. He never defended her or promised shit." She bites her lip, eyeballing me before continuing. "I'm not entirely sure what happened. She's being secretive. Which is dumb since I dragged her away from her apartment with blood dripping down her face."

My hands ball up before I even realize it. What the *hell* is he doing hurting her so badly she bleeds? Everything I noticed the past few days was discreet, at least enough that she could cover up. The mistreatment had a line drawn. Blood dripping down her face is undisputedly abusive. I don't know what fantasy world Myla lived in, but he's pushed well past the Dom perspective straight into abuse. I grip the desk, leaning in closer to Laci. "What the fuck did he do?"

Her brows shoot up, and I'm sure she's surprised by the anger in my voice."I don't know, honestly. She gave us - me and Anita - bits and pieces of a story. She's dodging, which is totally in character for her. She kept asking about you, like I know something about your life."

Interesting. She might be more interested in the club than I realize, but I still have my concerns. She needs to rest and evaluate whatever happened before considering a sex club. The next question slips off my tongue before I think to stop it. "She's staying with you?"

Laci shrugs, her body turning to the door. "Yeah, for now. Liam doesn't know where I live. She might go to our friend Anita's later in the week. There's no set plan."

Of course there isn't. I should go check on her and see what the bastard did. In days she could look drastically different. By next week she can cover it up and lie about what happened. I don't want her to lie to me.

She has my number now, which changes things. If she's so eager, I need to wait it out and see what she says. The ball is in Myla's court, and I can't push her until I know what's going on.

It's part of my dynamic. If I'm considering taking her on as a Submissive, and her inexperience is shining through, then I need to be prepared to lead the way respectfully. We can do plenty of sinful, dirty things when the time comes. But her mental health and comfort has to be the priority right now if Liam just beat her up.

I need her address. I won't ask Laci now, not when our dynamic is so fragile. But I need the damn address. It's time Liam stops fucking around and learns the consequences of abusing his place in the relationship. Myla gave over too much trust to someone who didn't deserve her.

Silently, I watch Laci leave with a brief wave, letting my thoughts stew. He has to be handled. Uninformed and overconfident wannabe Doms cause issues in the community. Submissives and innocents get hurt due to carelessness. People are mentally and emotionally scarred from this. He can't be allowed to just get away with it. Not just for Myla's sake, but for everyone's.

~~~

I'm still fuming over the problem after work when Myla messages me. I don't need an introduction to know this is her.

Don't tell my friends about my sex life. The card isn't that discreet.

I chuckle, walking the short distance to the parking garage. The work day ended on a brighter note, even if I'm simmering with rage everytime Liam's face flashes in my head. My hands itch to wrap around his neck, not in the way I'd hold onto Myla, but in the way he held onto her.

I don't cushion my response. I'm more irritated than necessary and I blame Laci's half-assed story. *Don't lose something I give you unless you don't need to find it again.*

Her response doesn't come until I'm in my car. *I*
~~~

didn't think I would need to message you. I didn't see things going the way they did.

And what way is that, Myla?

I leave her message open as I hit the street, hating the rush hour traffic. There's construction up ahead, like there always is in Jefferson county. I'm stuck for a solid ten minutes, letting the bass in my car drown out my thoughts, before glancing at her response.

I don't want to get into it. Laci blabbed enough already. I'm not with Liam anymore I guess. That was your requirement. When can I visit the club?

I smirk, wondering if she ever realizes the situation she's getting herself into. I should go home, maybe work out to wind down, blow off some steam. But I want to see her, evaluate what he's done, see the damage myself. I want to feel her curves under my hands and ensure he didn't do anything else.

Shooting her a text, I wonder if she'll be ballsy enough to jump on it.

When can you be ready?

7 MYLA

Laci is certain I'm in over my head. Anita will have a fit when she hears.

But the moment I walk into the club, a sense of wonder envelopes me. David warned me ahead of time the scene can be overwhelming, and promised we would leave if I feel like I can't handle it. But I've waited days for this, since the moment he caught me fingering myself at my desk. I don't care that the security guards give us bemused smiles or that I'm twirling like a lunatic in this grand entranceway looking at walls dripping in expense.

It's beautiful. In my mind, sex clubs are on opposite ends of the spectrum; either gorgeous establishments with high class standards like this one, or seedy places in the back of a sex shop that needs to be deep-cleaned.

As a joke when we were in the Springs years ago, Laci and I stopped at a well known one. The second I touched something sticky and some dude started eyeing us, we bolted out of there.

This is nothing like that. The opulence is everywhere, from pretty glasses to clean carpets and walls draped in silks. There are several hallways, the very front dominated by this beautiful entranceway.

David gave me a rough breakdown on the drive over. He quizzed me about what happened with Liam, but I'm set on keeping the details to myself. I don't want to think about him tonight, or the gash beneath my new DIY bangs. I want to enjoy myself.

There are rules to follow here, which he drilled into my head three times. The weekdays aren't busy, and he said there's a training tonight so there won't be much focus on people coming in to play. He said if I'm not overwhelmed he'll show me the halls, the play rooms, even the shop.

I shift the top of my red dress, a little number I stole out of Laci's closet. You're supposed to dress nicely, so I had to find something appropriate. It's too loose in the top portion and tight at my hips, making it rise higher on my thighs than hers. It'll work, and I've placed a cute scarf around my neck.

She's got a buttload of questions about what I'm out here doing, which should be interesting to dodge when I get back to her apartment.

David eyes the scarf critically, but I don't want a bunch of people here seeing the marks and looking down on me, or worse, looking at David like he did it. He claimed as we walked in that he knows enough of the members but that isn't an issue, but I have my doubts.

Everyone is a judge. Just because they are open about sex here doesn't make them less judgmental.

"We're here to observe, Myla," he says, watching me curiously as I take in the luxury once more. He's still in the suit from work, jacket gone, the top buttons of his shirt open to show off a smooth expanse of skin that I want to run my tongue over.

It's been a wild twenty-four hours. Yesterday Laci abducted me from my apartment. As the hours went by I realized Liam might've drugged me, or at the very least gotten me drunk enough that I blacked out. I don't remember much of what happened from the time he handed me a glass onward, and I almost want to keep it that way. We must've had sex. My lingerie didn't end up in tatters by itself.

But while I was unconscious? It leaves a bitter taste in my mouth.

I accept a glass from a girl dressed in a racy suit, the bodice cut high on her thighs and the top just a hair lower than decent. She has a name tag, but doesn't stay to chat. The men working have similar attire, but they don't wear shirts.

This could be a strip club with the way the staff looks. The security guards all wear proper suits, but the inside is something else entirely. David's hand rests low on my waist as he guides me down one of the halls, into a wide open space.

My feet catch on the rug, which ends at a hardwood floor. There's an array of tables on one level, elevated platforms at the back, and a stage up towards the front. The room isn't full, and I guess that's to be expected during a weekday. There are perhaps a dozen people standing on the stage upfront, and my eyes zero in on them.

A training class. David made fun of me on the ride over, but he said he wants me to observe. There's no hard boundaries between us, and so far as I can tell he's trying to play it safe. He's more reserved than he's been throughout the week, but I don't want to consider why. Anything akin to pity will shred the eager bit of confidence I've got going on.

The heels are Laci's, and I can barely maneuver across the too-smooth floor to a table off to one side. Most spots are barren, though a few men and one woman sit in the crowd. I barely notice the glass in David's hand, eyes turning to gaze up at the stage and zone in on whatever the trainer is saying.

There's a lanyard around my neck. David has one too, which I think would get in the way at some point. It's deep maroon while mine is green. I guess green is what people wear during the trial period. Maroon is the color of a Dom, black is a Master, Red equals Submissive, and silver is for Slave. A matching color is clipped to the lanyard if you are partnered up so people don't bother you.

There are other colors too, but he didn't go further into the details since I was hardly paying attention when we walked in. David called sometime before we arrived to get me into the club, and I'll only have one more trial visit after this before I either partner up with David (and waive the fee if we're together) or pay up. It's too much to think about all at once. I clench the neck of my glass tight, wary to drink after yesterday's... whatever yesterday really was.

"It's important to use your words," the man onstage says. He's well-built with dark skin and muscles that ripple with every movement. He's in the same outfit I saw the bartender in, so I'm assuming he works here. "Trust is earned, not expected. If you do not communicate, your Dom and Master cannot fully understand your needs. To the same extent, it is their job to listen to what you have to say, and respect any hard and soft boundaries. Your dynamic is different than someone else's, and comparing will do you no good. If you aren't going to exchange a contract, verbal discussion is key in order to stay on the same page. It doesn't matter if it's scene play or a twenty-four/seven power exchange. You have to respect one another or this isn't a partnership at all."

I glance at David. The low lighting in here keeps the attention on stage, but I can't help wondering if he agreed to this on purpose. I decide to end a messy relationship, and somehow the club is having a training session on communication.

Of course it is.

He leans closer to me when he notices my attention, pointing to the stage. "That's Nate," he explains, pointing to the man that has been speaking. I realize I haven't seen Nate's face yet, his attention being firmly fixed on the people on stage. "He leads all the lessons regarding communication and permission. It's a big thing for him."

"Why?" I ask, genuinely curious. David has the same mentality, but he isn't leading a lesson on a stage about it.

"It's important when he regularly shares his Submissive."

I jolt; the idea was wild to me. He just chuckles and points to a pretty dusty-blonde girl to the side of the stage. I almost blush, for some reason both embarrassed and excited at her display. She isn't shy, parading around as Nate continues on about boundaries in nothing but a pair of pasties.

And I do mean nothing else, other than a collection of beautiful tattoos on full display and a pair of large sapphire earrings that dangle as she walks. There's no embarrassment in her steps, her bare feet quiet across the stage. She pauses beside a girl with short-cropped black hair, who's struggling to keep from fidgeting. Her hands lightly rest along her bare shoulders, saying something into her ear, and the woman relaxes.

Strange. Everyone up there is scantily clad, but it's obvious that Nate's woman commands the stage. People seem to calm when she pauses to show them a proper hand placement, or give an encouraging smile.

I glance at Nate's back again, noting the tattoo across one shoulder. He's obviously entirely at ease with her walking around like that, and the idea that he willingly shares her with strangers is too much for me to take.

I cross my legs, and notice David eyeing me again. His blue eyes study me for a moment before gesturing back to the stage. "Callie loves it. She's fully aware of what Nate wants, and they've been known to put on a show in the rooms. Sometimes on stage. She's always present when Nate leads a training session."

It's a bizarre concept for me. I pictured a BDSM club being all about suspension, blindfolds, and bondage. Not classes on permission and a model-esque chick with a why choose kink.

I'm not certain what I expected anymore. The club is lush, gorgeous, and gives me an odd sense of comfort in a scene that should be uncomfortable. Sipping the drink in my hand, I try to pay attention again.

There's a lesson on posing, a submissive pose I've never even seen. Knees spread, hands up, staring up from the floor, evidently at your Dom or Master. It should be erotic but I'm too keyed in on learning.

My eyes flicker around to the men in the audience, and the one woman. Not every person onstage is a female. There's three men, and I have no idea who is partnered up with who. There is one couple onstage; I can tell as the man continuously leans forward to whisper something in the girl's ear. She isn't as young as Callie or the woman sitting in the audience, but she beams every time the man leans away again.

David must notice my interest. "She has a praise kink. She's out of a longtime abusive marriage. Damien is onstage because otherwise she might panic. That's why training sessions don't happen on the weekends. That time is reserved for shows and demonstrations."

I stare openly at the couple, and he taps my hand as the lesson goes on. Gaping is rude according to the rules David rambled off, and I'm doing exactly that throughout the session. I try to absorb what Nate is saying, but between the array of people, the nearly naked individuals onstage, and the fact that I'm *sitting in a sex club*, I feel out of my element.

When the lesson ends, Nate turns to kiss the woman who assisted him, Callie. It's the first time I see his face, and I imagine his jawline can cut glass as quickly as those eyes can melt hearts. He's gorgeous. "Tomorrow's lesson is suspension ties. The class is limited."

He doesn't seem to speak to anyone in specific, and I watch as two of the women rush offstage to greet audience members. One is enveloped in a hug, another bows before a man who locks a chain around her neck. I stiffen, unsure why anyone would crouch down for that.

There's not even a collar. It's just that. A *chain*.

"They are a Master and Slave, Myla. This is part of their routine. Don't stare like that, it's rude."

I grip the glass and look away before either of them notices. Glancing down, I peer through my lashes as she crawls out on her hands and knees, looking utterly satisfied, the man whispering praise as they go.

Maybe I'm out of my element.

My eyes drift to the only woman viewer, and a

man from onstage who walks to greet her. She kisses him deeply, wrapping a collar around his neck before they leave together. He's still tugging on a shirt as they go, handling the entire training session in nothing but sweats.

Huh.

David rubs my elbow, and I follow him silently out of the space. The rush of excitement is slowly turning to confusion, and I have no idea what I feel now.

Is this what I want? To be trained publicly onstage and then collared when I return to my partner? Is that the price you pay for a Dominant/Submissive relationship?

My skin crawls at the idea of doing something like that with Liam. The flaws in our relationship are starting to shine through to me, and I'm regretting turning a blind eye for so long.

"You're overthinking," David says, leading us back towards the front. He veers to the left, hand still low on my back, and we enter a new space.

I know I'm gaping now. How could I not? His finger taps my jaw and I manage to close my mouth, looking around.

It's a pleasure room. Or space. Or maybe just a decorated hallway. There's a few plush chairs, and toys line the walls as we walk. Toys I've never even tried, from oversized dildos to knives, ropes, and things that I could never trust Liam with.

My eyes glance to the side, eyeing David. Can I trust him?

He's oddly quiet, letting me get a feel on my own. I study the wall, unable to move past the room. People use these on each other, here?

"Everyone is different," he says, walking just behind

me. His breath tickles the skin behind my ears, and I hadn't realized how close he's standing to me. "Each relationship or partnership follows a specific set of guidelines. Protocol. Some keep it very linear, some verge into romance and it works for them. Some only want to be taught."

Blinking, I turn to stare up into his eyes. There's no guard up for once, and I can clearly see the lust in his gaze. It's reminiscent of the hungry way he looked at me at the office, only now if he spreads my legs I'll let him have me.

I've wanted David to train me from the moment he brought this up, but everything happened differently than I expected. I wanted to learn to please Liam.

When would that have worked? He would've lost it if he ever found out about David, and my trust in Liam is gone now. The reasons behind my interest should vanish with it, but if anything I'm more compelled than ever to try this out properly.

It was never really about Liam's pleasure. It was always about mine. *I* needed more to get going. I craved someone who would take control and give me exactly what I need, even when I can't say it myself. Liam is self-assured, but he's never been after my pleasure, only his.

I've chased orgasms for months. The BDSM attribute was a last-ditch effort to get things to work out. So many couples online rave about the successes in their relationships and oftentimes their marriages. They worked together and formed something beautiful. Liam only looked at the possessive, controlling aspect of the partnership. He wasn't overly concerned about how I felt about things, and my fingers subconsciously touch the scarf around my neck.

David's fingers are at my sides, rubbing circles

along my hip bones. It's a soft touch, maybe even verging on the side of loving, and my eyes flutter at the tender feeling. The bruises on my hips don't bother me too much now.

His voice steals me out of the tranquil reprieve. "Take off the scarf."

My eyes snap open again, peering into his. He's focused, certain of the statement. I touch the material again, thinking about the ugly marks underneath. "David-"

"No one is around," he reasons, stroking his fingers along my neck. I lean into his touch before I can help myself. "And those that are here tonight know I didn't put the marks there. Let me see you."

For some reason, removing the scarf is more intimate than I realized. Baring a part of myself I'm ashamed of is frightening, even if David's seen it before. Now he has an even worse opinion of Liam, and the levels of shame that bubble to the surface threaten to throw off the careful mask of calm I've been working on since getting into his car.

I'm rattled. Liam was supposed to be someone I could trust. But he's taken advantage of me, and he doesn't care if I'm responsive or not to get what he wants. My fingers shake, reaching up to clutch at the black material.

He catches my hand before I can pull, leaning in. "I don't like it around your neck because *I* would never place it there. I would use this to tie your hands in front of you, so I can watch you fidget while I slide my fingers up your thigh. This dress barely hugs your ass, and I've had my eyes on you the entire night."

Good lord, he's not making it any easier to focus,

but his praise is a needed distraction.

Flicking the material, the loose knot comes away easily through the silken fabric at his touch. “It’s just strong enough to restrain.” He slides it gently off my neck, and the material is so much more sensual when it’s gliding between his fingers. He drags it down the bare space between my shoulders, and my skin lights up at the touch. “If I could ball it up it might make a halfway decent gag, but I won’t take away the sight of you gagging on my cock first.”

My eyelids flutter again, nearly closing. I can’t even focus on my exposed neck now. I thought he'd be ashamed to waltz around with the rings around my neck, but he doesn't seem to view them the same way I do.

“I could tie your hair back so you can give me a nice, sloppy blowjob,” he breaths, his fingers playing at the base of my head. I stiffen and he moves on, fleeting thoughts of Liam’s punishing grip dancing through my memories. “Because I want to see you be my little mess. You can mouth off all you want to at the office, but here, you'll listen to me. The only reason your mouth should gape is if it’s waiting to take my dick down your throat.”

I moan, and I’m stunned this is getting to me. I’m not even that fond of head. It’s cruel in my mind’s eye, and although Liam claimed I was wonderful I didn't enjoy it.

David presses closer to me, and I can feel his hard length pressing into my stomach. His free hand rests along my back, keeping me upright. “I don’t know how wide that boytoy of yours stretched your mouth, but your jaw will hurt when I’m finished with you. I can’t wait to feel you struggling to take me, Myla.” His finger swipes my lower lip, the scarf in his hand trailing over the exposed skin above my breasts. “But I know you’d learn how to swallow my cock like a good girl."

I need him to stop talking and start touching. Grasping his shoulders I shift my legs so I can straddle one of his, pressing up onto the balls of my feet to reach his lips.

I haven't kissed David before, but kissing always happens at the beginning of sex, at least in my experience. I barely manage to place my lips against his before he steps back, leaving cold air between us.

A hard dose of reality smacks me in the face, and I've never felt this stupid. He's eyeing me from a foot back, twirling the scarf in his fingers.

"I'm not doing anything with you tonight Myla," he clarifies, pocketing the scarf. I watch it go, unreasonably sad to see it disappear. "Not after the last day you've had. This is a demonstration, nothing more." His smirk is back, eyeing me all over again. "And a teaser. If you are committed to this, and really want to learn, I'm willing to train you. But I train fully. It's a lifestyle to me, to a certain degree. I won't meet you here five days a week. You'd stay at my house during the duration of training, so you can learn exactly how I like my Submissives."

That knocks me back into place. I'm stunned, and I know he can see it. I'm not sure what I expected David to say tonight, but flat out refusal and rigid guidelines weren't what I had in mind.

I'm still basking in the beauty of this place, getting caught up in something I may or may not be ready for. I wet my lips, unsure what to say.

Training. I don't know how the word makes me feel. All those people onstage were training, but what are their lives outside of this? Do they go home and live vanilla lives or do they keep it going all the time?

I can't fathom how you turn it off, like the flip of a switch. My skin burns all over and other than watching a demonstration, and listening to David put all of Liam's dirty talk to shame, I can't imagine just switching in and out of rolls like that.

My indecisiveness must seal the deal. He gives me a somewhat strained smile, nodding his head to the space behind me. "Come on, I'll show you the rest of the place before we go."

Following along, I find it difficult to focus on the tour. There are some private rooms, more toys, and when we loop around I discover there's a flight of stairs up to the roof, as well as a flight down to more private rooms and something called a chamber. It's for darker play, a setup I guess makes sense at a place like this, but none of it affects me.

His words bang around in my head, from the breathy seduction to his admittance. We never spoke of rules and guidelines, he only ever hinted that he's into the same things I am.

But training, at his personal home? It's almost too intimate to even humor. We are work colleagues, and school rivals, nothing more. I don't think David even gave a damn about my existence until this week.

What would staying with him even entail? He won't kiss me, so how could we -

"I thought you learned something from the stage demonstration," David sighs, and I realize we've come full circle back to the entranceway. "You have to speak up about your thoughts Myla. I'm not a mind reader. I don't know nearly enough about you to figure you out."

I hesitate, subconsciously touching the wound at my neck as we walk past others to the door. No one really pays attention, but I'm still on high alert. The cuts are exposed and I feel vulnerable.

My answer doesn't come until I reach the car. "I don't know how I feel about having to live with you for this. We didn't discuss it."

"No, you thought you could date someone and learn elsewhere. This is different. Even if you're only here to learn, you're still entering a partnership. Trust is sacred between a Dominant and Submissive. If you can't trust me to learn and follow your limits, and I can't trust you to set them and believe in me when I give you a parameter, this won't work."

All that does is fuel my vault of questions. "How do you figure out my limits?"

"You tell them to me." He turns the key as I slide down into the passenger seat, welcoming the heated seats after the crisp evening air. "In black and white. If you're still learning your limits we build from there. But most people have hard limits that set the endgame."

"Such as?"

I can see his eyebrow cock up in the streetlights, and I take it as a good sign that he appreciates me talking back. "Blood, taboo, anal, breath play-"

"Ah!" I cut in, surprised he can just rattle off an entire list. That's more than enough possibilities for me. I rub my legs together, thinking it over in the silence. Some of those things I don't like right away. Others I have no idea.

"You aren't expected to answer the questions tonight Myla. You have plenty to think about. There's a reason I won't fuck you without a discussion." He shoots me a look as the light changes to red ahead of us, and my body is still twined to go. My core isn't on fire, but

I'd be down to keep going. Too bad he's set on getting an answer first. "You need to consider this carefully. I won't do something you don't want. But I also have my requirements you would need to meet for the duration of your lessons. Think it over."

"And what, I just text you when I have an answer?"

He smirks as we pull onto Laci's street, and I must've been more lost in thought than I realized. "You can show me. Actions speak louder than words."

I'm thrown off as he pulls into the parking lot. "What am I supposed to show you?"

"You'll think of something Myla, I know you will. You're smart." He parks beside the curb, turning off the car and getting out. I'm almost too flustered to realize what he's doing as he comes around to my side, and I scramble to undo my buckle and open the door. He still catches the frame and pulls it open for me, closing it in my wake.

He's charming when he wants to be. Another disarming attribute from David. I wave my hands around. "I can head up from here."

"I'm walking you to your door," he states, gesturing for me to lead the way. I don't bother fighting him, and begin the trek up three flights of stairs in these monstrous heels. If he didn't come up I'd kick them off, but having him walk just behind me spurs me to keep them on. Laci did joke that a great set of heels gives your ass a little extra lift.

Liam never walked me up to anyone's door. That thought lingers with me until I'm there, turning to thank David.

He catches me off guard, drawing me in for a hug. I thought maybe he wasn't affectionate when he dismissed my kiss, but the possessive look in his eyes keeps the words in my throat. "I'm serious Myla. Think it over. It's not a one night stand. It's a commitment and a level of trust and understanding. If you aren't ready for it after your breakup, don't push. It won't end well, it never does."

I scowl up at him."I'm capable of making my own decisions, thanks."

David shrugs like it really doesn't matter to him. "I'm sure you are. But that's part of my role as your Dominant. I take some of the stress and worry off of your shoulders by handling certain choices for you." His lip twitches, and he hesitates before speaking again. "I'm ready to teach you. But you have to be ready for me."

Damn that sultry voice. The words tumbles out of my mouth before I can think twice about it. "I am ready."

He smirks, leaning in closer to speak into my war. "When you're *truly* ready, you'll call me Sir."

8 DAVID

True to her word, Laci keeps Myla out of the office the rest of the week. It's a tedious pain for me; I've grown accustomed to shoving off work that's too time-consuming onto her desk. But she won't be in, and I'm starting to realize it's kind of a dick move on my part.

I keep thinking about her, her responsive little cries and curvy ass. She looked decadent spread out at her desk, and even better sitting on mine. If she didn't have issues with her ex, I'd have brought her to the club sooner.

I'm careful about who I introduce to the lifestyle. Rarely I meet someone there, and I usually bring my partners in. I haven't had a partner in some time, and Myla is becoming more and more alluring with each passing day.

But she's complicated, and it'll require finesse. Laci eyes me critically all throughout Friday when she's back in, and I wonder what terrible things she's picturing.

Myla is willing, supple, palpable. Laci looks like she'll jump at the chance to yell at me for bringing her best friend somewhere like that.

It's ridiculous, but I can see her doing it.

I don't trust Liam, and I dislike that Myla is skating around the issue of what happened to send her running. She's agreed to nothing yet, and it is not my job to dig and pry into her life unless I'm her Dom. Right now, we're only on speaking terms.

Still, that little number Laci gave her was a straight up sin. Her feisty best friend knew exactly what she was doing when she picked that red dress out. I saw the snide look in her eyes when Myla disappeared through the door to her apartment.

I want to be her Sir. Before it was an amusing idea, and the fun of corrupting someone held merit, but it's more than that now. Everything is twisted, and I need her to feel how good she truly can with a partner that cares.

And not just any partner. She will be mine. I've caressed her lips too many times to give her up without a taste. The kiss I pulled back from taunts me all day. She's like a candy, tempting me to take a bite each time we're close. Her submission will be hard work, and I know there will be obstacles from her past, but it's all part of the dynamic.

D/s should be a pleasure, not a chore. I tell my best friend Emilio to keep me posted about Liam's whereabouts. His background as a private security guard makes him ideal for this, and all I had to do was mention Liam's mistreatment to get him to hop on board and help. He's been sending me updates every day.

Myla's latest message flashes across my phone screen, successfully distracting me from the little work I've managed to complete today. *I don't know how to feel about giving you full control of me. I still want to do things I prefer. I like reading, and cooking, and binging cooking shows and bad reality TV. Freedom is important to me.*

At least she read the list I sent her about different types of partners. She doesn't want a harsh Dom, just someone firm. I knew that before she said anything. I've no interest in giving her a list of things to do or keep her on target. Hard Doms work for some dynamics, but Myla wants to be finessed, not repressed. If I allot her a certain amount of time each day for her own pleasures she will revolt, but I never expected her to go for that.

It's not her style. And it's not mine either. All she wants is real sexual gratification. *I'm not your boss Myla. I would only be in charge of your pleasure and withhold if you've been bratty.*

I like having these conversations in person, not where they can be misinterpreted through a text. But she's hiding now, fear or shame playing a part in her hesitation. I saw the interest shining in her eyes the entire time we were out together, and watching her gleefully check out the toys at the club did nothing for my aching dick. She's on a roller-coaster, and as fun as it would be to fuck some sense into her I don't like where things left off with the boyfriend.

Something happened, and neither woman feels like telling me what. I'd throw caution to the wind, but the red marks around her throat remind me Liam did that. I will do nothing to remind her of him. Still, I need answers about the gash in her forehead. Even those new bangs of hers can't hide the wound.

Laci catches my arm on the way out at the end of the day, and I'm almost worried that we aren't behind closed doors. Discretion is not her strong suit. "I know Myla's going to pretend everything is alright when you go out again, but it isn't. Her ex is blowing up her phone every day, and he's making all these threats. She pretends it doesn't affect her but I know better. She's upset with how he's reacting."

A burst of anger shoots through me, simmering just beneath the surface. Guys like him hold on longer than necessary. Of course the manipulation would extend past a break up. The hold he has is strong, and it's something else that needs to be broken before we can progress. "Did you suggest she tell him off?"

She gives me a cold stare as we march to the elevator. We're actually leaving on time, and a few of our coworkers give us interested looks. Laci is at least smart enough to not say something incriminating until we're out on the street headed for the garage. "Yes, a lot. He's trying to ping her phone to find her."

Of course he is. I'll mention that tidbit to Emilio, but I'm certain if it worked he already would've told me. "Talk to her. You know her best."

Laci nods, but she's jumpy this afternoon. Her hands grip together in an unusual show of apprehension, and she's gazing around like she expects to see someone, probably Liam. "I have. She doesn't want to be mean, which is ridiculous after-"

She cuts off, and I guess I won't be getting a story. I observe her as we walk down the block, and she's definitely on edge. Her shoulders are tense beneath the light sweater, and her heels tap restlessly against the concrete with each step.

She's jittery.

"Myla said something about staying with you."

Ah, here we go. I didn't expect Myla to bring it up so soon, but if she's mentioned it to Laci she's at least considering. With her little ex dicking around I'd rest better knowing she's safely at my house.

Preferably in my bed. Wrapped around my cock. "Does that make you worried?"

"No. Not really." Her response is delayed, which is weird since she wasn't like this upstairs. Her nerves are on end, and if I didn't know better I'd swear she's walking closer to me. "You can't be as mean as Liam."

Bold. Laci doesn't truly know me, neither does Myla. It's a blind leap of faith. I keep one eye on her as we walk, wondering what could possibly have her so tense. "You're certain?"

Laci's gaze hardens, the anxious little nerves slipping away as she straightens her shoulders to glare. "Positive. If I ever have to see him again I'll wring his neck myself."

~~~

When I do hear from Myla, it's barely an hour after the office closes. She sends a message that catches my immediate attention. *I want to start training.*

Full training?

Yes.

I wait to see if she'll catch on, but nothing else comes through. We'll have to work on it if she's serious. I'm not going to bring it up over a message, but a Sir tacked on at the end would do wonders. We aren't there yet, and I need to tread lightly.

Casting off my dress shirt, I remove the rest of the stifling work uniform. My bare feet pad across the carpet in my room, I can get away with tailored jeans at the club, and that's all I want to wear.

Myla is the focal point of my days this past week. I should exercise some restraint, but the side that craves her beneath me is impatient. If her ex used sex as manipulation, the best way to fix that is showing her all the spots where he fucked up.

I need a contract with her, or at least a well-worded outline. Myla is hesitant and needs clear representation of what getting into any sort of relationship with me
~~~

entails.

I hate surprises, and I'd like to avoid freaking her out the first day.

I told you an in-person offering is best. Texts are ambiguous. You could be lying through your teeth.

I haven't had the chance to see you! When Laci is gone, Anita is here. They don't trust me to not run back to Liam,

Another issue. She'll think of no one but me when we're together. Before I get a message out she's typing again.

What about the club? Laci said I can borrow another outfit to match the atmosphere. I couldn't get to the office and I don't want to wait until Monday. I don't have my car here. There's no way I can just come visit you.

I smirk at the phone. At least she's being straightforward. My instinct is to go grab her and bring her here, so I can start removing whatever influence Liam left behind. But she hasn't proven her devotion yet, and if she's going to back out and have second thoughts I need it to not be on my bedroom floor. It'll ruin the image of anything we might have together.

The club is a madhouse on Fridays. Saturdays are overwhelming because of the shows. I already planned to go there to unwind; seeing Myla will be an added bonus. There will be infinitely more people around, and she won't be able to shy away. The excess of people could be stifling.

Perfect. She can see how others react, and decide for herself how she would like to proceed. If she's willing and ready I'll bring her back here. But only once she's ready.

I'll pick you up in thirty.

~~~

Myla is confident in an emerald dress tonight, the top cinched lower than yesterdays, with a sheer overskirt adding some non-existent length. This time the scarf at her neck is loosely tied, like she knows I'll be removing it.

The club is packed, and her gray eyes zip around as a waitress hands off two flutes of champagne for us. I don't like champagne, and Myla is too busy taking it all in again to pay attention.

There's more life in her eyes, and an eagerness as we walk. The stage is barren tonight; unless it's close to the holidays shows rarely take place any day aside from Saturdays. I walk her to the bar where Nate is working, and she does a double take as he reaches out to shake my hand.

I've known Nate a long time, longer than this club. There are rules to follow, and if Myla wore a collar or had a ring connected to her lanyard he wouldn't touch her. She's still carrying around the visitor color. This is the last time she can come without being on her own membership, unless I take her on as a partner.

My eyes flicker up to the office above the main level. Vinny watches everything with a keen eye, and his wife is well-known for keeping track of any outliers in the club. They run a tight ship here. There's a reason the club isn't open to just anyone. Safety throughout is key. They'll know when Myla's trial period ends.

I glance back at Nate, who is busy looking between us. Something passes in his eyes that I can't distinguish. "Callie busy tonight?"

He laughs and makes my standard scotch, nodding briefly to Myla. He's going to knock out my drink limit
~~~

for the evening before we do anything. There's no getting drunk here. "I sent her off to play with Tyson. She's restless today."

Glancing over my shoulder, I spot the duo. Myla follows my gaze and spins back just as quickly, chugging her champagne as her cheeks color. I resist the urge to smirk. Thursday was tame. The club has a whole new life on the weekends.

Tyson and Callie are right in the middle of play, which is what I expected to hear from Nate. When he does share her with others, it isn't some bullshit romantic serenade. The couple is in the middle of going at it madly, her blonde hair knotted in his hand, the mask she's wearing obscuring everything but her nose and lips. Not a look I care for, but Callie is big into degradation. Her ass is red, and there's one or two members watching to pass the time, and a newbie off to one side that looks like she's going to pass out at the sight. Not everyone who visits appreciates the lifestyle.

Callie's pasties are purple tonight, covering the new bars I know she put through her nips sometime recently. Nate mentioned last week they were bothering her. It's the only reason she would choose to cover up.

"You must be new," Nate laughs, nodding to Myla as she fans herself. She not so discreetly keeps peeking over her shoulder to watch, like she's suddenly embarrassed. It's not a bad thing; Callie doesn't care and Tyson likes putting on a show. Her eyes zero in on him again, and I glance back at Nate.

I don't care if she watches. Observing is a good way to know limits she hasn't tested yet. Nate catches my eye, amused as she stares at the scene. "Her drink?"

I don't know a damn thing about Myla's tastes,

except she'll drink champagne like water when nervous. She's still hyper focused on the view, paying us no mind. "Rosé ."

The papers in my pocket burn, and I need to take her to one of the rooms. I didn't mention bringing a contract, but I don't want to scare her off either. Contracts mean commitment, and I expect a level of commitment to see this through. Not the all-consuming control she has on the brain, but we need hard limits mapped out. If she refuses to tell me about Liam, I need to know where consent ends. Undoubtedly, there will be things not discussed that come up. I just hope an outline will help her breathe a little bit easier.

She's still enamored with the scene, her wine an afterthought as she observes. Her breathing is heavier, eyes a little darker.

Good. A healthy dose of lust will help her relax before we talk. If she's too uncomfortable reading the contract with me I suppose I can call on Vinny or Jo, but we're both attorneys. We know how to read the fine print

And I'm pretty sure Myla will read every detail.

Nate is off working again as the space fills up, couples and groups separating as the night picks up. Myla glances my way and I smile at her, running my fingers over her bare shoulder blades. I'll give her another moment before it's time to go.

My gaze shifts to Emilio. He's chatting with Jo, a tall, modelesque woman who knows her worth. There's a reason she's married to the owner. They chat by the doors, Emilio swishing the drink in his hand. No updates since earlier today, and I doubt her ex even knows this place exists.

Myla catches my attention, following my line of

gaze. Emilio is intimidating, which serves him well working for his father's security division. We've been friends since we were kids. My dad always hired out security, and Milo regularly came with his father on jobs.

He's taller than I am, wider at the shoulders. Other than work, his only pastime is working out. He does side work investigating when people contract him, like me. Although he's been a member here for a long time, he's only had one Slave.

None since. It was hard when she passed.

Myla drags me out of my thoughts with a question. "What does that do?"

I look over at Callie once more. She's opening a package, more members looking on now. I recognize it immediately.

"It's a discreet vibrator," I say, leaning in closer to her. Callie is completely into it, audience or not, as Tyson stands behind her, spreading her cheeks. She's still red from his hands, and at some point he had put the collar around her neck. She's opening the box by feel with the mask on, handing it back blindly without seeing. He pushes her forward hard enough her knees slide off the couch into the floor. His hand is in her hair, keeping her head up as they slide off. He shoves the toy between them with little grace and she moans, as he slaps her ass again.

Myla stiffens, glancing towards Nate. He peeks up as he works, but is unfazed. If Callie is uncomfortable, he'll know. He'd be over the bar already. "Isn't she-"

"She's alright, Myla. I told you, she likes degradation. Tyson is someone she's often with. Callie has absolute control of where this ends if he pushes her too far."

She's unconvinced, and it's the first sign of doubt

I've seen. Callie cries out, but I'm watching Myla now and not the couple.

Her fingers around the glass grip too tightly, and her breathing is uneven. The lust in her eyes is still there, but fear is creeping in. Something about it sets her off.

I planned to take her to a room, that was the point of coming here. But if she's going to have a breakdown, it'll ruin the mood. And I don't need her thinking I don't care about her comfort.

Setting her glass aside, I shoot Nate a look as we leave. "Let's get some air."

The rooftop is popular. This building is a high rise, so neighboring skyscrapers can't see onto the roof. There are people up here, but also a hot tub and seating, and I drag her to the farthest set of chairs, pushing her to sit down. "Breathe."

She nods, and even in the mood lighting I see her embarrassment. People always assume the lifestyle flip comes naturally. That you can just embrace your dark side and run free, but it's actually an adjustment, especially when you harbor past trauma.

Even if she isn't looking at it that way, it is. *Trauma.* Liam was an ass, and it'll affect how she moves into this mindset.

After a few breaths, she gives me a shaky smile. "Thank you."

I nod stiffly. "No one here is going to be hurt unless they wish to be. The club offers a safety net of security. Guards are in each area, whether or not you've noticed them. Private rooms have cameras. It's to ensure no one breaks the rules."

"What are the rules?"

I shrug. "It's different for each couple. When you

join, there's a form with preferences you fill out. When you take a partner, you fill it out again. We don't see each other's forms. The idea is that we've discussed our dynamic prior to signing. Doms and Subs have a specific set of expectations within their own dynamic. Masters and Slaves often have a greater reach than that. But if you consent to pain, you have to have safe words in place. Many Doms learn, and should learn, the language of their Subs. Sex is an experience. You learn hard limits and boundaries through experiences. The goal is to never need the safe word. It's there if it becomes too much for one party. Safe words are a way to stop a scene or play before someone is hurt. But some couples enjoy pain play. Things like blood, knives, even the risk of guns. Consensual force like CNC. But anything risky like that requires notifying the club beforehand or security will step in. There are only two couples right now who don't have a safe word, and they are intense to watch. Sometimes too intense for me."

She looks less on edge, rubbing her hands along her thighs. It's not cold in August up here, but the breeze ruffles the edges of her dress. "Would you ever have to safeword me?"

I chuckle. "I would be surprised. I don't think our limits are the same."

Myla nods, smoothing the dress in place. "If we agree to this, I'd have to sign forms here too?" She's biting into her lip. "I don't want to pay for a membership."

"You won't. We would be partners so long as you require training. The only reason we would sign here is if you want to play at the club."

Her head is bobbing before I've finished speaking. "Yes."

My dick twitches at the admission. I want her in my house, but I don't know if she's ready. If she's even willing to try it out tonight, I'm willing. We can test boundaries before signing anything with the club, but if we intend to make a habit of it, Vinny will require signatures. He likes things in order.

My fingers skirt up her arm, brushing at the little strap along her shoulder. It topples off to expose more of her chest than I think she realizes, but Myla is only focused on me. I shift in my chair, feeling the heated lust return. It's only been a few days yet I feel deprived of her. "You're ready to learn?"

"Yes."

Smirking, my fingers slip up her shoulder to cradle her head. Leaning in, I watch her eyes follow my every move. "Yes, what?"

I need to know she can submit. This won't work for me if she doesn't want to be mine. I gave her my guidelines before. She knows what I have to have to agree.

Her lashes flutter, her fingers brushing over my chest. "Yes, Sir."

Perfect.

I drag her to me, kissing along her jaw. I don't go for her lips, because then she can't observe around us. My hand slides up her dress, wanting to touch her again. My cock throbs when she arches into me, and it's all I can do to keep from lifting that dress up.

The contract burns in my back pocket. There's no rule that she has to sign first, only if it's continued. My brain wants me to stop and hand it to her, but the rest of me needs to feel her.

I don't get to overthink it. She's bolder than I expect, or maybe just too horny to care, but she reaches across us to grip my aching hard on over the tight fit of my jeans.

I moan. She's going for exactly what I had in mind, but I don't want her in charge now; maybe another time I'll let her guide. Clasping her hand with mine, I rub along the length.

She moans in response. My fingers find purchase in her hair, swallowing the sweet sound with a kiss. She tastes better than I expected, the mix of her wine and her lip balm sending all thoughts south. The hand on my cock picks up speed, and I'm plenty happy to help her.

Giving her freedom of control might help, but I'm still in charge. I swirl my tongue along her lips, gaining easy access as I push the other side of her dress off.

She leans back a hair, speaking against my lips. "David-"

"Red," I growl, dragging my fingers up to push the top away from her breasts. "If you don't like something, say red. I will check on you if you seem uneasy. If I miss something and you want to stop, say red."

Myla leans back, flushed cheeks a brilliant contrast to the emerald dress pooling beneath her breasts. The stars popping out overhead compliment the softness of her skin, and even the uncertainty in her eyes is alluring. "Promise?"

I catch her chin with my fingers. If I show her the contract now, the mood is gone. "I don't take advantage if you don't want me. All you ever have to do is tell me what you need and I'll answer. Your submission is given, not granted."

Her eyes shine, and I'm certain Liam told her the opposite. I expect her to keep asking questions but she's satisfied, leaning in to kiss me again. I keep a firm grip along her chin, mindful that I need to firm up on her terminology.

I tease along each hardened nipple, feeling out her reactions. I like my partners to be over-sensitive, and Myla's already there. She's eagerly responsive when I flick one bud, her back arching under my touch. The shyness from a moment ago disappears as she moans, and I press a hand to her mouth with a smirk. Her eyes shoot open again.

"Shh, darling. Just because we're high enough that people can't see doesn't mean they won't hear. Be a good girl for me, or we'll have to pick this up inside."

Wide gray eyes stare up at me, nodding a moment later. I like that she's ready and willing, and even the clumsiness of her delivery is sweet. She's eager to learn and that's what matters.

I hold her gaze, hands locking at her waist to pull her up out of the chair. She gasps when I set up on my lap, my dick pressed to her through a few thin layers of fabric. Her fingers grip at my shirt, and I let her hold on.

I'm not breaking out every toy in the rooms downstairs for one session. Training takes time. It's different from establishing a partner; you have to be willing to feel out and guide.

I've only ever trained if I intend to take the Sub as mine. It's not in my nature to train for the sake of it. Myla is my outlier, and I don't know what I will do with her when the training is over.

My eyes stay with hers when I lean forward to nip around her areola, and she bows in my lap. My other hand stays at her back as she pants, keeping her in place so I can glide my tongue over the sensitive spot before sucking, tensing my teeth over her nipple.

She's panting in my lap, and my hand digs into her side to keep from dropping her. She tenses a little and I relax my grip again. Her back flexibility is impressive, and I'll be using that. I release her with a pop, and she cries out.

"Doll, be careful, or I'll have to fill that pretty little mouth."

She moans again, and I wonder if she's tempting me. Her hips rock into mine as I repeat the action on the other side until her nipples ache, and when I release her, I grab the scarf that's come loose around her neck.

Myla didn't even notice, panting too hard on my lap. I slide the dress up until there's nothing between us aside from a pair of blue panties that I eye, loosely fingering her neck.

She liked it when I choked her before, but it could also be a trigger. Liam took terrible care of her. My fingers flex along her jugular and she leans into my touch.

But I want something from her first. She has to be a willing participant. "I can feel how wet you are for me darling. I'll spread that pretty little pussy for me soon so I can fuck you right. But you're going to do something for me first. I know you can be a good girl."

My fingers brush over her lips, and it's like she goes on autopilot. She's off my lap before I can say more, sinking to her knees on the unforgiving concrete. She fumbles to slide her knees apart, pressing her hands up to face skyward. It's the position she studied on stage earlier in the week.

Briefly, it reminds me of her crumbling when I grabbed her wrist. I like her eagerness but not the fear-induced submission. We'll have to work on the differences.

I run my fingers through her hair, and she's already reaching for my fly. I should make her wait, but the Dom in me is more interested in learning what she already knows. I can correct and change a different day. She isn't asking to stop yet, which is a good sign.

My fingers reach into her hair as she pulls down the zipper, releasing my aching dick. I've thought about her lips all week, and I'm curious what kinds of hidden talents she's been keeping to herself. "What a good girl. You know I want to feel your lips around my cock. Are you going to be good and take all of me?"

Myla bobs her head, and I catch her hand when she doesn't speak. "No. You'll respond to me when I praise you, just like we discussed."

Her eyes sparkle at the reprimand. She does want someone to take control. "Yes, Sir."

She's taking me in with her eyes, working her fingers down the length of my cock. Her eyes widen as she studies me, and I assume that means I've outsized her ex. It's not the first time that's happened. Her fingers wrap around me at the base, her middle finger and thumb not quite touching. Those expressive gray eyes of hers are widening again.

"You look worried, doll. Am I larger than that ex of yours?"

She bobs her head, catching herself, eyes flickering up to me. She's caught the mistake. "Yes, Sir."

She's fast to learn. "Good girl. Are you thinking about me spreading your lips to fit?" She nods, and I continue before she assumes it's a mistake to not respond. "Good. Because the first thing you'll feel from me tonight is my cock stretching your cunt wide to take me." Myla moans, and I grip beneath her hand at the sound.

"Open."

Her response is instant, the head of my cock pressing to her tongue. She doesn't need coaxing, lifting her head to accept as much of me as she can. Her eyes stare down, away from me the entire time.

I can feel her mouth stretching around me, struggling. She's not used to it. Her tongue keeps pressing against the head, which feels good, but it's in the way of my goal.

"Relax your tongue. It'll make your gag worse." I grip her hand gently, lifting her head. Her eyes look up and away again, and I hate it. I tug on her hair a little and she looks up again, sprinkles of fear in her gaze. "You'll look at me when my cock is inside that pretty mouth of yours. I don't care if your eyes are watering or spit is dripping from your cheeks. I want you just like this."

It's harder for her to fight and maintain my gaze. He must've taught her to not enjoy looking at him. Her tongue is in the way when I start pumping my hips. "Tongue, relax. If it's too much, tap my thigh and I'll stop. The more you overthink the less you'll enjoy."

I give her a second to argue, and when she doesn't take the bait I plunge straight down her throat. She gags on the intrusion and I stroke her cheek. "Breathe through your nose. Relax your jaw. Let me do the work. Just sit there like a my personal fuck toy."

She's more resistive, I wait to see if she'll surrender. Her eyes are watery and she's still gagging, but after a moment the tension in her shoulders lessons. She's not comfortable, but I don't see signs that she's quitting either.

"Squeeze my thigh if you're good, doll." It's instant, and I'm hoping she isn't the type to lie to avoid disappointment. "You can tap anytime it's too much."

Myla tries her best, but I don't think Liam had much to offer. She's gagging every time I move my hips, and though her hands fist on my legs she's not backing out.

Her eyes are watery, but there's the edge of fear when I pump deep into her throat. It feels like heaven, but the look in her eyes diminishes it.

She won't tap. I told her to let me know and she's not doing it. Her eyes struggle to stay with mine and it's instinctual to keep looking down. She's not going to tap and ask me to stop. He's either taught her to take it, or she doesn't believe I'll listen.

I let her up, watching her inhale sharply. Her eyes are still heavy with lust, but she's more guarded now as she looks up at me.

It won't do. She's not trusting me. It's exactly why I have a contract in my pocket, but my cock is aching now and I need a release. I'm thinking with the wrong head, and I don't want this to blow up in my face.

I pull her up and spin her around so she's facing out towards the rest of the roof. There's one or two people I recognize watching, I'm sure in part because of the ring around her neck, but several others are too busy with themselves. Her back stiffens as I pull the remainder of her dress to pool at her waist. Her nipples have pebbled up again between my mouth and the cool breeze and I brush my hands over them as I lean in to speak in her ear.

"You're beautiful this way," I say, pushing her legs apart. She's shaking against me, but I don't think it's fear. Her nails drag along the naked expanse of my thighs, her toes no longer brushing the ground. "Wet, wanton, willing. You took me so well down your throat. I've seen you waiting on me, wanting more. I'm going to teach you the skills your ex lacked."

She's breathing heavily, but there's no fight. There are security guards up here the same as everywhere else. Myla presses her ass back against my cock, and I smirk against the curve of her neck. The scarf is behind her, and I'll be needing it before we're through. The guards are only watching because of the wound.

My fingers play with the sides of her panties before sliding the slip of lace to one side, one long stroke from her clit back getting her to moan loudly again. With the scarf in my hand I ball it up and stuff it into her mouth until she gags, stilling. "It's only there to keep you from crying out when I stuff your sweet pussy full. You'll take all of me because you deserve it. You've more than earned your orgasm. And you'll cum when my balls hit that tight little ass."

She moans around the fabric, and I know I made the right choice. I rub her clit as I adjust her to take me, keeping a hand braced against her torso instead of knotted in her hair how I like.

It makes her too tense, and she needs to be relaxed to take me in one go. I should be nice and work in, but she's doing things to me without even trying.

My head pushes against her dripping entrance, and I drag her down my length all at once.

She cries out loudly, even over the gag. I slap a hand over her mouth to quiet the noise. She's *tight.* Tighter than I expect for someone having regular intercourse. Her ass is firm against me, the smallest tremor sending her whole body buzzing.

Did he just not bother to *ever* stretch her out?

Still I feel her walls contract around me, a rush of

heat hitting me again.

She takes instruction well. I told her when she would get to cum, and it was enough to *get* her to cum.

I give her a minute to adjust, gently bouncing her against me. She's not crying in pain, but her shoulders are tight again. I press a kiss to the space between her shoulder blades to calm her racing heart.

Eyes dropping as I wait, I notice something new. Myla doesn't wear anything with a low cut back, least that I've ever seen. There's two uneven marks on her mid back, and I drag my fingers over them as she adjusts. I can feel another mark against my groin, something raised and new and probably from this week. The two I stare at are nothing but raised, white lines.

Scars. Uneven little marks. They could be from anything.

But as I stare at them, I already know who put them there.

I wrap my arm around her torso again, holding her to me. I need to not stare at those while I fuck her or I'll only see red. My other hand slides along her throat, testing the waters.

She's the ideal trainee, willing and eager.

"You can tell me whatever excuse your ex made up for those marks later," I growl, unable to help myself. He's trying to leave his mark where it doesn't belong. "But when I am inside you, you think of only me."

Her muffled gasps fill the space around us, and she's moving her hips in time with my half strokes. She nods against my hand at her neck, and I wrap each finger around her throat as I increase the pace.

When we finish here, I'm giving her the contract. I won't risk one of the bystanders making a play.

She's mine.

Keeping my grip at her neck, I pump into her at a faster pace than before. I can't give her full strokes like I like at this angle, but it doesn't seem to matter. She's moaning openly around the scarf, either oblivious or uncaring about the small audience we've drawn.

I didn't mean to shove my cock in her up here, but she was in the right mindset to try, and I'm not arguing.

My arm lets go of her torso, giving her better mobility to arch and squirm while I fuck her. My hand drops to her sensitive, swollen clit again.

She likes praise, has a little kink for being told what to take. And maybe a hidden adoration for being told when she gets to cum.

And I'm going to test it.

Raising my hand, I speak into her ear so she's the only one to hear me. "I bet you dreamed of me slapping your needy clit after I got you off in the office. Let's do it again doll. You'll cum for me, now."

I slap over the skin and she's bowes up in my lap, lifting off my thighs. The hand at her neck lets go to press over her mouth again.

She's a screamer. But only for me. Her hips spasm around me unevenly, breaking the rhythm, and I pound harder into her as she comes undone on top of me.

I let her go as long as I can, before pushing her off my cock. It’s only for a moment, and I barely need my hand to reach the end. She rests on my thighs, free of my hands for the first time, and I mark her back, hitting each of those scars as I go. I barely have time to register the fresh welt on one of her cheeks, like he recently broke the skin there.

She sinks back into me, and I pull up her dress as a

barrier. I'd like to look passable when we leave. I kiss her cheek as she leans into my chest, one word slipping out of my lips.

"Perfect."

9 MYLA

I'm in a daze when David hands over the contract in his car. Embarrassment shot through me after the high of sex, but he was quick to make my insecurities vanish. I was halfway off his lap before he stopped me from leaving, fixing the straps of my dress, sliding my panties back into place, smoothing out my hair. The scarf he shoved in my mouth did little to keep me quiet, but even the makeshift gag was erotic. It's stuffed in my clutch after I told him to not throw it out.

He didn't wait for me to slide off his lap, wreck my knees on the concrete, and clean him up. He did all of it without question.

I thought BDSM involved rough men, strict rules, and toys. I've never given a lot of thought to being an exhibitionist. Liam would never even try, and I'm usually too shy.

But David made me forget we were out on a roof. Even turned to face the onlookers, I couldn't focus on them. His hands on my skin, his cock stuffed as deep in me as anything's ever been, I couldn't even tell you how many people were outside.

And the *orgasms*. I sound like a smutty fangirl in my own head cheering him on, but goddamn. I can't remember the last time Liam got me off even once, let alone *twice*.

The dress clings to my back, and it's probably just

nerves, but I swear I can smell his cum on me as we drive. I haven't read the papers he handed me, resting my head against the cool window, his jacket over my shoulders.

It's not cold. He didn't need to hand it to me. But he did anyway when he noticed I was uncomfortable passing all the people that watched us.

And it gave me such a thrill. I never pictured myself being bold enough to do that. I didn't think I would cum so hard from being told what to do either. I figured he'd tie me to a bed and spank me with paddles until I was officially trained.

This is nothing like I expected. And the toe-curling, heart-stopping orgasms are the cherry on top of my very decadent cake. I should be reading, I should be taking careful stock of what I've just done and how it's going to affect me.

I half expected to have a mental breakdown. The last time I *thought* I had sex was burned in my head, and I worried I'd forget where I was when David started playing.

David, however, is unforgettable. The way he whispered in my ear, took control, manipulated and owned my body, I couldn't confuse him with anyone else. Liam is not the same, and the dull ache between my legs from the new size is nothing short of a miracle.

The slut inside me wants to do it again. In his car. Maybe in front of Laci's. I'm craving him like a glutton, and I don't even recognize myself.

Is this what I was supposed to feel all along? Because Liam really missed the mark if this is what a true D/s relationship is supposed to be.

"Tell me what you're thinking."

I blink, pushing off the window. It's dark now, and

I can't make out much about his features in the dim light. I press my lips together, his words floating around in my head. Do I still call him Sir? "Um, well, Sir-"

"David. We aren't playing right now. If you would like to address me as Sir, it should be to start a scene. It's a clear queue. You don't need to feel obligated to use the term every time we talk."

Some of the air in my lungs disappears. Right, of course. It's an amateur mistake. "I'm thinking how different this is."

"Than?"

"Than Liam," I say, glancing at my hands. Fear clings in my throat, wondering if he'll dig for the truth now that I've mentioned him. I haven't told him much about what happened, at least the things I recall, and I won't even go into our ongoing debate through my messages.

But David saw the scars. I didn't even show my friends those.

He *knows*. Shame claws at my mind. Liam left those not too long ago. I didn't think there'd be a time anyone else saw them.

"It's supposed to be different. I'm not pretending to care. I know what I'm doing. And I don't see a need to scar you to get a point across."

My lip twitches. It's like he read my mind. He's pissed. I don't know what else I expect. Even if this is a mutually beneficial situation, I guess seeing scars on anyone is triggering. I eye his knuckles, tight and white against his steering wheel.

I didn't expect him to turn me around. I figured I could hide them for a while. Subconsciously my fingers trail over the marks on my neck. I saw the curious looks when we left the club. Even David's friend Nate shot him a look. I don't want to give him a bad rap. He didn't leave them.

He hates them. The scars on my back are small and easily hidden. I'm hoping the fading red ring is soon nothing but a bad memory.

"You don't need to feel ashamed," he says, filling the silence where I fail. I grip at the hem of my dress, ruffled from playing. "It's in the past. But I won't be adding to them. Your neck is the last set of marks you'll bear."

His words touch a spot inside me I didn't realize was hidden. The marks just became part of the process with Liam. I didn't contemplate when they would actually end.

But there's conviction in David's voice. Like he won't accept anything less.

"Am I taking you to Laci's?"

The question startles me. I didn't think there was anywhere else. I don't have anything to collect from her place, save the set of laundry in her wash. Everything is still at my apartment.

Part of David's deal included living with him, but I haven't signed anything yet. I've been so lost in thought I haven't even looked at it

My heart picks up, worry setting in. He said the club offered a level of security because someone is always around to stop you. I don't see David taking things too far. Even during oral he sensed when I'd had enough, disappointing as I'm sure I was. But staying at his house is a world unexplored. We still work together. Won't that make things awkward?

I grip the contract, another thought flying through my head. "I can't read this at Laci's."

He shrugs. "I want you to read it tonight Myla. We can talk and change things accordingly. You can turn away without consequence. But I want you to have the full picture tonight. I don't want to keep pushing it off." He runs a hand through his hair at the light, dark locks blending in with the night. "I wanted you to read it before I fucked you. Raw nonetheless." He scoffs, like that's insane. I was so lost in the moment I didn't even think about it until now. "We need to be on the same page. It's crucial in order for this to continue."

My heart pulls at the idea of this ending when it's just getting good. I want the training, I do. I have no idea what I'll do with it now that I can't return to Liam, but I want it. And David makes learning so much fun.

"I can read it in the car before I go up."

He's unimpressed, giving me a look. "You don't think your nosy friend is going to show up and ask questions?"

I think about Laci interrupting my one woman show in the car on Monday, and I know he's right. She thinks David is a hell of a lot better than Liam, but she's still cautious. She saw the state I was in on Wednesday. If she hears David wants me to sign a contract she'll have a fit.

I bite my lip. I do want to read it, even if I have to take pictures and check it out discreetly on her couch. "What about texts?"

"No. It's an in-person type of thing. You will have questions. I don't like texting about this to begin with. Things get screwed up through messages." He rubs his jaw. We're only a few minutes from Laci's. "You can come to my house if you want."

Panic sets in, immediately. "I haven't agreed-"

"I didn't say to stay," he snaps, pinching the bridge of his nose. "I meant so you can read it. Ask questions." He glances my way. "Clean up. You can wash Laci's dress before you return it to her and explain what the stains are."

My cheeks burn at the thought. I think I'll just pay her for this one. It's not an awful idea to go to his place, but the nerves inside still don't settle. "If I get uncomfortable can I leave?"

"You're not a prisoner Myla," he groans with a sigh. "You're free to leave if you see fit. Hell, text Laci the address if she'll feel better. But *don't* invite her in."

I smile at the image. Laci would just waltz in if she thought she could. After a moment of hesitation I nod, pulling out my phone. There's another dozen unopened messages from Liam, and I can see the log of missed calls. Ignoring it all, I send Laci a quick message that I'll be out longer with David, and turn the phone over. Still, I manage to catch sight of the latest message coming through.

He's getting crueler with his messages. Wednesday he couldn't figure out why I didn't come back upstairs and he kept asking what the problem was.

Laci lit him up. That's when I took my phone back and tried to stop checking messages. She was enraged, claiming he must've drugged me. I don't remember what all happened, and thinking about it makes me numb. I try to shove him out of my head, but he's there, prying into my thoughts and making me doubt what I just did.

By the time we reach his house, my insecurities are back in full force. He must notice, eyeing me carefully as we walk up pretty stone steps, and I'm a little upset all of this is his.

I remember high school. David was one of the popular kids, and money isn't an issue when your dad's a huge stock market guru. If he suffered from the 2008 recession, he bounced back with grace. I always knew he was better off monetarily than me. But the sweeping family-sized home in a gated community with a fresh-cut lawn and three car garage is so suburban I almost think we're at the wrong house.

The inside is just as grand, but I can't focus. The paperwork in my hand is a little damp from my sweaty palms, and I nervously tap my borrowed shoes on the hardwood floor as he flicks on the lights.

He makes coffee, even though it's verging on eleven. I expected wine, liquor, something to set the mood. I guess the club has a low limit on drinks, but my one glass of wine and champagne didn't make me all that tipsy. The coffee is still brewing when he turns to me, settled on the island watching him. "He sent something to you."

I sit straighter. Am I that transparent? "How did-"

"You got upset after you looked at your phone. I'm guessing Laci wouldn't make you feel that bad."

His intuitive nature is becoming annoying. I can't hide anything from him. I tap my phone on the counter, unsure where else to put it. The tiny little bag Laci handed me for my ID doesn't fit my phone and my slim wallet with the scarf stuffed inside. "And if he did?"

David sighs. I'm pretty he's getting tired of going rounds with me. "My job is to train you Myla. That's what you wanted. Part of training is ensuring you understand your own self worth. You should have some self-assurance for these things or people like Liam will get under your skin. You broke up because he did something awful, right? Don't let him continue to get away with it."

"I can't just shut him out. All my things are still there-"

"Then go get them," he interrupts, like it's just that easy. "Put them in storage. Stash things at Laci's. Do something so he has no control over you. If the only reason you still check messages is to protect your things, remove them and the problem is solved."

I press my lips together. That's not the only problem, and he knows it. But I'm not ready to share tonight.

Sensing that I'm through talking about it, David mutters under his breath. He makes two cups, and I'm surprised when he puts in a good amount of cream and sugar without asking. I take the cup with wide eyes, gaping at him. "How do I know how I like my coffee?"

"You're joking," he replies, sitting beside me. "I can smell that sweet shit from my office. It's heaped in sugar and cream. You may as well skip the coffee."

I laugh, because it's true. Laci takes hers darker, and I only vary when she's the one bringing me caffeine. I sip the hot drink, unusually giddy that he noticed such a small detail about me.

I'd be lucky if Liam remembers I like coffee.

He taps the papers in front of me, still folded tight. "Read. That's why you're here. And stop fidgeting with that phone. If it's that big of a deal, block him."

I bite my lip. I considered it, but what if he says something I need to know? My uncertainty is obvious, and David slides the phone away from me and the contract forward. "Just read. He's going to keep blowing you up either way." He flips my phone over, and I panic.

"Don't look at them!" He raises a brow, and I

swallow my outburst. Is that out of line? Am I going to end up reprimanded now? "Just, don't open my messages. Please. They're private."

For a moment I think he's going to argue, but it passes in silence. He sets the phone down and starts walking around the kitchen. "Fine. But don't read anything else either until you've read each page."

Okay, fine. I'll read it. He's insistent that this is important. I thought he did a magical job understanding me earlier, but maybe it gets more intense. I flip the papers open and for a moment it's like I'm having an out of body experience.

Play Contract. I can't believe that's what the pages say. It's a neatly outlined document, going over the terms David prefers (Sir) and any hard limits he has (taboo, sharing, etc) as well as what he expects from me (not running back to my ex).

I can't believe he actually penned that in. It's a requirement. He wants me to sign that I won't take what I learn and go back to Liam.

How can he demand that? He isn't my boss. He's a Dom. A *Sir.* Once the agreement is over, he has no say in what I do.

Besides, he's said on more than one occasion this is for training purposes only. Even lost in lust I could still tell when he was teaching, showing me how to react or how to swallow his cock better. I didn't feel like he was ever upset with me. Just teaching. Instructing.

Ensuring I know what I'm doing.

I have no idea why it takes as long as it does to move past that stipulation. I don't want to go back to Liam, not after what's happened this week. But it's like agreeing that I'm putting him in my past, and it takes me a long time to move on.

The rest of the contract is fairly simple. He wants me to stay with him throughout training to see how partners can interact throughout the day. He doesn't expect me to call him Sir unless I want to start playing. He doesn't have the desire to boss me around and turn me into a maid.

Those are his words. He literally states he has no interest in *domesticating* me.

The second half of the contract is for me. I get to list things I'm not okay with, names I like, and if I want different safe words. I get to tell him my limits in black and white, and they do not change unless both parties agree.

Once David feels my training is complete and I'm satisfied with what I've learned, I'm free to go. There's no date, but it's based on the idea of completion. I don't know what I'll do with this knowledge when I'm no longer learning, but it's an arsenal I want to have.

I'd never felt more alive, idolized, *desired*, then I did sitting on David's cock, screaming when he slapped my clit. I want that high again, and I'm going to ride it as long as I can.

Thankfully, we have the same dislikes. I don't want to play with guns, partake in a 24/7 power exchange, get my skin sliced up, and I've never fantasized about golden showers, getting locked in a cage, or pegging. My nose wrinkles at the idea. Everyone can have their pleasures, but I'm thankful they are nowhere on his list.

Anal is though. My one experience doesn't have me vibing for more, but I leave the option open. Maybe impact play. Who knows, maybe I'll feel differently in a week or two.

The last page past our signatures is a list of things we can try out, from exhibitionistic play to bondage, breath play and similar activities. There's options for paddles and whips, the stuff I envision when thinking about BDSM.

But there's more to it than that. David's made that clear. And I'm not going to turn down the option to learn.

When he turns back, I'm holding out the signed papers, and he looks surprised I agreed. I know how to work my way out of a contract if necessary. The only detail left to discuss is my living with him, the only line I didn't initial.

He doesn't even look through the stack, eyeing me. "I still want you here."

My hands grip the island. He always cuts to the chase. I squirm in my seat, eyeing the high ceilings. "Do you have a guest room?"

He looks offended by the question. "That's not the point."

I hold his gaze, not backing down. I won't jump in all at once. "Do you?"

He's glaring at me, but it's more irritated than anything. He sighs and waves a hand. "Yes. It's across from mine."

Good enough. Tomorrow is Saturday. I'm off. David is off. Laci is off. I can run back to her place like a coward if I need to. "If I can sleep in there, I'll stay."

10 DAVID

I wake to the smell of bacon. It spurs me out of bed, down the stairs, to my kitchen, where I find Myla wearing my shirt as she gracefully dances around my kitchen, which does nothing to cure my hard on. I tried to jerk off before giving up and coming downstairs. It can be a lesson. She still falls into the submission position uncertainly. It's a very basic pose that her confidence doesn't meet. We can practice, and I won't have to spend way too long upstairs getting rid of my erection.

I'm irritated, which is irrationally unfair. She slept across the hall from my room all night. It's the closest I've had her, and I knew for certain no one had their hands on her the entire night.

But it wasn't right. I need her in my bed. In my arms. Wrapped around my cock and tangled in my sheets. I would've pushed last night, but self doubt ruled my kitchen before bed. Liam's got his claws deep in her skin. She's apprehensive. I can't push further than I have.

I eyed her room before I came down. It's pristine, like she didn't even sleep. The bed is so perfectly made I could bounce a quarter on it. That's definitely not my half-assed bed making skills.

She didn't need to do it. I don't give a damn if her space is neat or messy. I know it's part of her habits, another to break. The bed can be made without the need to tidy up the rest of the room before breakfast.

Myla spins around the kitchen, and I eye her neck. It's looking better everyday. I spotted Nate's concerned look when we left, but everyone on the roof witnessed I didn't do that.

Vinny spotted us. I'm sure he'll have questions whenever I next go back, Myla or not. Abuse can't be tolerated.

She's prepared a whole breakfast, and though I'm not upset that my morning meal doesn't have to come from a toaster, I didn't expect her to do anything.

Instead of ruining her flow, I step up behind her as she finishes the last pancake and starts cleaning. I'll wash the small collection of dishes she's made. Everything doesn't need to fall on her shoulders. My hands grip the oven handle on either side of her. "Leave it. I'll wash them later."

Her back stiffens, and that won't do. I press a kiss near her pulsepoint, mindful of the marks. I want to clean them today. It's time they heal so she can be done with them and learn to move on.

She sees them when she looks in the mirror. She tugs every shirt or scarf she can up to cover them. The sooner they heal, the sooner the visual reminder is gone.

After a few chaste kisses, she relaxes. "I just wanted to do something for you."

"Why?" It's too damn early for this, but we're going to talk. She shouldn't be having concerns this early in the bloody day. I can hear the undercut of worry in her voice. "You did plenty for me last night."

She turns, rubbing every curve of her body against me. If she's not careful I'm going to bend her over the kitchen counter. She's frowning, her teeth pulling at her lip in a way I don't think she realizes is seductive. It's way too much of a turn on. "But I didn't make you cum."

I blink, confused. "You took a shower because you were sticky. I don't know what you think happened, but-"

"With my mouth, " she interrupts, her brows knitting together. "I - I meant I didn't make you cum when I gave you a blowjob."

"I didn't expect you to," I reply, frowning as I lean back. "Fun as that would be, you weren't going to last through it. You were already overwhelmed. I'm not training you just so you can give me head. You were struggling, and that's fine. I'm not mad that you didn't get me off just so I could fuck you after."

Okay, she looks more troubled than before. This is something I worried about. Myla is an award-winning overthinker. We went to bed well past one, with the smell of my soap dancing along her skin. I let her shower alone, which took more self control than I'll admit, but she needed some time to herself. And I was confident she wouldn't be looking through her phone in there.

I wondered what she'd do this morning. She relies on other people boosting her up. I don't mind doing it, but eventually she has to be able to do it herself. Her self-esteem can't take another blow like Liam.

Her fingers tap nervously together, but I don't help with her unease. Whatever she's thinking she needs to blurt out. The lusty haze is gone, and her real insecurities are blossoming. Now I can start pinpointing the problems Liam created.

It feels like a millennia before she responds, and I'm starting to lose my patience. Breakfast beckons to me.

"But it's my job," she mutters, looking away. "I can't fuck you right, but I can give head. I mean, I give head *okay*." Her cheeks burn as her gaze avoids me. "It's...

you're different from Liam. More to take and I wasn't prepared and-"

"It's not your job," I snap again, cutting her off. "I didn't tell you I expected you to finish me. It's not the expectation, especially if I'm intending to pound you after." I grab her chin when she won't look up, my grip firmer than last night. She needs to hear me. "You didn't fail me. That wasn't the expectation."

"But I couldn't take you right, and my eyes watered-"

Releasing her chin, I grab her hand and tug her after me. I need air, preferably so I don't break one of my cabinets listening to this. The sliding glass door opens to my deck and I tug her outside with me, the warm air inviting compared to last night.

I run a hand over my face. I don't think I did something to set her off, not from the way she reacted last night. But I saw her phone on the counter, and king dickhead could've caused the issue.

I don't know how. But it's possible. I stopped her yesterday because she was getting overwhelmed, not because she was bad.

When I look at her again, she still looks unsure. My shirt is big on her, but she's gripping the edges to keep it from rising in the wind. I almost laugh thinking about her spread last night. "Why are you self-doubting? I gave you the notes I felt necessary. I didn't say you disappointed me."

She's biting her lip again, and I drag my fingertip across to get her to release. She's gonna draw blood. "I just, I was thinking about it."

Bullshit. "Or Liam messaged you."

Her cringe is all the answer I need. I'm sick of her

putting up with his shit. She seems aware that he's toxic, yet she still gives him openings to get under her skin. I should talk to Emilio again. Something has to be done about him.

When she doesn't answer, I've had enough. "Go get your phone."

She frowns, eyeing the kitchen. "But, breakfast-"

"You just finished it. We have a few."

Myla hesitates, her tangled locks blowing in the wind. It's not as bad as it could be since she showered, and I like the messy, sleepy-eyed look on her. After a moment she listens, and I sit in the nearest chair. The table on the porch will block her.

I don't personally care, but it might make her feel better. She's quick to come back, and I take the phone from her. "Kneel."

She stays upright, wide eyes looking around. She isn't so carefree when her head isn't clouded with lust. "What?"

"You wanted to learn. You're making a point of it. So kneel. I'll show you what I like without an audience. You can tap out at any time." I flash her phone, which I discover doesn't have a lock or code, and that's just criminal. "And we'll see what Liam said to fuck up your head."

She tenses. "Don't-"

"You aren't taking care of yourself if he's still manipulating you," I interrupt, knowing she's going to fight me. "You've done a good job shutting me out of whatever he did, but I can only teach you so much if I don't know what makes you so fearful. I told you before, you have all the makings of being great at this. Liam holds you back. He doesn't get to touch you anymore, the only control he has at this distance is making you feel like shit."

She's ready to fight me, balling up her hands. "So I need to blow you while you look through my phone."

"It'll distract you from stealing the phone," I reply, wiggling my eyebrows. "We can both learn something."

Her hesitation almost makes me second guess the choice, eyes skirting around my backyard. These are spacious yards; dad ensured I'd have plenty of privacy when he picked it out during college.

But she drops to her knees, hands gripping the shirt as she opens her thighs. Staring up at me, those gray eyes hold too many questions. "Sir?"

"Good girl." I give her more leadway this time, biting my tongue before I comment on her lack of security on her phone. That's for another time. Checking the first message, I can tell he's doing whatever he can to make a dig.

"You don't have to read it out loud," she whispers, before pulling down the sweats I tossed on and wrapping her fingers around me.

I forget to teach her when I open the messages. She's doing good despite still struggling with my size, and I'm too focused on what Liam sent to give her pointers.

I need to keep my hands to myself. I'm pissed, flipping through his endless tirade, and I don't want to push her too far down and hurt her. So instead I'm gripping the phone, hoping it doesn't snap on me.

Or maybe it should. He wouldn't be able to reach her.

The ones from this morning are all along the same lines. He wants to know whose dick she's hopped on and how quickly she's going to crawl back to him.

Myla is hesitant, and I run my hands through her hair as I scroll. Even if I'm pissed I don't need to make her feel bad. "Good girl. Keep that pace."

She likes the encouragement, but I'm distracted. His messages are endless, everything from begging to gaslighting. It's exhausting to read. One comment sticks out though, and I'm debating throwing her phone.

Don't you want to see the video? I'm sure you'd like to know what I did while you were sleeping. I've got several.

Incriminating as hell. I slam her phone face down on the table, startling her, and she looks up at me.

Her eyes are full of fear. I hate it. I'm not doing my job at all, but the words sear into my mind and won't let go.

But if she doesn't make me cum this will be a problem the rest of the morning. I grab her head, though I haven't uttered a word from her messages, and pump her down my length.

It takes longer than it should to empty my balls, but I can't focus. Myla is a trooper, and I try to keep from misting her eyes. I want her to feel accomplished when she's finished, not used.

When I do finally cum, she surprises me by swallowing. I didn't encourage it, she just does it. Her mouth pops off of me and she looks up, eyes dancing with confusion.

I'm blaming this on her ex too. He shouldn't be fucking with either of our heads. He's out of the picture.

But what the *fuck* is on that video? I have a sinking feeling it's whatever sent her running. I glance at her forehead, the cut in her skin a constant reminder. The DIY bangs do okay covering it, but I still know it's there.

My fingers dance over it, making her shudder. I've

already made a decision before I speak, and I hope she'll go along with it. "You've got to get your shit out of the apartment."

11 MYLA

I think Laci is gonna have a stroke. Or offer to ride this guy. I don't know, but I don't want to be around for either.

After breakfast yesterday I tried to adjust to David's place. It's weird not being cramped or living under the expectation that everything will be clean. I don't walk around feeling like a visitor. Oddly his house is more inviting than mine. He games, reads, and does normal things on his days off.

We don't go to the club. I want to so I can let go, but he reminds me my guest visitation is used up, and I'll have to make a decision next time. If things don't work out with us for training, I doubt I'll go back. I have to pay my own membership or sign the consensual paperwork that we're a partnership. Signing with David is one thing. It's private between us. The club is too much for me right now, and trying to mesh with any of the other members sounds surreal.

It's better anyways. I need to go to my apartment, and Liam works on Sundays. We're going in the evening, because it's the only way I will go there. And I refuse to send David and Laci together. I have secrets to keep.

David is bringing along his friend Emilio, whom we meet on the way over there. He's only coming along partially because you need two people to move moms heavy antique tables, and partially because David's betting Liam doesn't go to work.

Emilio is a wall of muscle, rippling, strong, and all he's missing is rain to be every girl's wet dream. Short buzzed hair, wide shoulders, and get-on-your-knees hazel eyes. I briefly recall seeing him at the club.

He's dreamy, but he doesn't do it for me. Laci though? I'm pretty sure if we weren't there she'd ask to sit on his lap.

Emilio - *Milo,* if you're a friend - seems to find it greatly amusing. He thankfully doesn’t mention anything about the club to Laci. I haven't brought it up yet, but if she's interested in him I have to mention where I've seen him.

Which means I'll have to admit that I've gone to this sex club shamelessly, and I let people watch David fuck me.

It was so much hotter than I imagined. I want him to do it again, but maybe after this apartment fiasco is settled.

But first, I have to open the door. We've been standing here a good five minutes, David to one side, Laci to the other. She might be mentally sleeping with Milo, but she's staring at me.

I know David read that text about Wednesday. I was surprised he sent it when I surfed through texts yesterday, and it started a domino effect. I didn't think David would be so stern about Liam's influence, but he's hellbent on destroying it.

If I could mask my feelings better, this may not be today's problem. But David is insistent I get my things and be done with it, and Laci is completely on board. Battling both of them is too exhausting, and with four people moving out will go fast.

"Open the door Myla," David says, coaxing me as the seconds drag on. If Liam is inside then there's no avoiding the inevitable.

I take a breath, and turn the key that's been sitting in the lock waiting for me.

Surprisingly, the apartment is silent. It's messy since I've been gone, boxes of old food sitting around and a bunch of beers and soda beside Liam's favorite spot on the couch. He's obviously been gaming a lot.

I start to check the apartment, and David isn't having it. His hand catches my arm before I can hurry off. "Hold on, let's look."

My heart leaps, thinking about the bedroom. "No!"

Three curious sets of eyes stare back at me, and I regret nerves winning out over reason. "I mean-"

"You can walk with me then," David interrupts, gesturing to my sad one bedroom apartment, "while I check each room."

Terrible idea, but at this point I'd rather he see my sad bedroom attempts than Laci. Gesturing to the kitchen, I give her a pleading look. "Pack mom's China?"

She shoots me a wink, wraps her hands around Milo's forearm, and drags him into the little kitchen.

We aren't quiet, and I'm not surprised when Liam doesn't turn up. I leave the pair in my kitchen, knowing Laci knows what's what, and face my room.

I don't know why I thought Liam would clean, but he hasn't. The set of torn lingerie rests on the carpet, although I feel like I threw it out, and the collar is back too. There's a box with the new one I purchased, mocking me from the packaging.

David is tense when we step inside. The sex swing is nondiscreet, but it's the most unused item here. I'm staring at the bed, left untidy like I assumed, and the little fingerprints of blood on the desk glare up at me. Between that, the ruined clothing, and the collar, I'm batting a thousand here.

I blink, having completely forgotten about the blood on my side table. There's something similar on the headboard but I don't recall that at all. David walks beside me, but I already know Liam isn't in the bathroom. Still, my feet carry me there. I pause inside the space, out of line of the hall door, and place my hands on the counter with a shaky breath.

Why is it affecting me so much? I can feel my heartbeat picking up, nerves on end. Why am I so overwhelmed? Liam isn't even here.

His hands are in my hair, massaging my scalp. I glance up in the mirror. This is undoubtedly David, and I stare back at him in the reflection. "Breathe Myla."

This is stupid. I've got to pull myself together so we can be gone before Liam comes home. I don't believe for a second that he's at work.

David taps my hip, and I halfway turn to him. His gaze is hard, and I can't read his expression. It's nothing short of a miracle that he hasn't spotted the bruises on my hips at this point, though it can't be much worse than the marks on my back or the gash still healing along my head and ass. "Let's play, darling."

I can feel the color leaving my skin. It sets my anxiety on high alert. And it takes me someplace dark, to the last time I was in this room. "No! I can't-"

"We won't do anything sexual," he interrupts, grasping my chin firmly in a way I've come to crave. "But you need to go on autopilot before you slip into a breakdown. You aren't going to let me kick you out to do this myself, and you're going to lose it if Liam walks in." He lifts my chin higher so I can't look away. "You aren't ready to face him."

He has a point, but I don't know if I can shut off and just get things done. Is this part of my training? I wet my lips. The need to dry heave is strong, and I force the bubbling panic down. He's waiting for a response. "Yes, Sir."

David doesn't offer his trademark smirk. Instead he leans forward, lightly kissing my forehead. It feels more intimate than anything we've done so far. "Pack your room. I'm pretty sure I can figure out what's yours in here."

It all blurs together after that. I manage to convince him to knock down the sex swing before Laci storms in, set on packing up my closet. I toss the swing under the bed for dignity's sake, and try to ignore the spots of blood around my bed that David hasn't commented on. The lingerie I swore I threw out goes in the trash a second time, along with the collar of my nightmares and the new one I don't want to think about. My mind is set on getting out.

I knock everything off the side tables, the only pieces of furniture I intend to take. David helps me put knick knacks I should leave behind in a box, stuffing clothes around it.

I change when Laci is busy instructing Milo to handle one of the tables with care, and I know David has the other to carry out. We'll leave soon, and I'll never have to come back again.

My sweats and tank are like silk on my skin, and I pull another scarf on. Even if everyone in the living room knows I have marks on my neck, I'm not broadcasting to the neighbors.

When I come back out, David is staring at my sex toy drawer, and I feel my soul leaving my body at the sight.

Dear lord, no. I drop the makeshift outfit I've been wearing combo-ed between Laci's dress and David's jacket, and let out an indecent screech.

His eyes meet mine immediately. "What?"

The drawer is right by the bathroom, and I'm ready to slam his fingers if it means I can close it. He grips the edge, and he fights to keep me from moving it.

I don't try hard before giving up. I've seen firsthand that David is stronger than me. "Don't look in there."

He scoffs, glaring at me. He hasn't looked at me like this since early last week. "I was trying to pack. You didn't tell me what I couldn't open. And there's no point in waiting around if you're trying to get out quickly."

Biting my lip, I glumly acknowledge he's right. I don't know why I thought he'd miss this, but the evidence is clear when I drop my gaze.

We didn't own anything expensive. He's already seen the collar cast-off that I trashed. The welt that's healing on my ass protests the sight of the cat-o-nine trails that's still discolored from where it sliced me, and the cuffs he liked are broken in the middle where flimsy metal snapped.

David's fingers are on my hip where it's still sensitive, sliding to my side when I hiss. He's turning me. I don't really acknowledge it until I'm tucked beneath his arm, a strong whiff of his cologne sucking me out of dreamland.

He's pissed. I can feel the tension in his finger, the stiffness of his posture. Even if his scent is grounding, it doesn't distract from the anger leeching off him. "I don't know what you plan on doing when we're done with training, Myla. But I'll burn this place to the ground before you come back here."

I choke, the sound strangled in my throat. I don't try to think that far ahead. This is my home I'm running from. I have no plans after training is finished, just wild ideas. I can't focus on it.

Someone clears their throat, and I can't lift my eyes up from his chest. The toys I once accepted loom dirty and cheap compared to what I've seen at the club.

Emilio is telling David something about the time, but I'm not focused on it. My eyes drift up to the top of the dresser, little useless things I'm just going to forget and leave behind littering the top above the drawer.

My eyes catch something that looks out of place, and on instinct I grab it. I need to continue packing, but I can't focus.

I don't remember this bottle. Liam's against going to the doctor. If there's a pill bottle it's usually mine.

I turn it around. There's no label, just something scribbled in sharpie. *R. Hypnol.*

That's not mine. I'm not even sure what it is. There's a nagging voice in my head telling me what it is, but that's impossible, so I shove it away. I'm about to open the bottle when David snatches it out of my hands, turning to me.

"Where did you get that?" he snarls, startling me from the daze. I don't know what it is, but it sounds like he does. He's gripping my arm firmly now, shaking the bottle. "Did Liam give you this? *This*?"

Shaking my head seems like the wrong response, but I'm not sure what he wants from me. "I've never seen it before. You know what it is?"

David lets go of me, squeezing the bottle so tight he's going to dent it. His eyes are narrowed to slits, and he shakes his head. "You've never seen this?"

I'm supposed to be on autopilot. But it's hard when he's looking at me like I've lost my mind. The creeping feeling is back, but Liam can't be that awful of a person. "No. I don't know what it is or where Liam got it. It's not mine. Now tell me what it is."

David scowls, before putting the bottle *in his pocket.* "I'm going to get Laci to help you finish. Tell her the top drawer is empty."

He's ignoring me. It's a dick move, and I'm ready to resist. I don't care if I piss him off. This is my problem and now he won't even answer my questions. "No, we're not done here-"

"Right now, we are. I'll get Laci. Talk to her." The rage radiates off him as he leaves. He's out the door before I can keep the argument going, and I simmer beneath the surface.

I get that I asked for a Dom. I even behaved and called him Sir. But when do I get to rebel? Because this bossing around act and him always having the final say isn't going to work for me.

12 DAVID

Myla doesn't come out of her crappy headspace until I take her out. I refuse until Wednesday, because she's shutting me out.

I'm barely reigning myself in. I took the bottle out of her hand, ignoring the obvious stain of blood on her headboard, and had Laci help her finish packing up the dresser drawers.

I needed to be out of that room before I started breaking shit. She's living in denial, but I knew exactly what was in that bottle. She claimed missing memories and had a bloody head wound. I don't need her to go into detail about her problems with Liam to put the pieces together.

Emilio caught me walking out just in time to spot me punching the wall outside her apartment. My hand stings from the impact, but it was better than wrecking the place. She wants a no-conflict break from Liam.

I can do that for now, but I'm not finished with him. I already spoke with Milo. Laci claims to have been invited over rarely in the past. I see why with all the evidence laid out. It was hard to miss the bloody fingerprints on the table I picked up, the way she looked down in shame when I noticed.

It makes me wish he had been home, so I could bash *his* head into the headboard until he stopped moving.

The pill bottle sits in my office at home. It's evidence, I know. My inner lawyer is having a fit over the removal of evidence, but if I have it my way this problem will never reach a courtroom. It was a stupid ass choice but leaving the bottle behind was out of the question. When I spotted the label I knew it had to go. Any woman Liam brings back to the apartment would be in danger.

I doubt Myla will report anything. Pride and denial will be her downfall, I'm banking on it. Liam could go through the justice system and maybe be tried for violence, but it takes time for cases to work through the system. Myla is in complete denial that anything would fall back on him. I work as a lawyer to right wrongs. So does she.

But our main focus is on car accidents, unsightly divorces, things like that. But spousal abuse? DV and assault? Sometimes prison doesn't fit the crime. You can just as easily destroy someone outside of the courts.

If Myla figures out my endgame, I'm not sure what she'll say. But I'm sick of her sad glances and uncertainty. Liam did this. I don't know enough about her history to know if she actually had any other influences before him. The bottle of rohypnol didn't just end up in their bedroom accidentally. He either left it out when she disappeared, or it's been hiding in plain sight the entire time.

It doesn't really matter which it is. I'm positive he gave it to her during their relationship. We talked some on Sunday, and she described the loss in time, *vaguely*. He's a violent type. She's either forgotten due to a drugged influence or she's disassociated.

I think it's a little bit of both. The only highlight at the beginning of the week is Phil singing her praise. They had a meeting Melissa skirted around and Bridgett missed about Myla's position. He's dangling a promotion that probably doesn't even exist in front of her eyes, and she's following along all too eagerly. It grates on my nerves, but after a year of working here I know how Phil works. When there's less going on I'll tell her the truth, but the initial pick me up comes at a good time.

She doesn't improve outside of work and I finally cave and take her out. She gives me a curious look when we arrive, wearing a long casual dress with a slit. I told her to wear whatever she wanted. I gave her no direction, and I could tell from the moment I mentioned dinner she was uncomfortable. I know she wants to go back to the club, but it won't be a simple visit when she goes back for a third time. I know Vinny wants to question her neck, and Jo will hunt us down to sign the paperwork.

I didn't tell Myla what to do for this evening and the uncertainty leaves her hanging. My instinct is to pick her outfit and keep her guessing, but she's so on edge I almost just tell her the plan. She gruels me throughout work, Laci shooting us non discrete looks. The outfit Myla changes into for dinner is sweet, not seductive, and I still want to rip it off of her.

For living in my house, I get very little time with her. Sex hasn't been on her mind the last few days, and I haven't wanted to push her into anything. We might have a deal, even a contract, but just because I'm the Dom in this relationship doesn't mean I get to ignore what she actually needs. Training is more than just showing someone how to freely take and earn pleasure. She has to know she deserves it too. And it's her decision when and if it happens.

I could make her, but it wouldn't do it for me. I like my partners willing and undistracted. Neither thing describes Myla this week.

"You didn't say black tie," she breathes, fiddling with the high neck of her dress. A pretty scarf is draped over it, the wounds little more than calluses and scabs now. It's better, but not perfect, and she still fears anyone seeing.

My gaze flickers to her forehead and those makeshift bangs; the wound seems to be healing. Her friend Anita messages daily and Laci checks in, too, even though we see her at work. Their concern is almost suffocating, and Myla must've exhausted herself dodging questions about Liam over the past year.

Milo even asks how she's faring, keeping a constant eye on Liam for me. He also checks in to see when I intend on putting my plan into action.

It's undecided. I'll need to clean the bottle and return it to the apartment if she wants to report. Between now and then I can make my move, if I want to. If she doesn't want to file any sort of report, I can move forward with my contacts. I have my ways to get what I need to see the plan through. Working cases with Melissa has never worked out better for me.

"It's not black tie," I reply, my guiding hand resting at her waist. She studies the interior, lush decor and sweeping ceilings with ritzy chandeliers. Some diners are dressed to the nines, but others are more casual like us. It's expensive, but not black tie. She fiddles with the neckline again, and I grab her hand. She's got to stop second guessing everything.

Somehow, she manages to avoid looking at me until it's time to order. Her eyes look around the room, biting her lower lip. She taps her fingers on the table, readjusts every few minutes, and checks her phone. If she gets any more nervous she's going to break the glass.

When the waiter is gone with our order, I'm ready to toss her phone out with the bread they offered. "Stop looking for his responses."

She frowns. "I'm allowed to look at what I want."

Letting out a sigh, I ignore the little spike of defiance. Myla is a brat, though I haven't yet called her that out loud. Her determination is admirable, but she could put all that focus into a worthwhile cause. "It's illogical to keep checking it. You know he's mad. He's not going to change. Looking at the messages only hurts you."

Myla scoffs, gray eyes flickering away from mine. If we were just in a partnership I'd pick on her for disrespect. It's part of the role play. But I think she'll go off about it now. I haven't reminded her to call me Sir in days and it's really beginning to cut into the agreement. The need to slip in a *brat* comment grows the longer we talk. If I'm not training her, what are we even doing here?

Her chin juts out defiantly when she responds. "I asked you to train me. Not to whip me into obedience."

My brows lift as the waitress reappears with an appetizer, and between their twin blushes I'm not sure who is more embarrassed. "I'm not whipping you into anything. I told you before this started I like my partners Submissive. I'm not beating anything into you." I straighten, offended. I haven't done anything to challenge her this badly, yet she's acting like I've started controlling every aspect of her life. "You know, I always thought you were a bit of a brat, but your colors are really showing through. If you think I'm beating submission into you-"

"You told me what to do at the apartment," she snaps, leaning forward. She reminds me of the spitfire

I'm used to working with, not the hidden Submissive she longs to be. "Told me to go on autopilot. Told me what to do there. Like I'm not already aware of Liam. I don't need you bossing me around. And I'm not a brat."

I narrow my eyes. "Yes, you are. And are you really that mad I bossed you around at your apartment?"

"Yes! You just..." she shakes her head, gripping the tablecloth. "You took over and told me what I couldn't do."

My frown deepens. "I'm not Liam, Myla. I told you to go through the motions so you didn't have a breakdown with Laci there. I don't think she knows how crooked your sex life went." Her blush returns, and I take the advantage I've gained before she tries to plow through the conversation again. "I'm not trying to control you. I'm offering you an escape when it's too much to handle. I told you what to do because I didn't need you having a meltdown at your apartment. Liam may have returned before we left."

She scoffs. "So what? He knows I've been there. It's only a matter of time before he finds me anyway."

I press a finger to my temple, my patience slipping. I'm not sure where the downward spiral came from, but I'm not a fan. "Why are you so sure he will?"

"Because he promised," she whispers.

It's the oldest threat in the book. Leaning back in my chair, I glare at her. "Then I'll take care of it." I shrug when she lurches forward, her drive to fight returning. "Or you can. But if he raises a hand..."

She cringes, and I let it hang in the air. If Myla wants to face her demons, more power to her. But I'm not just going to stand in the background and watch him hurt her again either. She's still mine to care for, even when she's bratting. I won't let him harm her again.

It's strange, thinking about the conditional contract with Myla pulls at my heartstrings like no other partner has. I don't like to consider things going past this agreement, because then things get complicated. I have no idea what I'll do with myself when the partnership ends.

She's tapping the table again, eyeing her phone. She keeps checking it every minute or so, her nerves working against us. She hasn't relaxed since the apartment, and until I can wedge myself beneath this shield she's created I won't make any headway. But I don't like her reading his messages while we're out. "Leave him on read until dinner is over."

Myla glances up, surprise dancing over her features. "It's not Liam." She worries her lip, and I start doubting she'll share. "It's my mother."

Interesting. Other than heavy ass side tables, I haven't heard her talk about her parents. In high school I didn't pay much attention to her familial setting, and I didn't care anymore in college. I don't know if she has siblings, if her parents are together, nothing. "Do you talk to your mother much?"

She's confused, staring at me for a beat before responding. "Not really, no. She's usually busy with her family."

Frowning, I sip the wine I had the waiter bring. She's twirled her glass, but so far hasn't drank or eaten a thing. Her nerves are frayed. "Wouldn't it be your family?"

She sneers, and I know I've touched something sensitive. "No, hers. This is her new family. She got married when I was nineteen."

"And you don't like them?"

Rolling her eyes, she picks up the glass and tosses

back the entire thing. "They don't like me. It was just the two of us all throughout my childhood. My dad knew about me when she was pregnant, he just didn't want a kid. That's all I know about him." She shrugs. "Ronald just... appeared. She fell in love with him. Waited until I was done with high school to marry him. She dotes on her stepkids." Her nose wrinkles at the mention. "Ones in high school now, one in middle. They have one together in elementary. It's the perfect little family she couldn't have with me."

"She doesn't invite you or you don't want to be a part of it?"

The empty glass slams down on the table, and I grip over her hand before she squeezes again. "I'm not invited. It's a brush off. Mom *knows I'd* rather spend time with Laci and Anita than go on a cruise with them, or get locked up with all of Ron's inlaws for the holiday. She sends my birthday cards a week late because the middle child's birthday is two days before mine and she doesn't want her to feel overshadowed."

I'm beginning to see how she fell in with Liam. Her mother found a man that suddenly made her life perfect and she ditched the old one. Myla either tried to do the same thing, or run in the opposite direction.

"So you don't see your mom at all?"

She shrugs. "Mom doesn't have siblings. Her mom died of cancer when I was six. I didn't know her. It was always just the two of us. Now she has a huge family that welcomes her every holiday and watches her kids when she's tired. I'm just an outlier." She picks at the plate between us, but I've lost my interest in dinner. It's not a peaceful distraction. "I think I saw her three years ago? She wanted to congratulate me on my bachelors.

I finished it the year before, but she just sort of forgot about my graduation invite for a year."

I feel bad. My parents are emotionally distanced, but at least they chimed in when I did something in my life. I lean back, taking her abandoned glass with me. "My dad tries annually to convince me to be a stock broker."

She snorts, staring up at me from the roll. "At least your dad remembers you exist."

"Of course he does. He wants me licensed in New York so if he ever gets caught with fraudulent funds he has a lawyer on speed dial."

Her jaw drops. "You can't be serious."

"Very. It's why he funded my degree. He was annoyed when I wouldn't transfer to NY. He's rarely in Denver anymore. Mom comes through in the summer, but this late in the season she's down in Florida or off in the Caribbean. She'll fly back to NYC for Christmas and New Years before she heads off again. My sister is typically in upstate New York with her boyfriend."

Myla stares like I've told her something fascinating. I doubt she knew I had a sister (she's eight years younger), much less what my mom does. They both just coast comfortably on whatever funds dad sends their way. I wanted something separate in case this goes south again.

"I guess you don't spend much time with your family either," she muses quietly.

I shake my head, digging out my phone. She's bitter about choices her mom made, but it's not a jaded, shady history like I started to fear. Her mom is just a grade-A bitch that abandoned her kid when she found something better. I open my pictures, showing the last family picture we took together. It's a few years old now, you can tell from the length of my hair. "A couple years ago I went to

New York for the holidays like they wanted. It was fine, but the life they lead isn't mine. I don't want to live out there, I like the mountain air and national parks around here. I like distance between us so they aren't always digging in my business, finding out my habits, or the clubs I frequent."

Her eyes widen, catching my meaning. I like my family but they can stay out of whole sections of my life. Reaching out I brush my fingers along her knuckles, the rolls forgotten. "We make our own families as we grow. Fill our lives with what makes us happy. The lines our parents set for us don't determine who we will be. Sometimes to blossom we have to leave behind their expectations, and their disappointments."

There's a sheen to her eyes. I wonder when the last time was when she thought about her mother's dismissal without thinking it was her fault. It's her mom's fault for giving up on her, as well as the new husband for doing nothing to change it. You can't blame the faults of a parent on the child.

Our waitress appears, looking strangely between us, and I slip the phone away. It's not as hard to chat after that. She's less hostile, distracted by food, and I slip what I've learned of her family away for later. I'm sure Laci knows, but what's being done to remedy the loss of family comforts?

By the time we slip home, she's in a better mood. I bought the remainder of the wine, which she happily carries off towards the guest room.

I catch her waist upstairs, in the hall between our rooms. "Stay with me tonight. You can use my shower. It's a lot better than the hall."

Myla frowns, stiffening in my grip. "It's OK David, I

don't mind the hall."

Cooking my head to the side, I don't let go. "I don't mind you in my room. You'll learn nothing sleeping across the hall from me."

"It's okay," she stresses again, the tension returning to her shoulders. "You don't have to open your room up to me."

My eyes narrow, watching her fiddle beneath my gaze. She was tense at her apartment too in the bedroom, even before we found the bottle. She won't meet my gaze, glancing towards the door she's so familiar with.

I suspect it's more about the bedroom itself than the fact that it's mine. I run my hands down her arms before capturing her chin. "We'll shower, darling. You can choose to sleep in your room or mine after. I won't force you to. But I want to feel your skin slick with more than your cum."

Her flashes flutter, and I know I've struck the right chord. Myla is a difficult puzzle to decipher, but I'll figure her out yet. Beckoning to her room, she nods and slips in, and I go to start the water. I need to feel her again. Once is absurd. If I had it my way I'd be buried inside her every single night.

For now, this'll have to do. If she doesn't start to trust me soon there will be nothing left to show her. You can't teach the unwilling, and Myla is slowly slipping back into her shell.

13 MYLA

"What do you mean you're still sleeping in his guest room?" Laci growls.

I snatch the file out of her hand, setting it on my desk. Kathy, the file clerk, and another receptionist stare openly at us. I want to face palm.

The rumor mill is hard at work. I've driven with David to work the past few days, because it's stupid to leave at the same time to go to the same place every day separately.

Plus, David's car has a remote start, which means the heated seats are already toasty when we get in. And he *offers* to drive instead of guilt tripping me into it.

I'm getting comfortable, which is the opposite of what I had planned. I'm supposed to be learning, but that feels stagnant since the apartment. I refuse to talk about that little bottle we found, and I haven't gotten up the courage to ask David where it went.

He would tell me, I'm nearly certain. But he's all about communication and using my words, and I've done neither since Sunday. He's not forthcoming.

The training hasn't ceased. We still do things, but not like the club. I want to go back, but again, I haven't asked. David took me to dinner at some posh restaurant he tried to downplay, but we haven't gone back to the club.

I don't know if I miss the atmosphere or the

openness to try new things more. I'm comfortable with David, but there's one glaring issue every evening.

He wants me in his room. It's not that different from sleeping in the guest space, except my clothing is tossed haphazardly in there. I told him I don't want to be woken up with anything inside me, and he took it to heart.

"I want to be awake when sex starts. It's important to me, Sir."

We hadn't done anything. Laci was still downstairs after getting back from the apartment; I just wanted to explain for later in case I got tired. David stares at me, setting down the pile of clothes he was collecting.

Sweeping a finger over my lips, he held my gaze. "Of course. Even if you hadn't said, I will stop if you ask. I'm not going to force you into something."

Shrugging, I step out of his reach. Being emotional before going downstairs won't do. "If you say so. Just... if I don't wake up, please don't continue."

I didn't stay around for his answer. David eyed me the next few days carefully, but he hasn't brought it up again. Not in so many words. He asks each night if I'll sleep beside him. I just can't make myself walk in there.

I like the control of sleeping alone. The bedroom door locks, and David told me to lock it when I see fit. I do it each night and he's never said a word.

Controlling what happens when I'm not alert is important. David doesn't push, but I see the frustration in his gaze. He wants me in his bed, in his room. I can't make myself take the step yet.

"I'm comfortable there," I hiss, forcing a smile at our audience. There's a rumor that we're sleeping together. It's annoying but not unfounded. Neither of us plans on changing the car situation, and I don't need to worry about Liam walking up to me on my way to or from work if I'm walking with David.

It's strange to consider that after more than a week Liam has no idea who I'm staying with. Even though they had the confrontation in the office, I'm not sure David has ever crossed Liam's mind.

Laci wiggles her eyebrows, sitting in the way of Kathy's curious gaze. "I'm sure it's also comfortable in his room-"

"Lace-"

"With those pecs-"

"I'm warning you-"

"And those abs-"

"Laci, don't-"

"And I bet he's packing beneath the belt."

I hesitate, the stress of the last eleven days settling in. I don't have it in me to lie anymore to my friend. And David's never turned down the rumor mill. "Well, he is."

Roaring with laughter, she hops off my desk with a little dance. I think Kathy's jaw might break with how far it's fallen, and the other receptionist is green with envy.

It's actually kind of nice. People are jealous I'm with David, no matter the arrangement. I always told myself Liam was a catch, but no one ever gave me a death glare because I called him my boyfriend.

I guess it's fair. They weren't missing out on much.

"Then you really need to explain why you aren't naked in his bed," Laci hisses, gathering up her hair. It's humid for the end of August, and she looks hot in the stifling office air. We walk out of the space, towards the desk she's supposed to occupy. "The guy moved you out of your controlling, abusive ex-boyfriends house. What else do you need?"

I bite my tongue. Laci knows nothing about our dynamic and I want to keep it that way. I don't need her judgment on the matter, and shutting off during sex is easy for me. It's not like with Liam where I zoned out completely. This is more like... letting him lead. He tells me constantly that everything stops if I want it to. And after the apartment he isn't pushing.

It's nice. Almost too nice. Liam’s texts have lessened, but I'm not a fool. I dropped the entire lease on him and ghosted him on a Sunday afternoon. There's no way he'll just let it go.

David is gone at court with Melissa probably for the rest of the day.

Phil keeps me busy, but I think I've annoyed him. We had one chat about my position before things went south with Liam, and nothing since. I know he has the hots for me, but a relationship rumor about me and David shouldn't stall my progress at work. I jumped right back in after being out last week. I know he's against office romances, but it's not affecting our ability to work.

I've proven myself. I have no idea why he's suddenly uninterested in having me sit in for cases. I wanted to go to court with him next week. What happened to that?

"I'm adjusting, Lace. I wasn't planning on a breakup."

She shrugs, picking up a file left there for her to handle. She flips through and sets it down again. "You just wanted to shack up with David and keep Liam strung along?"

That makes me sound like a terrible person. "I would never-"

"Good," she interrupts. "I'm glad you're finished

with him. And David's a great upgrade." Winking, she pokes my side. "I knew you'd never do that, by the way. I see the way David checks you out. You two are like fated love."

Immediately, I try to shut that down. There's nothing romantic with us. He's teaching me submission, and that's all I can focus on. It's not the building blocks for some star-crossed-lovers romance. "Hardly. Things just worked out. We have mutual benefits for each other."

"Oh yeah, cause every guy totally lets their coworker hide out at their house *in a gated community* for benefits sake." She glares at me. "And his garage is filled with your shit."

I scratch the back of my head. Yeah. It doesn't make a lot of sense without the other details, but even if I do decide to tell her about those I wouldn't do them here.

"Laci!" She scowls as Marcy comes into view, white and gray bun pulled tight as usual. She looks pissed as she eyes Laci, who picks up the file she's been ignoring. "You went to the bathroom almost an hour ago."

I shake my head, leaving her to her own fate. I got Laci this job because she got fired from the last, but I don't think she's reception material. She's way more interested in gossiping with me than answering the phone.

~~~

I almost think it's going to be a regular, boring day. The kind I had before David discovered my secrets and set everything in motion.

The thin veil of comfort I've settled around myself is ripped away by a single voice, and the tremor that shoots down my spine is almost worse than turning around.
~~~

It's barely four. On a Thursday. He should be at work. If he hasn't already been fired.

"So you are alive."

I spin so fast I almost knock over the binders I've meticulously set out today. My fingers lock over the edge of my desk as I stare at him, and I hadn't even heard him come in. I assumed it was a coworker.

"Liam." I'm impressed by my own voice when it doesn't shake. His eyes narrow a hair, but otherwise he's keeping his mood in check.

For now. He always knew how to play the game. I've spent enough time with David to see that now.

He looks the same. I almost wish he looked worse, so I could see how his life had fallen apart without me. But he's no worse for wear, same relaxed outfit, messy hair, smug look, those light and ruthless brown eyes I've grown to hate. At least he doesn't look better.

Holding out his hands, he looks around. "Here I am thinking something terrible happened. You run off with your little slutty friend, you don't take my calls or respond to my messages. And then I get home today and find out you've run off with all your shit."

It's Thursday. He hasn't been home in days. I shake my head, that fact irritating me more than it should. I cross my arms and straighten my back. I don't feel the confidence my voice holds. "We weren't working out. We haven't for a while. I wanted a fresh start." I nod my head at the end, convincing myself too. "It's for the best. We don't work together."

His hand slams into the corner of my desk, sending the binders I've worked on flying and I flinch back. I hate it, a dark side of myself rearing up in the back of my mind that I'm letting him get to me.

I'm at work. There's a camera he doesn't even know about focused on this very spot. Fleetingly I recall the videos of myself and David, and the last time with Liam. Those are gone now, but anything and everything he does now will be caught on tape.

He can't get loud. It'll draw attention. So will violence. His presence is unnerving but there's a limited amount of things he can do at my damn job.

This is the only day since last Monday that David hasn't been in the office for a good chunk of the day. Liam claims to have not been home since at least Sunday. I left the apartment last Wednesday. Yet he knew I hadn't been home, and his messages never changed so I just assumed he was mad about everything, not that he was so out of the know.

How is it that the one day David is gone he just so happens to visit me at work?

"Stop shitting me, Myla," he growls, getting in my face. I lift my chin at him, the fresh wave of fear sliding down my spine. The office isn't empty, but it's not like it was a few hours ago. He drags a hand over his face, as though he can smooth out the lines of anger. "We work fine. Your friend is in your head. Stop listening to her nonsense and come home. This little game is over."

He reaches towards me and I'm jump back. I don't like that I can't stand my ground, but I don't want him to touch me again.

"I'm not," I say, glancing at the door. I ball up my hands as he tenses, digging in my heels. Someone will walk by sooner or later. His back is to the door. If anyone happens by, I'll see them first. These offices are at the back of the law firm but eventually someone will spot us. "It's not a game, Liam. We weren't working out. It doesn't have anything to do with Laci. It was my decision."

"You don't know what you're talking about," he says with a scoff. He digs out his phone, dangling it in front of me for reasons unknown. All our messages are the same. "We're going home."

"It's not my home anymore, Liam. I'm not fighting you for it. The apartment is yours-"

"Ours," he snarls.

It just makes me think of all the messages he's sent to my phone in the last week.

You think you can just run off and sleep with someone else? No one will love you like I do. They won't humor your sick kinks like me. You're going to miss out on the only man who could ever want you.

If you can't even take care of me, what makes you think you'll be good enough for anyone else?

Whatever lies you told to slide into someone else's bed won't save you when they learn the truth. You're nothing without me.

No one can get you off. You're impossible. And no one will care if you enjoy it or not. I've taught you how to enjoy what you can.

They are all just words, contradicting what David says. I shake them out of my head and point to the door. "You need to go. This is my job. I don't interrupt you at yours-"

"You don't even come to mine!" His rising voice banishes my hopes to keep this private.

"I didn't need to, Liam," I snap, the weight of the past year slipping into my voice. I put up with him because I thought it was part of my submission. Now I'm thinking he used it as an excuse to keep me quiet. "I don't care about going with you to work to watch you flirt with all your coworkers and make out with them when you think no one is around to tattle." I roll my eyes, taking a step back from him. "Do you think I never knew about Hillary? Bianca? The tattooed redhead at the bar last month? I always heard rumors but didn't see it. I brushed off the proof. But I'm not doing that anymore and I don't want to pretend your excuses make up for the lies. We're done."

He steps towards me and I backtrack at the same moment Laci appears. She halts, wide angry eyes staring at us. Liam doesn't notice her as he walks closer to me, waving the phone about. She tenses, and I hope my eyes plead with her.

Laci is all spit and fire. But Liam hits hard and I don't need him getting near my best friend. This is a damn law firm; there's security for the building and a handful of employees who can intervene. At this point I'm betting on Liam fighting Laci before backing off. He wants to blame her.

She turns and quietly hustles off, and I'm glad she's listening. Or I hope she is. Liam gets my full attention again when his hand flies up to my face, and I duck out of reach.

I miss David. The thought makes me realize I'm becoming entirely too reliant on a guy who's training me, but there's a level of comfort whenever he's near. I'm unsure if Liam would plan to come by when David isn't around, but it's too coincidental. Or else the universe is out to get me.

I need him back here. The strength I've grown to associate with him requires his presence. And Liam isn't backing up.

"Come on, Myla," he snaps, "don't you want to see

my last video of us?"

Pausing, I try to remember any time when Liam took a video. I don't like when he does, it could come back as blackmail later. I always said no. It felt like a power move in the relationship, but now I'm left wondering why I humored the idea that he wouldn't try something crappy like this. I never agreed to being filmed, despite the year long relationship. I didn't want him using something against me at any point in time. I thought submitting was enough, and Liam always tried to one up me.

Shaking my head, I decide to call his bluff. I need to buffer the next few minutes until Laci returns, hopefully with security. If he gets closer I will start screaming; someone's bound to show up. Andrea in the desk a couple rooms over will pound anyone into the dirt without question. If Laci doesn't pop back up in the next half minute I'm calling for help, pride be damned.

Maybe I could get a good punch in before he tries to choke me, but I'd rather avoid that scene at my job. My neck is still tender as it heals. I won't irritate the marks.

"There are no videos. I explicitly told you to not film me."

He chuckles, a dark, rumbling noise that he usually wouldn't make. "You think I listened? Come on, Myla, stop showing your ineptitude. It's fucking easy to set up a phone and hit play. I've got lots." He twists his wrist, showing off the shiny case I got him last year for Christmas. "Come on, don't you wanna see what happened to the lingerie?"

It's like he's dumped a bucket of ice across my skin. I try not to think about last week too much. The bottle David took and the torn clothes left little to the imagination, but I don't like thinking about it. My voice catches in my throat, fear threatening to take over. "I told you to leave me be when I'm sleeping."

Shrugging, he clicks his tongue. "I never said you were asleep, love. You were there, at least enough to matter."

I think I'm in a daze, debating whether or not I can cold-cock him with my stapler and get away with it. Before my fingers can wrap around it, the idea of seeing anything he did or didn't do to me causing nausea to work its way up my throat, Laci returns.

She isn't quiet this time. Her heels stomp on the checkered floor, and Liam huffs out a groan as he turns to her. He doesn't lose the angry set of his shoulders, or step back from me. She's jabbing a finger his way, her voice hitting new heights as it vibrates off the walls. "Get away from her!"

Liam laughs, and I think he should take things more seriously. Laci might look like a real-life Barbie, but she's a force to be reckoned with. The idea that he might strike my friend spurs me forward to catch his shoulder as he advances. "Liam-"

He spins back to me, getting in my face. His hand catches my wrist in a bruising grip. "She *knows* something, doesn't she? What lies are you whispering to your little bitch?"

"Oh, don't you even-"

Laci is cut short, her nails digging into Liam's shoulder. I stare past Liam as I try and pull his hand off, my eyes going wide as humiliation settles in my stomach.

"What's going on here?" Phil asks as he rounds the corner, one of the security guards in tow. Another attorney is with him, Cash, and I'm not surprised to see that they both look equal parts upset and mad.

We're almost on the top floor of this skyscraper. It's supposed to help eliminate the problem of excess drama, and I've personally delivered my own dosage here at the office.

Liam lets go, glaring at me as he does. Laci makes a self satisfied noise as she takes her claws out of his shoulder, shoving him out of the way with her hip to link her arm through mine. Her grip is firm, stabilizing, and it's the first time I realize I'm vibrating with energy.

Or fear. Panic. Rage. A toxic mixture of it all. Seeing Liam is a cold wakeup call I didn't realize I needed. Before he can make a jab about this being a misunderstanding, I meet Phil's inquisitive glare. I'm going to have to give some type of explanation. "Please remove him. This is my ex, and he's not welcome here."

Phil looks shocked, but the expression quickly morphs to indifference. Cash, ever the enigma of the office, remains stoic. With a nod to the guard, Phil gestures to Liam. "Come on then. We won't be having the staff disturbed. You can speak with Myla another time if she's interested in talking to you."

Liam scoffs, tossing his hands up in the air at the guard. His eyes zip to me, little green orbs of hate. "Fine, whatever, I was just leaving."

Laci mean-mugs him the whole way out, and when the space is no longer littered with Liam's hostility, Phil turns to me. Cash walked with the guard escorting Liam out of the building. He looks between the pair of us before stabbing a finger over his shoulder. "My office. Now."

It's like when you would get in trouble at school and the teacher marches you down to the principal's office. Only Phil is both the teacher and principal, and every pair of available eyes watches the three of us walk into Phil's office, his door slamming shut.

He glares at us as he sits at the desk, and I'm scrambling to come up with an explanation that doesn't delve into my entire past with Liam nor leave the impression that I ever want him back here. Phil isn't patient, his desk piled high with the teleconference crap I've been prepping for court tomorrow. This is another stack I'll need to handle. "Explain, Myla. Why was there a disruption?"

He's berating me like a child, but before I can comment I glance out the window and do a double take. Liam, a distant figure I recognize even in a crowd, is navigating his way by pushing through the crowd to the parking garage down the street. There's metered parking right out front, but I don't see his car.

What I do see makes my stomach drop. Laci and Phil debate behind me, and I think she's trying to cover my ass. But I don't look away as David, and presumably Melissa and their client, wade through the afternoon foot traffic.

Right past Liam. I may as well be watching my own show. Fate is a cruel beast, bringing Liam here today and letting him walk right past David. They only met for a few moments. He doesn't seem to recognize him.

David, though, must realize this is Liam. His figure pauses, and I see the moment happening in slow motion. At first Liam gets by scott-free, walking past David. Then he does a turn, and I see Liam pause.

My jaw drops open when David clearly drops the briefcase and socks him directly in the jaw, sending Liam flying.

Right into a parking meter.

14 DAVID

"I don't intend on this being a problem."

Myla flutters around, checking the bruised knuckles on my hand, avoiding Phil's scathing gaze. She somehow flew down from the fifteenth floor in record time. She saw me punch Liam square in the face from Phil's office window.

I wasn't planning to. I didn't know he was nearby. No one said a word to me about it. But I recognized him from that day in the office, tearing through the crowd with a perma-scowl on his face. I almost let him pass me to avoid a conflict. But it was his words that caught my attention.

"She's stubborn. I even told her about the video I made and she's still defying me. Someone fucked with my good little slut and I've got to fix her up all over again."

The sting in my hand is nothing compared to my satisfaction listening to his nose break beneath my fist. Once I recognized him, there was no question in my mind who he was talking about, and the callus way he spoke of Myla had me seeing red.

I still am. Going over specifics with Phil is tedious but necessary. Liam is now banned from the building, and Melissa is gung-ho about representing me if he presses charges. She caught some of what he said too and didn't like it. Even our client overheard. He wasn't being discreet.

To be fair, she didn't know it had to do with Myla at the time, but after the coy smile she shot my way when I hugged Myla close to me, I know she knows it's got to do with her. Just the particulars escape Melissa. It's annoying that the entire office is now in our business, but there's only so much to be done when the jerk shows up to cause issues. I didn't think he was ballsy enough to do it in the middle of the day.

Phil is massively annoyed, which is a tremendous pain in the ass. He wanted explanations, which is invasive when it isn't my story to tell, but Myla smoothed it out with a censored version of her issues with her ex. She stays close to me, insecurities on full display. She smells like his cologne, like he spent too long pressed into her personal space. It's making me unreasonably mad.

He's a lot more than controlling, but she left it at that. We're supposed to be smoothing things out after an ambulance, the police, and a news station were all called. His head bounced ever so perfectly off the metal parking meter, and there's a gash in the back of his head as well from smacking into the concrete. It was a spectacle for sure.

Phil glares at me, reminding me I could be slapped with a lawsuit if he presses charges. I was working when I decked him, and I made a scene for the local news team. I'd love to go to court over this. Even if I lose I'll enjoy making a jury see that he's a piece of shit boyfriend.

Ex-boyfriend. He didn't deserve her in the beginning and he clearly doesn't now.

All this drama over a girl I'm supposed to be training. People think we're in a relationship now. I don't do relationships. Emotions get too messy. Physical needs are easier to give up in the end. You let go of the feel-good feelings and move on.

Emotions cloud judgment. They make you do reckless things, like punching someone into a parking meter.

Despite the news station turning this into a fued-worthy headliner, we manage to hide upstairs. They're making a dramatic story out of it, and I'd be unsurprised if someone talks to Liam to get his side of the story. I refused questions, so did Melissa, who ensured our client was not caught in the crossfire. Unfortunately people put the pieces together and they know I work up here, so a reporter stood in the waiting area for twenty minutes until security removed them.

Liam jumped up from the ground, going off about me fucking his ex. *A hot shot attorney always steals the girl.* I wanna roll my eyes at the line all over again, a headache forming in my temples. If he wasn't such a tool, he wouldn't have to pull out the dramatics.

It's not like I could lay into him like I want on a crowded street. I can't bring up a mysterious pill bottle with a crowd. I was working, and I'm not airing out Myla's business like that. I need time to talk to her. The little pinched look on her face bothers me.

We haven't been alone this entire time. Laci fusses over Myla like a mother to her firstborn, and Phil has more off the wall questions than *Jeopardy!*

I want to check her myself; she looks shaken up but otherwise physically fine, rubbing occasionally at her wrist. But her confidence is rattled, and I need to hear what he said to her.

He made a dig, I'm positive. Her shoulders droop, her confidence holding on by a thread. She was just starting to make progress, and his entitled ass had to step back in and ruin everything. I want to run my hands over her skin, to ensure he didn't somehow do something worse. I want to quiz her, figure out what he said to deliver that blank look back into her eyes.

Now if Phil could just stop with the questions.

By the time we escape it's past five, and Laci shoots me a concerned look before heading out. I wrap an arm around Myla's shoulders, tossing concern to the wind, and we walk silently back to our set of offices.

When everything is gathered and we're sitting in my car, I quiz her. The reporters scattered for a more news-worthy story by the time we headed out. "Tell me what he did."

"That's not-"

"Myla," I snap, gripping the steering wheel without driving. I need to calm down first. "Just tell me. No games, I just want to hear what happened."

The fight in her is gone, so she tells me. He questioned her, intimidated her, made her question herself and her abilities. There could be absolutely nothing to his video threats like she says. Or there's damning evidence on his phone that needs to disappear.

Either way, I listen until she's finished. My eyes glare down at her wrist, but it's impossible to say whether or not the skin will bruise. When silence envelopes us again I manage to drive out of the parking garage. My mind is scattered. I should try and reign in the anger and focus on her. It's difficult when my hand burns, questioning why I didn't keep going until he stopped moving, client or not. The problem would be gone if I just took care of it.

Walking into the house, I expect her to slink off and hide. He's good at destroying progress, and Myla's eyes swim with the same problems that have weighed her down since the beginning. I've just tossed my keys on the table, tugging my tie when she's on me.

Literally. Her hands lock behind my neck, heated kisses pressing to my lips as her body presses into mine. I catch her hips, keeping her a scant few inches from me as I meet her lips. I only kiss her a moment before reaching up to grasp her chin, tugging her back.

She doesn't wait for my question. "Sir, please. I don't want to think about Liam anymore. I don't want to think at all."

Myla wants an escape I can easily offer. Kissing her again, I let my hand brush her cheek. She's tense but not pulling away. I can study her as we play, and ensure he doesn't touch what isn't his. He was close to her. I can tell without asking as I kiss her.

"You'll tell me if he did anything when I ask," I reply, thinking of the backhanded commentary. She's eager to nod, and I do nothing more until she speaks.

"Yes, Sir."

I tap her thigh before hooking my hands behind her legs, and she effortlessly wraps her legs around my hips when I lift her. I want her with me, beneath me, moaning for me. But I want to do something different this time.

My stairs are familiar, wide, and easy to climb even with her clinging to me. I don't stop until we reach the master bath, setting her down on the tile. She gives me an odd look as I toss off my tie, pulling up my sleeves to fiddle with the water.

"We're gonna shower?" She asks, confusion clouding the heat in her voice. I eye her when the setting is right, moving to the buttons of my shirt.

"You reek of his cologne. He's soaked in that shit."

I'm halfway done before she steps forward, finishing off the buttons to trail her fingers low on my stomach.

She's eager, uninhibited, something she hasn't been at my house since she started staying here. The idea of my bedroom makes her shy away, the same with the bathroom. She's fighting whatever war plagued her before, probably to mentally tell Liam off.

I'm not about to tell her to stop. I can analyze it later.

I may have torn the buttons on her top, I'm not sure. Her clothes join mine on the floor, and I back her into the shower with kisses.

I'm not training. I've thrown it to the wind. She doesn't need a lesson, just a distraction. One time with no rules and no foresight won't doom me.

She shudders when the dual shower heads hit her back, the slight sting of heat touching my busted knuckles. Running my hands up the curve of her spine, I can feel the little scars he left behind. The mark on her ass is all but gone, and aside from her neck I don't see any new spots.

I should've hit him harder. Dragged him up by his hair like he so fondly pulled her around, and slammed his head into the meter a second time. Or kicked him in the teeth while he was down. Something.

Myla kisses my neck, distracting me. "Sir? You're overthinking."

I almost laugh at the irony. Grabbing her hips I drag her to me, pressing her against my hardening dick. Her moan disappears into my mouth when I kiss her, wet hair slipping easily through my fingers.

Turning us, I push her to one side. There's a long built-in seat on one wall, perfect for partners. I push her down onto the bench until she's eye level with my cock, gripping her soaking hair.

She's eager, grabbing at the base to lick my head. I moan, placing a hand above her on the wall. Keeping my distance the last few days was crucial. I'll distract her all she wants but we're doing it my way. "Open."

It isn't as difficult for her to relax this time, maybe because there isn't an audience watching. My head brushes the back of her throat and she gags, but a few encouraging words is all it takes to get her to open wider.

"Look at how well you take direction. I knew you'd learn to relax for me. Good girl." My fingers brush through her hair, opposite the punishment Liam would give her. "You need this."

Her moans echo off the tiled walls as I slide down her throat. She still gags, but there's a determined look in her eye when I talk to her. She wants to be better, and practice makes perfect. I'll practice with her every day now until she doesn't struggle anymore.

When I let her up for air she gasps, saliva mixed with the water raining down on us. Her eyes are wild, legs wide open. I haven't touched her yet, her gaze filled with lust. Removing my hand from her locks I run my fingers across her cheek to brush her lips. Perfect.

She's eager, licking her lips. But I have other ideas. Kneeling down on the tile, I hold her gaze, brushing my tongue over her swollen clit.

Her cries fill the room, fingers scrambling uselessly across the bench. I keep a hand on her hip so she doesn't slide away from me, the other hand dipping to brush her wet little pussy.

She's dripping already, panting on the bench. Her eyes are wide, enormous, looking at me like I've offered a gift from God. I hold her eyes with mine, leaning forward again to lightly nip with my teeth.

Bucking on the bench, I fleetingly wonder if she'll bruise her ass on it. The water does nothing to distract us from one another, splashing into one side of our bodies. I run my tongue up her slit and she gives a strangled cry.

"Did Liam ever taste you like this? Could he be bothered?"

She's shaking on the bench as I slide a finger into her, watching her gaze grow heavier. She jerks her head as I gently tease in and out of her. "N-no."

Her voice isn't faring well, but I want her to answer me. I plan on knowing everything he's deprived her of enjoying. "No?"

Shaking her head harder, she bucks to meet my agonizingly slow pace. "No! Sir."

I tilt my head to the side. "Did he ever?"

Myla shakes her head again, arching up on the bench when I add a second finger. Her back leaves the wall, hands scratching at the tile behind her. She looks gorgeous, slowly coming undone for me, pressed to the tile. I click my tongue at her response, watching each move of her hips. "That's too bad. What a waste."

She cries out when I nip her clit again before diving lower. She's already soaked; working her up is all too easy. Dragging my tongue along her entrance she moans again, her fingers tentatively resting on my hair before pulling back. I hum against her for a moment, her body shaking against my lips before I pull back.

"Show me what you want darling. Everything you wished he would offer you. There's nothing you can ask that I won't give to you."

Myla moans when I return to her, licking her again.

She tastes better than I imagined, and her ex missed out on a whole experience depriving her of this. I suck at her lips and she cries out, thighs tightening and hands falling to grip at the longer locks at the top of my head.

She's direct when given the chance. Riding my face, she cries out every time I pinch her clit. She teeters on the edge of her orgasm, letting me lick and taste every inch of her I can.

My tongue is drenched, and I plan on sharing with her. If Liam was too much of a bitch to offer to please her, I doubt she's gotten the chance to taste herself in a long time. But fun teasing won't get her off, no matter how close she is.

Myla has a kink, one of my favorites, and I'm discovering she likes to reach her limits before getting off. I pull back, tapping my fingers along her exposed, sensitive pussy. She shakes looking down at me, eyes pleading with me.

I smirk up at her through the water. "Orgasm control is fun. Liam wouldn't fuck you the right way, now you think you have to wait for my permission. What a good little listener you are."

She whimpers when one hand trails up her side, the other hovering over her clit. I love that she's desperately waiting for me. I didn't give her explicit instructions to not cum freely, but she needs the push to cum at all.

I wink at her, and she unravels when I deliver a swift smack to her clit. "Cum."

Her cries echo in the room as I lap her up, her hips coming up off the bench. She craves permission to get off, as she desires submission in all other aspects. I let her ride it out, fingering her until her body relaxes back into the bench again.

She's panting when I remove my hand and stand, holding out my fingers to beckon her. Her posture is destroyed as she leans forward, falling against my torso. I don't think she's used to regularly finding a release. But her hot breath hitting my dick does nothing to help my erection.

I trail my fingers over her lips, but she's already getting the idea. "Suck."

Her eyes glance up, curious gray orbs holding my gaze. She can take them easily between her lips after struggling with my hard on. There's uncertainty back in her gaze as she licks my fingers clean. When I am satisfied she lets go with a pop.

"You taste amazing," I tell her, helping her to stand. I'm nowhere near done after today. "Liam's a fool for not taking a taste."

She moans into my mouth, and I can't get enough of her. I'll train her tomorrow. For today I'm enamored with her. I wrap my arms around her waist as I kiss her. "Grab."

Tapping above us, she notices the handlebars attached to the upper walls for the first time. Quizzical eyes stare down at me and I smirk. "I'm not going to hold you up. So you better hold on."

Her grip is immediate, and I have free range of her body without holding her up. She moans when I cup her breasts, dragging my fingertips over her nipples until they pebble, bending to flick my tongue over each in turn. She's a panting, rocking, hazy-eyed mess in a few short moments.

My cock is beyond hard, and I need to be inside her. The toys I keep aren't useful in the shower, and I'm too busy to detach one of the shower heads right now.

Guiding the head to her entrance, I use my free hand to press against her other hole.

She's tense but rocking against me at the same time. I'm gripping her hip just hard enough that she can't move freely. Leaning close, I speak against her lips. "I'm going to fuck you until those legs give out and your arms let go of the bars. I'm going to fill you until you can't handle more. And each time you want to cum, you'll ask permission. Understood?"

Myla moans, arching just enough to get some friction on her clit from the head. "Yes! Yes, Sir."

I smirk, and in one smooth motion I fill her full. She cries out, her body a little less resistive than last time, tossing her head back as I fill her with every inch of me.

"Good girl. You get better and better every time."

Picking up speed, I pound into her. My hand stays on her waist to keep from bouncing her painfully into the wall, the other teasing her puckered hole from time to time. She's resistant, and I won't take her in that way for the first time in the shower. She cries out on the end of my cock, legs gripping tighter and tighter to my hips.

It doesn't take her long to get there, like I assumed it wouldn't. "Sir, I-"

"Cum for me," I say, leaning up to kiss her lips. I pick up speed, crashing my hips into hers and she comes with a scream.

It's not enough. I need to hear her again. I grip her hip tight, nodding to the bars. "Hold tight or you'll impale yourself."

She's moaning, and I continue to tease along her ass. She's so lost in the moment she doesn't seem to care, arching up into me. I add a little pressure as I fuck her, and her head snaps up.

I watch her intently, waiting for her cue. She has to talk to me. "Words."

Myla wets her lips, panting. Her long hair is a mess behind her as she struggles to stay upright. For a moment I think she's going to resist again and make me question her ability to communicate with me. But as she struggles to keep up with my thrusts she nods her head. "Green."

Interesting. I expected her to say red and we would stop. Anal is not something I'd try the first time in the shower when she's proven to be tight. I like lube to avoid unnecessary pain or friction. But a finger won't break her.

Holding her gaze, I press harder until there's pressure. "Tell me when darling."

She whimpers but doesn't say much, holding my gaze. Her body fights the intrusion, and she's either never tried this or Liam (undoubtedly) had no idea what he was doing. I let go of her hip, confident she's holding on well enough to support her for a few moments, and adjust the shower temperature and angle it to hit her more directly.

I keep the same rhythm going, the focus of the shower more directly aimed at her throbbing clit as I pound into her. She gasps when I slip a finger into her ass, arms shaking on the bars.

She won't last much longer, and neither will I. Pumping up into her, I feel her resistance when I press another finger into her. Her panting fills the room as steam takes over, and I can feel my balls beginning to tighten.

"Sir," she begs, and it's the first time I've ever wished she used my name instead. "Sir, please."

I plunge deeper into her ass until she screams, her body clenching around me. She's right on the edge. I smirk, resting my opposite hand just above her clit. She just learned to cum without needing the final slap. "Cum on my cock Myla, with my fingers stuffed up that tight little ass."

Her cries echo through the shower and I'm just behind her. Slipping my fingers out, I catch her when her arms give, sliding her off my dick to set her on the bench. It takes barely a pump of my arm before I empty myself across her chest, bracing an arm on the wall above her.

The shower washes away the mess, and Myla has a content little smile on her face. She's spent, chest heaving in the cooling spray of the water. I give her a minute to relax, grabbing the bottle of soap off the shelf. She's half aware when I start running the sponge over her skin, eyes opening.

"You don't have to-"

"It's aftercare," I reason, giving her a look. "Learning submission isn't just about learning to do whatever I want. It's a partnership. You let me do dirty things to you and wear you out. Taking care afterwards is part of the exchange."

She frowns, her discomfort bleeding through. "I can wash myself."

"I never said you couldn't. But you're tired, and I'm the reason you need to scrub. Letting someone care for you isn't a sign of weakness. It's a power exchange. You submit for me. I care for you."

She grows quiet, thoughtful, and lets me wash her skin in silence. She's more hesitant when I reach for the shampoo, and when I think about why, my anger pitches again. She's stiff when I start massaging her scalp, but after a few moments she relaxes and leans into me, the exhaustion in her limbs evident.

Keeping a hand on her upper back when I wash it

out, she starts trusting me. The conditioner is faster, and by the time I'm finished she's halfway into a dream state.

I ring out her hair, wrapping her in a towel. Myla is more relaxed than I've ever seen her, but she still stiffens when I lead her back to my bedroom.

Her hand falls out of mine, and I study her. "I... I would prefer to go back to my room."

I leave her where she is, walking to the bed. Her eyes trail me. I didn't put a towel on my waist. It's for her benefit with the AC. I quickly washed myself around her, my hair leaving little drops on the carpet. "Why?"

Staying in here sets her off. She withdraws every time I've tried. Even now she's fighting it, when the hazy call of sleep beckoned her moments ago. Fidgeting by the bathroom door, she eyes the doorway to the hall.

Her body says it all. She feels trapped, but I don't get why. I'm not keeping her captive. It must fall back on Liam, but I don't think she'll offer anything more today. It's not late, but the day was long and tiring.

I'll leave her be for right now. She needs time alone with her thoughts. I shrug, gesturing to the door, and she nearly bolts to it. "Find something to wear. We'll order in."

15 MYLA

David hasn't pushed, but I know he wants to. He was on the phone with Milo last night when I overheard him in his office. It's a basic room, with a few files and mostly holding a laptop and safe he pointed out when I was snooping. He isn't hiding things from me.

I didn't ask what he was talking about. I didn't go back to sleep in his room either. Memories of Liam plagued my sleep, but I can't go to bed next to David.

I didn't mention the video again. If Liam does have something it could work as evidence against me. I haven't shared with David, even though he stresses that I should tell him my concerns. I guess it's another part of the line of communication, sharing and letting him carry some of my burdens. I guess he knows about some sort of video from Liam blabbing and getting punched, but he isn't interrogating me about it.

The office is abuzz after Thursday. I'm all too eager to run out Friday evening, the long holiday weekend.

Labor Day weekend. Usually I drive down to the Springs at the asscrack of dawn to watch the hot air balloons lift off there. It's one of the best events in the state. We watch balloons, drink coffee, and stop for breakfast. We always go on the first day of liftoff.

Laci called it off. She stated the Liam issue was more pressing, and claimed she needs to spend time with her brother. He's in town for the weekend before his next semester starts, and I don't intrude on her sibling bonding time.

I'm pretty sure it's an excuse to not intrude on my time with David. No one says anything, but everyone buzzes around, waiting for us to kiss or something. I don't want to impose on him so I don't. That will ruin the learning curve.

Friday evening passes in a blur of sex. David told me I can initiate, so I tried it out on his couch. It worked wonders, and the leather is finally breaking in.

Saturday, we go back to the club. I can't believe how giddy I am. David held off coming back, but I'm all too eager. He said they do a suspension show for the holiday, and labors of love.

I don't know what any of that has to do with each other, but here we are.

I get to wear something sparkly he picked out. It's silver, glittery, and long with a slit that almost reaches my hip. The underskirt doesn't do much to cover me. But I'm not worried. Sexuality is embraced here, giving me an extra sense of power.

Callie smiles my way when we arrive. She's actually wearing something akin to a top this time, a sheer slip of fabric with beads all over. Her hair is up in two tight pigtails, and the collar on her neck is glittery gold with space for a key.

I stare at it when she hands me my drink. It locks on her. She winks and catches my hand before I can pull back, following my gaze.

"Got it from the store," she explains, gesturing to a mirrored space I assumed held more toys. David never directly takes me inside there. "New. Shiny." She wiggles her eyebrows. "New designs too. If you want to check them out, the designer is in. I'm sure David would show you."

I blink and pull back, reaching towards my neck. We haven't discussed it. My neck is tender but nearly healed. I haven't humored putting another collar around it, not when the last one hurt me. David's hand plays along my back, and I glance at him.

He's giving Callie a pointed look. "I don't collar my partners until they are ready. Myla hasn't expressed the desire. We'll look if she decides."

Callie gives us a smirk before dropping her gaze. "Of course. But Rich is here if you decide to take a peek."

David shrugs, and I stay quiet as we walk away. I don't know what to do about that. He showed me the drawer he keeps specifically for toys, a much friendlier collection than the crap Liam and I used.

Everything he owns looks new. He said he doesn't reuse toys with new partners. It makes me feel better. A collar is absent from the collection. He didn't elaborate why.

We sit at a table off to one side, and I take in the stage. It's done up for performance night, and the room is packed compared to the sparse onlookers for a lesson. As we wait Emilio sits down with a girl I don't recognize.

I do a double take. She's naked save for a sheer cloth wrapped around her body, and she's sitting on the floor in the submissive position David showed me. She's wearing a collar, but not a glitzy one like Callie. This is leather like my old one, but significantly better quality. There are cuffs around her ankles and feet that look like they interconnect but are currently left loose, and a chain resting lightly in Milo's hand.

She notices me and winks. *Winks*. I down my drink

and wait for the show to start. Some things are still too much for me. David's fingers dance across my back, and I relax again.

The show itself is a spectacle. Glitz and glamor galore. I thought the suspension showcase would involve sex swings like the one David kicked under the bed at my apartment. This is nothing like that: hooks hang above the stage, and all across it with lengths of rope and elaborate ties. There's a man at the front of the stage, probably in his late forties, holding up each length of tie or rope he plans on using. The women performing with him are in various states of undress. Some are completely nude, some wear little slices of fabric, a few have glittery hooks and loops attached to their attire.

At some point I'm sitting forward, forgetting about the rest of the table. The man orchestrating the show is detailed. He shows the types of rope or cloth used, some of the performers he ties to the lengths hanging from the ceiling when the demonstration is complete. Some he ties with the separate pieces spread out on tables across the stage.

A few have hooks that he laces the ropes through, and suspends from the chains above. It's like a moving orchestra, girls lifting into the air as he demonstrates full body binds, and he attaches toys as he goes.

A whip in one girl's hand that she uses on another. A dildo in the next girl. Some cannot move, some have free reign. The women that can move twist about like aerial performers in sequin outfits or nothing at all.

The audience drinks it up. Some couples make out. I see one woman stripping for her partner. A man does the same on the other side of the room. A few are doing more than kissing.

No one bats an eye. No one interrupts. I'm noticing a theme around the room, even onstage. The Submissive partner, in almost all dynamics, wears something like a collar. Some have chains, some pretty, expensive embellishments like Callie had. She isn't part of the showcase, and neither is Nate. I've seen neither since we grabbed our drinks.

Wait staff buzzes around the room, keeping those who aren't at their limits well stocked. I don't want to drink more. I want to see if my inhibitions stay in place when the club is crowded but I'm not relaxed from drinking.

Eyeing David, the haze of insecurity returns. I haven't even humored the collar idea. I wore it for fun with Liam. Many of the people here wear it like a prize. I don't fear David the way I do Liam, but I don't know that I want to parade around with some gaudy neck piece while he's training me.

That's all this is, training. He very clearly drew out the lines for us. There's a finite amount of time before we go our separate ways. Buying or wearing a collar is more than teaching me a D/s relationship.

I might have my fears, but it tamps down my confidence knowing David won't ever offer. I want the full experience and I trust him. But I can't expect more from him if this dissolves when I'm satisfied with what I've learned.

How long can that even take? A few weeks, a couple months? When it is over I'd have to either give it back, or keep it and bear the memories.

Still, I wonder what it feels like to actually enjoy it. To know your someone's prize above all others. Not in the cruel, possessive way Liam was. But in a claiming, sexy way, like David is.

The rest of the show passes, and I try to focus. Every so often I see David and Emilio saying something to each other, but they speak low and quiet. It's a secret I'm not invited into.

As the lights come back up, the man onstage begins to help his partners down. No one assists, and first I think it's a jab until he releases the first, showering her in kisses and running his hands all over her, massaging along any spots that were bound.

I blink when he repeats it with the second woman, then the third. David stays beside me through the fifth before leaning down to speak in my ear. "They are part of a harem. They show up with Julio every few months for a showcase like this." His touch is gentle on my arm as he turns me, and I realize the table is vacant. "We give them some privacy after the performance. Julio is generous to his partners."

Following his lead, we walk back to the front. I want to go up to the roof again and test my exhibitionist curiosities, but he pauses out in the lobby. My eyes drift to the area Callie indicated earlier, and I want to put the brakes on the part of me that's curious. I don't need a collar to wear, given by someone who's only interested in training me.

We pause when a man approaches, and I watch his attitude. Most everyone here is mindful of each pair's dynamic. I've noticed differences between Dominant and Submissives compared to Masters and Slaves, but I can't figure out this guy. He's tall, clean cut, probably in his thirties. There's tattoos along his neck and the tops of his hands. Everyone is dressed to impress, but he's wearing a suit jacket without a shirt, his tie loose on his neck.

"Vinny," David says, his voice tense. It takes a moment to remember this is the club owner. Vinny flashes a set of pearly whites and winks at us.

"David, I see you found yourself a playmate. Is she planning to hang around?"

He nods, eyeing me. "Yes, we're learning." He tugs me forward, showing me off. His hand rubs gentle circles on my back. "This is Myla."

Vinny turns his attention to me, and holds out his hand. I take it, but he doesn't kiss mine or shake. He bows, eyeing me as he does so. His smile is genuine when he stands, nodding to David. "If teaching is all you want, that's fine. We just need to fill out the proper paperwork and ensure all is consensual."

I almost laugh out loud, but that would probably be in poor taste. Vinny is more concerned that David and I have a good standing relationship than Liam ever was about our intimate one.

I've started looking at Liam in a different light. Distance offers perspective, and what I used to assume was commonplace I'm now realizing was abusive. Doing things I couldn't remember, starting sex while I was asleep and waking me in the middle, bragging about videos I don't recall. It's manipulative.

David makes me feel good about myself. My fears of sleeping in bed with him absolutely stem from Liam. He wants a verbal explanation so we can move past it. I can't form a relationship with anyone without being able to lay beside them and trust them, and he may not push but he's pointed it out a couple times.

"Jo will come by to have you fill out the forms," Vinny explains, catching my attention. His chocolate eyes are hypnotic, drawing me in. He's patting David on the shoulder like an old friend, and they turn to go.

My heart picks up. I've never been alone here without him. But David just smiles, and I recall we fill out forms separately.

Callie appears from nowhere, back to her favorite nude form. I give her a strained smile as we sit and watch passer-bys, but no one is playing up here. I want to walk further in and explore, but I have to get this tedious part over with. When the forms are signed, I'll be David's partner until they are voided out. I won't have to pay a membership and I can come or go as I please.

"Jo is nice," Callie explains, flashing me a winning smile. "Vinny just runs a tight ship. He hates to see anyone be mistreated."

She's eyeing the marks on my neck, and subconsciously I touch them. It's nearly healed, and I think I may even avoid scars. Any other marks are covered, and though my wrist is tender it never bruised. "It's not what you think. David didn't-"

"Oh, hon, I know he didn't." She shakes her head, the soft expression in her eyes turning hard. "Permanent marking is frowned upon. Very few people truly enjoy it here. Blood play is dangerous. Even the dungeon downstairs has limitations. The guards usually stop couples who partake. It's difficult to watch someone be manipulated like that. I've known David for years. He isn't into marking." She shoots me a wink. "Claiming is completely different. I'm sure he'll keep you around."

"He's just helping me learn."

She laughs, patting my exposed knee. "Keep telling yourself that."

I don't get to argue. A woman wearing an oddly extravagant hat appears, a sheer gown the only other coverage, though I can see straight through. Her face is youthful, and she has surprise dimple piercings that contrast the softness of her strawberry blonde hair. "You must be Myla. Come, let's get this sorted so you can enjoy the night."

Callie gives my hand a squeeze of encouragement before disappearing. I look around but David isn't back yet, and the newcomer must sense my unease. "Vinny is old friends with David," she continues, trying to soothe my worries. David had spoken with me about needing to sign with the club to continue coming and while I was adamant I wanted to, actually doing it is another experience. "They seem to be taking their time filling out David's forms. We have you fill them out separately for safety's sake; ensuring you're both on the same page and no one is being manipulated." She smiles warmly. "I'm Josephine, Vinny's wife. You can call me Jo. Come, you can review anything he signs, and I'll show you the agreement. We've seen you two together a few times, so we believe you know what each other wants. And of course we keep your forms confidential."

I'm surprised how candid she is, following her into a cramped room with a loveseat and two cushy chairs. It's sparse, but I doubt this is used for much. The forms come out instantly, and they all look pretty standard.

I almost laugh again at the *defined relationship* line. I put in Submissive, and add trainee at the end. I don't miss the curious look in Josephine's blue eyes, but I don't question it. David never claimed to want me as anything more than a student.

It's almost a copy of the form I filled out with David, only this one has some of the rules of the club. You can't bring in outsiders without express permission beforehand, which made me realize that David had to call ahead the first time to mention me before we arrived. Background checks are run to ensure safety, medical records are required so there isn't a concern of spreading anything to other members, and anyone has a right to end their contract at any time. I already knew this. David gave me the protected email to send my records to after Vinny evidently gave him hell for not having me send them over beforehand. When my contract expires, whenever David is finished with me, I can decide to stay with the club and shell out the money for the membership fee.

I haven't thought that far ahead, so I push the thought away. I don't need to overthink.

A knock on the door interrupts me as I'm filling out preferences, and Vinny appears with a form. Right. We don't see each other's answers. This is how the club knows that we've agreed to everything consensually without coercion. I finish up and hand mine over, and Josephine gives me a dazzling smile that highlights her pierced cheeks as Vinny leaves.

"I think you're good for him," she explains, assembling a neat stack. "David always brings his own partners in, but you're the first one to stick. He never brings girls back after the first time."

The unsolicited statement shocks me. That's an odd thing for a membership-wielding sex club member to do. This is my third visit, and I hope it doesn't end. "Oh."

"I can tell he's fond of you," she continues, leading me back towards the front. "He's careful with you. It's different."

I'm not sure it's her place to comment, but I forget to care when I spot David. He's chatting with Emilio again, that woman still sitting happily at his feet. She seems utterly content like that and Milo gently strokes her head. David smiles when he spots me, wrapping his arm around me again.

I lean into his touch. I'm yearning for it. I'm pretty sure that isn't really how a Submissive behaves, or not one that I've watched. Outside of sexual pleasure, I realize I know little about what I should be doing.

Like the shower incident? I still don't know what to do with that. I had no expectations that David would clean me up. That's always been my job as far as Liam went.

David walks us away when they finish talking, and I'm too lost in thought to focus. We walk past the shop, and he points towards a display. "If you want one, I'll pick one for you."

My shoes catch on the dress and I almost fall over. "What?"

He raises a brow, keeping his hand at my elbow. "A collar. One that I don't find at the dollar store." His fingers brush over my neck, and lord help me as I arch into him. "If you want one. When you're ready."

This feels out of the trainee territory, but I don't argue. Gripping his tie, I fiddle with it and drop my gaze. "You want me to wear one?"

His grip on my chin is firm, and when I meet his blue eyes they are full of intensity. "I've wanted to replace his since day one. Collars are meant to be a symbol of pride, not shame. If you choose to accept and wear one, it's an honor. I want mine around your neck so anyone daring to look at you knows you're mine."

My heart leaps in my chest. This has to be outside the realm of learning. His words are sincere, and I drink them in. "I don't want to wear something gaudy like the leather one."

"It wouldn't be," he reasons, brushing my hair off my shoulder. His fingers are smooth, a contrast to his healing knuckles. "You're lovely Myla. You deserve to be envied. I would pick one just for you, so you always remember your worth."

My mind leaps ahead of me. "With a lock?"

"If you wanted. But I'd be content with a latch." He brushes along my collarbone, ever so gently over what's left of the cuts, and I think I might swoon at his touch. "It would fit snugly against your skin. A mark of pride. But removable if it's too much to handle. Delicate, so you could wear it to court. Discreet, so only people who live our lives understand the meaning."

I think I'm panting. *Over jewelry.* "Would it be mine to keep?"

David holds my gaze, his next words stealing the breath I've been holding. "Always. I don't collar anyone freely. If I give you a collar, it's akin to a wedding ring for me. It's a commitment to our relationship, and I like mine long-lasting. If I place one around your neck, I do it with intent." His fingers tilt my chin up, and all I want to do is seal my lips over his. "You'd be mine forever. But only when you're ready."

16 DAVID

Myla will be my descent to madness.

I'm supposed to be training her how to submit. Not falling for the girl from the office.

I didn't buy a collar last night, even if every nerve inside me said to. Watching her integrate into my world, free and willing to learn, eager eyes searching for approval, I think I've met my match.

Which is fucking annoying, since my match still needs refinement.

Fuck it, she doesn't need a thing.

The only limits Myla had were the result of a poor lover. Liam limited her, repressed her needs, and turned her into the sex-seeking siren asleep across the hall. Her eyes shimmered last night when I mentioned my requirements for a collar, and I swear she nearly caved and gave in.

That's dangerous territory.

I took her to one of the private rooms, too impatient to wait until we reached the house, and bent her over the bed. Her ass glowed the perfect cherry red when I was through with her, and my wrist stung from striking too many times. But I didn't break skin, just got her endorphins pumping like you're supposed to. She came multiple times and I had fun finishing her off with my cock.

It really just adds insult to injury that I'm in here

alone. I want her in my room. Talking about collars is fine and dandy but she's never even sat on my bed. She runs in and out of here like I have the plague. She refuses to even have a chat here, no matter the time of day.

I turn the faucet again and take an ice cold shower. I plan to remedy that today, or, at the very least, find the root of the issue.

Maybe it'll distract me from the spot inside me that warms every time I think of Myla.

It's got to stop. The agreement is for learning. Not commitment. She just got out of a relationship with a controlling asshat. She needs freedom, not a new relationship.

I turn the knob as far as it'll go and hope my dick doesn't freeze off.

Thankfully, she isn't on another *let's make a champion breakfast* kick. The first day was enough, and I can't handle that much self doubt so early in the day. Maybe I'll cook her something. We don't have to work tomorrow because of the holiday; I could keep her up late.

The text from Emilio as I reach my kitchen ruins my mood, and I find Myla glaring glumly down at her phone.

Great.

I've barely grabbed a mug when she starts talking. "Liam's going to post the video he has of me."

Okay, we're starting off the morning with bullshit. I snatch up the coffee pot to fill my mug, drinking it black as I sit beside her. "So you'll sue him for unlawful distribution of pornographic images."

Her eyes shoot wide, and I'm gonna need a shot with my morning coffee at this rate. "I don't want to sue him. I just don't want him to have anything of me that he can share." Her frown deepens. "I don't remember him filming, ever."

My grip on the handle tightens, and I remind myself to not destroy my dishes. I should've punched him harder. On repeat. Until he didn't move again.

Revenge tactics aren't my strong suit. I'm a lawyer because it forces me to think one step at a time. In my own life I prefer to hit first and resolve later. Dealing with Liam should be either jail time or a bullet between the eyes. My instinct is to go for the violent approach, because then I'll know it's finished.

But that would leave my hands dirty, and even if I don't really care, I'd bet my membership Myla does. I need to be more tactful than that if she's still avoiding reporting him.

Milo is great at this shit. He gave me the inkling of an idea last night while she was distracted with the show. Now we just need to set the cards in motion. Liam will be his own downfall, and he won't be able to fight it in the end.

It's a punishment even Myla will approve of, if I tell her, but she's too in her head right now, and I rub softly at her shoulders.

Liam is a problem I can't fix at this moment. His impression on her, though, I can at least work on. "It's a scare tactic. He's hoping you sit here and fret until you give in."

"It's a good one." She's shaking her head again, self doubt reappearing. "I almost had a chance at the office to call his bluff. I should've. He was right there-"

"You were intimidated and frightened," I cut in, pushing her phone away. "You wanted to get away from him. And there's no way to know for sure if he's being truthful. Don't beat yourself up over it. I'd much rather you play it safely."

She gives me a sad look. "I'd rather know he doesn't have anything else to hold over me."

I would too, but her safety is more important. I keep waiting for someone to serve me papers for decking Liam, and I'm still surprised I wasn't arrested. Melissa saved my ass, claiming he was being degrading to her walking by. He definitely was being a jerk. If she hadn't known the Denver squad car that pulled in, I'd be waiting for someone to post bail.

It would've left Myla vulnerable, even if Liam has a concussion. I had Emilio check and that's what the reports state. He'll be out of sorts for at least a couple days. Or even more hostile than before.

Her mood doesn't pick up, which is exactly why I enlisted Laci for help. Having her number is both a benefit and curse. She's more than willing to come play distraction, even if she doesn't know what I've got up my sleeve.

She also wants to know all about Emilio. I'm not one of her gal pals. I don't know anything I can share with her.

I hope Myla doesn't either. Discretion is important when it comes to the club. She knows this, but turmoil loosens even the tightest lips. Emilio won't come by when Laci is around if Myla blabs about his involvement.

When Laci arrives, I slip out before either of them can come up with creative questions. I need to chat with Emilio, and don't need them getting overly curious.

Parking outside Myla's apartment, I stare up at the building. Liam's trashed SUV is parked in the spot I know she pays for, and he's going to struggle with rent here soon. The holiday might save him, but unlikely. Rent is due, and this town is expensive. He won't last long without her help.

I saw the messages he's sent. Myla's guilt kicked in when she saw him complaining about paying, but when asked, she told me she paid almost all of the rent.

Scoffing, I told her to let him burn. He didn't put her on the lease, apparently a tactic in case he ever wanted to evict her (which is not how that works) so he's the only one that's going to get leashed with the bill and the ding on his credit if he doesn't pay up.

Emilio's message pops up just as I'm debating opening a snack. I don't want to be here long, but I like doing my investigating hands on. He's sending over the information he picks up in Liam's phone. *Brunette.*

I watch Liam appear with a girl that could be a knockoff of Myla. She's a little shorter, heavier, same long locks, still beautiful but obviously a substitute. Her eyes are hazel instead of gray. People don't pick lookalikes of their former girlfriends unless they want to send a message.

I feel kind of bad for her. It's not her fault Liam is a tool. When I'm finished with him, he won't be a danger to her. She looks sweet. Young. Probably easy to manipulate.

Poor thing.

He keeps pointing to his head, probably looking for pity. His nose is bruised and there's a bald spot with a bandage where I imagine they shaved away the hair to put in stitches. The girl runs her hands up his arm and I'm debating throwing up. Claiming to want Myla back and yet banging her lookalike is just another weapon in his arsenal of abuse.

I wait until he's driven off, oblivious to me, before

hopping out. I put a beanie on, which I positively hate wearing, and pull at the sleeves of the too small hoodie. I haven't worn a hoodie since I was twenty.

I wouldn't call it a disguise, but I don't need to be obvious either. Liam's going to have a rough time soon, and I don't need anyone recalling me. I know from our last visit the security here is shit, and Milo double checked the cameras. Most are for looks, they aren't hooked up. The only spots with video feed are up front by the office, and this apartment is nowhere near that.

Walking up to the door, I pretend to knock and slide the scanner against the frame. It's discreet. I only need it to alert me when he's home. Everything needs to be timed to a tee to avoid suspicion. He cant stray from the norm too much when I intercept. I don't take his cruelty to Myla lightly; he will pay for abusing her.

When I get back, I plan on focusing on my room and why Myla runs away every time. Part of our agreement is that she sleeps in my bed, yet she won't even hang out in there. I don't want to push, but any relationship she enters will have that expectation, someplace down the line. It shouldn't be ruined for her.

And I have a decent idea why she hesitates.

I slip my hands in my pockets, sliding the other device beneath the frame of the window by the door. Out of sight, out of mind. I only need to see if he's got company. The gear is Emilio's, from his father's stock. I'm certain it's high grade tech. But I'm only borrowing.

Turning, I resist the urge to check in on Myla. She's perfectly safe in my house with Laci. And I just saw Liam leaving with someone else. Nothing is happening.

I'm anxious because I have to push her. It's now or never.

17 MYLA

Laci hung out late again at David's. We haven't had this much freedom to hang out in years.

Before I threw myself into college to make a name for myself. Before mom ran off into her new perfect life and left me alone. Before Liam fell into the picture and started cutting off my friends.

Before Anita started her residency, we would sit in my crummy old apartment and binge watch TV until I almost missed class and Anita was running late. Laci didn't go to university, so she typically got to sleep in while we ran around madly, soaking in one of the few benefits of working the late shift.

When she left, I'm almost certain David walked her out to the car. We were asleep, but Laci was fretful about getting home. I'm surprised she left at this hour. Her paranoia is high, and she's usually triple-locked her apartment door by now.

Anita and I have asked her in the past about the excessive security, but she won't budge. Something haunts her that she refuses to share, and I'm almost certain it's part of the reason she so adamantly ripped me away from Liam when opportunity struck.

I nuzzle against the softness to my right, fighting off the lingering dreams. I should get up and go upstairs to bed before I trouble David. He was out, but not so late that I had to go and fall asleep on his couch again.

My fingers press into the pillow. It's a lot firmer than I remember.

The cushion feels like pecs.

And the armrest beneath my knees feels more like an arm.

My eyes flutter open in the dark, and I stare up at a man.

He's holding me. Reasonably, realistically, I know it's David. I'm in his house. But sleep is a curious thing, muddling your awareness for the first few moments. My eyes flicker open, and for just a moment it's not David.

It's Liam. Sandy hair, pensive eyes. His hands are too tight, restraining in a bad way. I don't remember his touch ever being gentle.

The scene around me flashes. The old apartment ceiling, the ugly popcorn aesthetic. Visions of him walking with me, tossing me on the bed, telling me it'll be alright -

I gasp and jerk in his grip, and he drops me. Not on steps but a flat surface. I kick out and connect with his ankle, skittering back on the floor.

"Ouch - shit, Myla!"

I snap out of the hazy fog. David leans down in front of me, far enough I can't kick him again.

David, not Liam. What kind of idiot am I? Of course it's David. Liam would never carry me gently.

I don't recall the memory. It must've happened if I could confuse past and present, but I don't know what to do with it. I've been nursing a growing fear that Liam drugged me after we found that bottle, but I've just avoided it. I didn't want to consider it, but it makes sense. I don't remember getting the gash in my head.

But the memory is vague too, hazy like a memory

I can't quite grasp. Is that a sign of another drug induced incident?

"Myla." David's voice is commanding, firm. It snaps me out of my raging thoughts. He's gripping onto my ankle with a gentle firmness, enough to keep me from kicking him but not enough to hurt. "Myla, it's me. You're alright."

Humiliation bleeds into me. And not the fun kind that earns a reward. I choke back a sob I didn't even think I was holding, staring at him in the dark. I'm ruining his lifestyle. I can't function as a Submissive, and I can barely operate as a person. I have strange recurring memory loss and an ex with a control problem.

David must sense my spiraling thoughts, and he moves forward in the dark hall. I tense when he grabs me again, pulling me into his chest. "Breathe, Myla."

He smells good, the scent a familiarity now, even after only two weeks: Tobacco and cedar. It smells like coming home.

His fingers brush through my hair, and I rest against him until I relax. When my breathing evens out, he stands, pulling me with him. There's a vague outline in the meager light from his room, probably drifting in from the walk in closet I've seen. "Are you going to tell me what that was about?"

I start shaking my head, then hesitate. David likes words. And maybe if I use the right ones he'll help distract me. "No, Sir."

His hands tense around me, and he's gripping my chin before I realize it. "Don't start something you don't want to finish, Myla. It's late. You'll come to my room at this hour."

It's a terrifying idea. I've avoided his bedroom

pretty much since I arrived. The memory of Liam is invasive, and I should shy away.

But I don't want it. I ruined a perfectly good moment, and the longer he controls me it'll ruin others. David is kind, and warm, and dominant at all the right times.

I check out the windows even though it's absurd. David wants me in his room, in his bed. Liam couldn't touch me there.

Wetting my lips, I rush out the words before fear grips me again. "I don't like being in the bedroom with you because it's the only place Liam would fuck me. Sometimes I'd wake up and he'd gloat about how much easier I am to handle when I was asleep. I had no memory of it. He would only do things in the bedroom." I hesitate to continue. "It was easier to hide the blood and the toys in one room. I... I don't like being vulnerable when I'm sleeping. That's why I don't go to your room."

My sleep delirium is screwing with me. I'm vomiting out way too much for this hour of night. David doesn't want to hear about my mental struggles, I'm sure. It's just another sad little dot on my map of poor choices.

His touch gentles on my chin, fingers running up to cup my cheek and I lean in. "You're never vulnerable to being hurt with me, Myla. I won't take advantage of your Submission. And I would never give you anything to make you forget our time together. I intend to make you remember every second."

He's kissing me, and it's the exact opposite of what I expect but it's exactly what I'm yearning for. My body is instantly responsive, the ground-in fear of rejection slowly slipping. I like the way my body ignites when David is touching me. His words sink into my skin like a balm I've needed to find. I keep expecting him to turn up his nose to my past and be done with my issues, but he isn't disgusted or annoyed with my admission, and it gives me an uncanny sense of power.

I don't delve into the reasons why. David's hands are on the backs of my thighs, lifting me up off the floor in a demanding manner, opposite to the sweet carry he used to bring me upstairs. He backs me into his bedroom, and although the nerves prick at my insecurities, I'm not panicking.

David isn't Liam. He's safe. And he cares if I'm coherent.

His bed is as comfortable as it looked when I ran out of here the first time, his sinful shower making its debut in my dreams. The sheets are soft and silky, washed with something woodsy that reminds me of him. He isn't suddenly gentle and treating me like glass after my admission, which I'm thankful for.

I don't want the dynamic to shift just because I had a random act of courage and told him my fears. I like the way David treats me. I don't want it to end.

Pushing me back into the sheets, he eyes the oversized tee and shorts I pranced around in all afternoon. His gaze is hungry, dark, and he gives me the infamous devilish smirk he's known for. "Wait there. Exactly like that."

Watching him curiously, he wanders to his dresser. I know the top drawer is full of toys he briefly showed me earlier this week before I zipped out of the room. He's quick to unlock it with the keys he keeps out of sight, and I stay where I am on the sheets. He pulls out something dark and black, followed by a leather covered paddle I'm familiar with.

It's the main toy he used before. I expect him to be done but he's fishing more out of the drawer, my eyes widening at the assortment.

"Spread," he says, turning back. "Turn over."

He wants me up on my hands and knees. I learned this last time he set the demands. This is the type of BDSM I expect. I can't get into the masochist/sadist side, and bondage is a part we haven't done a lot with. But I can see the ties trailing in his hands as he returns.

Ties, not ropes. He asked my preference days ago and I told him the strength of rope made me nervous. I'd rather ease in before he pulls out the heavy hitters.

His fingers drag down my skin, across my back and over my ass, along the backs of my thighs. He's taking his time, which is a tease all on its own, and I want to drop down on my stomach as he teases a finger along my slick pussy.

He's hardly touching, and I'm still excited.

Something soft wraps around my ankles, and I stiffen and look back. Last time he was direct about the position of my head, this time he's less inclined. He lets me watch as the ties slip around one ankle then the other, disappearing to the posts on either side of his bed.

This angle seems wrong. I always thought the point was to keep someone spread-eagle. He tugs the restraints, and it pulls my legs wide in this position. He pushes me down on my stomach before I can respond, dragging a finger along my aching core again before he circles my ass. His fingers slip between my legs, and another tie seals around my wrists, keeping them together beneath me.

I can't adjust. My head can whip back and forth, but he has a grip on the other side of the strap, keeping me down against the bed. Leaning over me, he leaves wet kisses along my shoulder.

"I love making you squirm," he says, his other hand massaging along my hip. "And I do enjoy that mouth of yours. But I'd rather hear those screams instead of keeping you quiet. You won't be afraid of sleeping next to me, because I only plan to fuck you when you're wide awake. You can't sleep through what I do to you."

I moan, the fear ebbing away. He has a point. I could never snooze through him railing me. My body is too responsive, and I'd definitely notice his cock pulling me apart.

"Tell me what you want, Myla."

He's going to make me ask. I don't know if it makes me more horny or more ashamed. I turn down and hide my face in the sheets, uncertainty leaking through. I don't want to have another weird flashback and ruin the moment.

The smack on my ass is swift and firm, and I jolt at the contact of the paddle. It's much harder than his hand, leaving behind a pleasant sting. "Words, Myla. Don't shut down on me now."

I wet my lips, letting the sting ground me to the here and now. "I want you to fuck me."

He chuckles. "Is that all?"

"Sir."

"Hmm." He pulls back, and I can feel my hips moving to their own accord. He's made me a glutton for punishment, and my body is just too needy as I wait for him. There's no way he'd deny me now. There's a pause as he messes with something I can't see, and then something locks over my sensitive clit.

I buck against it, but he has me retrained. I can't move as the device turns on full force.

I scream. It's not a moan but a full blown scream that wants to drag my orgasm out with it.

Just as quickly as it turns on, it stops again. "You'll cum when I say so, Myla. And it won't be without my cock in you."

I miss the friction, but David is quick to fill the void. I don't know how he shut it off so quickly unless there's a button, but the thoughts leave me as his head parts my lips, and I moan as he sheathes himself inside me.

Taking David is an altogether different experience from Liam. Liam was uncomfortable, and I figure it's because I was never this wet. He was smaller, easier to adjust to, but it always ended so quickly.

David isn't in the mood to give me a break, much less let me overthink. I feel him bottom out in me, his groin pressed tight to my ass, but it's only for a moment before he's whipping his hips into me with a precision I can't match. Between my restrained ankles and the grip he has on my wrists, I can't rock back into him.

It's torture, and I cry out again when the device on my clit flicks on for a few seconds before cutting off. It's definitely a button.

The paddle slams down on my ass again and I moan. He hasn't used this many toys on me since we started, and it's got to be a distraction tactic to keep me from slipping back into my mind. I don't care what his reasoning is, so long as he doesn't stop doing it.

I'm shaking as he pounds into me, and usually David throws in some dirty talk. But this is ruthless, his hands digging hard into my hip, the paddle in his hand slapping against my ass every so often.

And that damn toy on my clit has me spasming and panting beneath him. I want badly to cum, but David is insistent I will only when he offers permission. I think he did it in the beginning to convince me to not hold out. Now it's a ploy to control how long this lasts.

I love it. Whenever he does let me cum, it makes my eyes roll.

"I'm going to overwhelm you until you're not afraid to sleep in here," he growls, and I can hear the edges of anger. It's not directed at me. If he disliked Liam in the past, this is full-on hate. "You're going to squirm while your clit throbs. You can ask for your orgasm when you can't handle it anymore. But right now I need you to take my cock so I can fuck his memory out of you."

I moan. It shouldn't turn me on but it does. If memories could disappear so easily, life would be better. I struggle to connect with his thrusts, crying out whenever he strikes my ass for doing so. My clit is on fire and I'm shaking in the best way possible.

I can hardly focus, and the soft ties around me keep me in the exact position he wants. I don't feel threatened or in danger. I don't feel like he's using me just to toss me off the bed when he's finished.

David is looking at me, all of me, and he sees the person underneath everything.

The toy on my clit clicks off, and I cry out at the loss of friction. "Cum."

My voice echoes through his room, and it's a good thing the neighbors are spaced out. I'm rocking against him as much as I can, and I can feel my body shaking as the orgasm washes over me. He doesn't need to strike my ass to get me there. I'm already over the edge, falling into a puddle.

David follows suit. He pounds into me at that bruising pace a few more times before pulling out, and I feel it splash across my lower back. I let out a strangled breath, my body stiff from the position.

David's hands are light on my skin, and the taut pull at my wrists releases. "I'll get you out of that. Give me half a second."

I don't know how long it takes. I'm too busy riding my high to care. A few toys and some ties and I'm putty in his hands. He unwinds the knot around my wrist, breaking the tension on both my ankles before the ties disappear. I feel him swipe something across my back before tapping my hips, and I fall to one side.

My eyes glance down. The toy he placed over my clit is a little rabbit toy. I've seen them plenty of times before, I just didn't realize how powerful they can be. He removes it with ease, and I realize it was never attached at all but placed. My legs were pressed together to keep it in place initially, and the stickiness of my cum helped keep it there. He removes it, running a warm towel briefly over my sore body.

When did he go get that? I didn't realize he was wiping me down, I thought he was just releasing me.

The cloth is warm, comforting, and it even feels good over my sore ass as I lay there. I should get up and help. He's a mess too.

Before I get the chance, he sets a TV remote beside me, and winks as a glass of water appears on the table nearest to me. Okay, I don't think I was that out of it but I didn't even know he had a glass up here.

"Drink. Pick something to watch. I'll go grab another glass." He leans in, kissing my temple. It almost feels too intimate for us. "You did wonderful. Now rest."

I'm in a daze as he steps out of the room, completely nude. He turned the lights up at some point, and he left behind a second blanket for me. I wrap it around myself, enjoying the pleasant ache between my legs. My gaze flickers around the room.

It's nice here; plain, basic. A typical guy's room. The infamous bathroom is to the right of the bed and I hope we'll be using it again come morning. We should make the most of our day off.

Flipping through streaming services, a weight settles in my chest. This is nice, perfect even. It's commonplace for a couple to sit together in the bedroom after sex and not make a big deal of it. Liam had no interest in me once the deed was done, but David is the polar opposite.

It makes me feel loved that David is still interested in spending time with me even after he gets his rocks off.

And that can't happen. Letting feelings sneak in will only lead to heartache. David is too good to be true, and I'm starting to wonder what will happen when it's time to let him go. I doubt I'll ever find someone quite like him again.

18 DAVID

People don't get served paperwork on holidays unless the matter is severe.

I avoid it until Tuesday, and the damn courier shows up at the office. I've already heard the rumors floating around, and it's no surprise Liam's bitch ass is filing.

Punching someone into a parking meter doesn't go unnoticed. The media story isn't getting a ton of headlines, it's mostly a joke article. I'm certain that angered her ex. But he wants to press charges for being unjustly attacked, and before I read too much into the situation I stride into Melissa's office.

Melissa is a force all her own. She handles hard-hitting criminal cases with a smirk and a wink at the opposing party. She's tall, nearly my height, and with her heels I know she surpasses me by an inch or two. I'm nearly six foot three, but she's more intimidating than I am in court. She uses her height to her advantage, talking down to defendants and turning sweet eyes to a jury. She's great at swinging the jury one way or another, and she does it all in her signature red outfits.

Not maroon. Or orange-red. It's firetruck red on her bronzed skin, and she kills it. When I pop into her office she groans and pushes the file away.

"I'm betting you finally got served?"

I show her the notice. Melissa can handle the

preliminary work, and I need her to get it dismissed or handled quickly. Having a pending case will really ruin my plans. I won't be caught, but the less attention that's on me the better.

She lets out a breath, dark hair pulled up into a wayward messy bun. She's shoved a pen into one side, giving her a younger look than a refined attorney usually has. She's the newest partner, and neither Phil nor Bridgett will go against her. Personal injury lawsuits payout when the time is right, but Melissa brings the media attention when she wins or screws over someone in a high profile case. Her place at the law firm is absolute.

Which makes her the best attorney money can buy to get me out of this. An error in judgment while he bragged about hurting my girl is too much to ignore.

I almost stutter when she speaks to me, the thought on replay in my head. When did Myla become my anything?

"You're going to need to appear sympathetic. Judge O'Connor doesn't care for arrogant pricks."

Scoffing, I sit in the chair opposite her. "I wasn't planning on punching him. I didn't aim for the parking meter behind him. Call it a happy accident."

She raises an eyebrow, folding her fingers beneath her chin. "I said sympathetic David, not smug." One side of her lip pops up, interest shining in her eyes. "I didn't know you cared so much about Myla."

Tricky. I don't like showing my hand. We're supposed to be a teacher and student dynamic, not romance. I'm teaching her submission as a Sir, not taking her out on fancy dates.

Except that one time.

"It happened," I say with a shrug, dodging. "I need

an airtight reason for punching him."

"Just because he's being a jackass doesn't mean you get to punch his lights out. A concussion means you struck him hard enough to cause damage." My memory flips to Myla, the mark on her head sewn up in secret by her friend. I could toss that into the evidence box, and probably earn mutiny from the girl in question.

I don't care that I'm in a tiff with the law. I hate the impression he's left behind on her, and listening to him gloat is out of the question. I simply cannot do it. It's difficult to deal with if I'm going after Liam, but that's the position I've locked myself into.

When I only shrug, Melissa tosses up her hands. "I'll call Sabrina in to draft up a response. You'll look guilty lawyering up so early."

"Or prepared since I work here."

She shrugs. "Either way. The judge would lean one way or the other. If you show remorse," she continues, glaring, "it could be dropped with a plea deal."

""I'm not getting a blemish on my record because of him."

Melissa glares down her nose at me. "Then use discretion. If you want to punch his lights out don't do it on a public street." She stops, running her fingers through some of the loose hair that's fallen around her face. "You need the charges to be dropped. People don't trust an attorney with a shady side."

Well, people will lose it then if I ever get caught. I've put precautions in place to avoid that, and the motion sensor and camera are ample for what I need. I'll be slipping into his apartment before he's evicted, and he'll be walking back out a changed man.

I had half a mind to trick him into falling off the

balcony. Police might still be too risky. The plan isn't fine-tuned yet, which is okay, since I can't do much until I understand his schedule more. It's varied since Myla left and I'm waiting to snuff out consistency.

Maybe he doesn't have any, but it'll make things easier if he does.

"The entry will be filed this morning," Melissa continues with a wave of her hand. "Now go work on something. I've got to finish prep before Martin shows up."

I can't remember who Martin is, and I take the cue to leave. Myla is stuck in prep today with Phil and a longstanding client, and I've got to sit in on the Schreiber call while interrogatories are collected.

It's too high profile to leave to just anyone. The paralegal on the case is skilled, but paying me to sit there and help out is more than worth it with a settlement working its way towards eight figures. This is the kind of crap that makes its way into commercials and seals someone's career.

I should be focused, but my mind is on Myla. She finally slept in my room on Sunday, and again last night.

I left her up there Sunday claiming to need a water glass. In truth I needed to step away. The bottle I took from her place burns into my memory whenever she tells me something about her ex, checking off another reason he needs to be handled.

She didn't want to sleep in my room for fear I'd assault her and she wouldn't even remember it.

I broke the glass because I threw it when I went for water. I needed to punch something, but I didn't want to tip off Myla so late in the night that I was royally pissed. She knows I don't like hearing it, even if it's necessary.

It's half the reason I tied her up and took her like I did. I could've dragged it out.

But I want her to have nice memories of sleeping in my room, to replace the sick feeling that's settled in her gut. She was terrified when she thought I was Liam in her sleep induced haze, and I did get her to tell me about the memory that surfaced in the dark.

Running a hand over my face, I sit at my desk. She needs help. More than I can offer with sex and lessons. She should speak with a therapist, dive deep into her psyche and figure out any triggers that linger.

Vinny thought the same. I didn't like telling him about Myla, but it's part of the rules. He didn't get all the gritty details, but I had to say something. Two weeks later the marks on her neck are mostly little red lines, but there's evidence of past hurts.

He wanted to know if she'd be an issue. It's not the first time someone with a turbulent past has stumbled into the club. Trouble could follow her, but I don't believe Liam has the capabilities of a stalker. He gloats too much and is more likely to show his hand than hide it.

I assured him she wouldn't be a problem, and made him agree to say nothing. So long as it didn't cause issues at the club, Vinny and Jo are happy to keep their noses out of people's business. Myla doesn't show signs of continued, ongoing abuse, and that would be the biggest reason to worry.

I didn't get to take her back to the club. I've selfishly kept her to myself since Sunday. I can tell she's eager to return, so we'll have to go this week. She wants to be up on the roof again.

Smiling to myself, I flip the file I'm avoiding open. Myla is a surprise I didn't see coming.

~~~

The week passes with little conflict. After the unending antics over the last two weeks, a boring few days is welcomed. Melissa manages to get me off scott free.

The judge is forgiving after meeting Liam. I don't go to court, just sit in with Mel for the teleconference on Friday. Liam can't shut up, and I get the feeling he couldn't afford the attorney. He could get a public defender, but I'm betting that he thought it was too low class. The case gets thrown out without so much as community service.

He might be intoxicated during the teleconference. It’s a preliminary hearing to decide if the case warrants a true hearing date or if it’ll be dismissed. This is just supposed to go over evidence and prep for the trial dates further down the line if necessary. But Liam is irate, blathering, showing off his true colors. It's a poor move to earn sympathy from anyone.

He tells the judge openly during the call what he was saying on the phone that day about Myla, almost verbatim. Honesty isn't the best option when you come off as an ass. He proceeded to complain that his girlfriend needs to listen and she's ruined his week. The best way to get a case thrown out before it begins is to show the judge your complaint is unfounded. I may have punched his head into a meter, but he ruined his chances of going to trial by squandering the initial appearance in court. Melissa opting to appear by phone for the initial status was perfect. We didn’t have to waste time showing up in court, and Liam looked like an even bigger idiot. At least that problem is solved.
~~~

I don't need to do anything; he's digging his own grave, but it's nice when problems solve themselves.

Melissa gives me a knowing look after the call. She isn't into gossip, but she knows something is crooked with Myla's ex. I don't worry Myla when we talk, telling her that Liam couldn't shut the hell up and talked me out of the case all on his own. It definitely wasn't unprovoked like he tried to claim.

Saturday comes around again. She sleeps in my room each night. Every day she's a little more comfortable. Her hairbrush is in my bathroom, and she added the toothbrush and toothpaste this morning. There's even a shirt and some socks on one side of my bed.

I almost tell her to put her things in my empty drawers, but that might be pushing too far for her.

That she's even in here makes me happy. When I step out of the bathroom she's kneeling in the Submissive position I taught her. Rarely does she use it, hands up as she eyes me.

She wants something, I can see it in the light bouncing of her foot. She's hesitating to share. The position is wrong because she's fully clothed, but I'll let it be a moment. Smirking, I lean against the doorframe. "Looking for something?"

She bites her lip, and I don't think women realize how distracting that is. "I was hoping we could go to the club."

My eyebrows fly up. I step away from the doorframe, circling her. She's still in the lounge wear from early this morning, afternoon chasing evening now.

She should be sore. I wasn't as nice this last time, and I thought she'd want the break.

Her body trembles as I circle her, trying to

see what's up her sleeve. Satisfied she's not hiding something, I crouch in front of her. "I love how you ask, darling, but it isn't necessary. You can simply say you want to go."

The smile she gives me is effortless, and not nearly as concerned as before. She pops up out of her position to stand with me, second guesses herself, and I catch her arm before she slips back to the floor. Curious gray eyes look up to meet mine.

I wouldn't usually correct her. I let my partners give into their own levels of submission. Some like to request permission for way too much. Others prefer it to be strictly sex-related. Myla hangs somewhere in between, wrapped in uncertainty. I kiss her hand when she stands, sending her a wink.

I'm not myself. I know it. Myla drags out a sweeter side of me that I rarely share. I used to be a little more carefree with my family around, but those bonds have long since severed. We're spread around the country and no one is interested in a reunion.

Thinking of Myla disappearing from my side brings a level of sadness I can't face. She's coming into herself, offering submission where she's comfortable and defiance where she isn't. She isn't marked by an asshole anymore. She requested, in the most submissive way she allows herself to, to go to the club. She likes the freedom it offers. She revels in the atmosphere, soaks in the pleasure surrounding her. She likes the club, even if the first few times had her hair standing on end.

Decked out in another dress I managed to pick for her, she's practically dragging me inside. She's excitable and I don't want to squander the joy she's found in the place. There's another show tonight she's eager to watch, and I let her guide us to the bar for drinks.

Callie gives her a wink, her customary greeting towards Myla now. Nate is busy mixing drinks, since Callie is shit at cocktails, and they fall into easy conversation. I watch them, unwilling to drag her out of the mindless chatter.

When she saw Callie with Tyson, I thought she might have a stroke. Now she's used to the busty blonde, and seeks her out each time we visit.

She absolutely *did not* like Emilio's latest attempt at a Slave. I don't know why he does this to himself. He has a strict set of expectations, and very few members ever meet his goals. The one girl who did is long gone now, and each hopeful is met with disappointment. I spy him walking into the club, stopping to chat with Vinny. He barely nods my way before disappearing.

Time is on our side. Myla is happy tonight, ready to drink in the euphoria of the show. I send a smile her way when she peers up at me, and force the thoughts from my head. Liam is a problem for next week. The cards are in motion. As satisfying as it would be to strangle him to death, Myla turns her nose up to violence. She might appreciate the sentiment, but I think she'd grow to hate me with time. Any violence on her behalf has to fit the crime.

Manipulation is the name of the game. Control. Liam wanted so desperately to control Myla that he made careless mistakes. The mistakes will cost him, and in the end he'll only have himself to blame.

19 MYLA

"Let's look."

I almost trip in my heels passing the shop. David agreed to fill our Sunday with sin and return to the club. Curiosity gets the better of me, and I've peered at the store more and more each time we go. I don't go in, because what's the point?

My eyes zip to his. He isn't joking, holding out a hand to me. We haven't discussed collars since Callie brought up the designer last week. His words float around in my head, taunting as they are intoxicating.

His. If he places a collar at my throat he intends to keep me. It would contradict everything we've discussed so far.

Akin to a wedding band. Those were his words. It's more commitment than a few weeks together learning submission, and that's something that scares me. He must see the conflict in my eyes, his jaw tensing. "We're just looking. You're curious. The shop is here to browse."

I do want to go in. I want to know why the windows show such elegance for what is essentially a sex shop. The gowns in the few windows are all glitz and glamor and in various states of undress. One is little more than a silver see-through shift. Walking to the entrance, I see the slip is set with little sparkling diamonds in the material.

The price tag makes me want to turn away, but David wants to look. His hand is low on my back, the dark gray outfit of the evening jumping off his skin. He looks even more decadent than usual, the tie he chose matching the navy of my dress.

He also chose that. I don't know where David, a Denver prodigy lawyer, picked up his keen eye for fashion unless he has someone who handles the details. I'd almost believe that, since I never see this man out shopping. Maybe he's an online shopper in disguise.

My thoughts waver as we walk to the cabinets on one side. There are sex toys here, various vibrators and stimulators that are entirely too expensive. It seems that's the name of the game here, and my eyes fall on the collars to one side.

Many are displayed vertically on figures. There's gold, rose gold, silver, expensive looking leathers. Chains, like the ones that David described to me, hang off the figures like body jewelry. They are beautiful, ending with the toys he's described. It's easy to see how they would keep you sensitized, the draping chains easy to pull and get instant stimulation.

I shy away. There are some for men to wear as well, but that feels even more controlling than a band around your neck. These decorate your upper body. It's beautiful as well as intimidating. My eyes drift back to the choices of necklace, more than I expected to be on display.

Some are discreet. David mentioned you could wear some as everyday jewelry and I didn't believe it until now. There are delicate chains, decorative lattice works that encircle the better part of your throat, little padlocks with a set of keys. My fingers touch my throat where nothing remains but faint lines. I'm not sensitive anymore. Even the mark on my forehead is faded. Which is perfect because I despise curtain bangs.

The padlock is a little much for me. I find the selection of more delicate bands, and David walks with me. We've only just arrived a little bit ago and I'm antsy to head to the roof. I'm pretty sure David told me once he doesn't come here on Sundays. But here we are. He even stopped to chat with Nate and Callie. Nate took an interest in me for once instead of letting me sit there, and he's nice enough.

Callie returned a phone cord to David she claims to have borrowed months ago. It's a weird thing to give back at a sex club, but I don't question it. He said he was never in a partnership with her and I believe him. There's zero chemistry between the two, and Nate is entirely unfazed by the exchange.

My eyes find a pretty, subtle option in rose gold. My favorite type, not that I ever have a reason to wear something gold. It's pretty, a thin lattice chain that sits at the base of the mannequin neck. A heart pendant dangles at the front. It's a little girly, but lovely. The polar opposite of the one Liam placed around my throat.

There's a matching ring, and my eyes widen as they land on the jewel. It's not what drew me here. The gemstone set in the middle is a yellow-brown color in the flickering lights, and I read the description. *Chocolate diamond inlay.*

Of course it's a chocolate diamond. What else would I pick?

David's lips brush against my ear, and I'd almost forgotten he was in here. This feels surreal, like when people go pick out their wedding rings preemptively.

The chocolate diamond glares up at me mockingly.

"I like that one," he says. "Much better than the last."

I blush. This feels intimate, out of my comfort

zone. Rings and collars are signs of commitment. My time with David fades with every passing day. He congratulated me yesterday evening on how far I've come.

It's starting to feel like he's preparing me for goodbye. There's a tint to his eyes whenever I look at him, like he's guarding something from me. I can't get a read. The confused feeling is off putting, but he's doing it on purpose. It's got to be a sign that the end is coming.

I'll deal with the fallout. I'm not supposed to be involved emotionally, and he's humoring my curiosity now. David doesn't need a trauma-wielding newbie as a real partner. There's plenty of women who walk around here fluttering their lashes at him until they realize I'm attached. Even the Submissives won't push boundaries inside the club. Messing with any partnership is grounds for termination of your membership. Sometimes I think a few of them just ignore the lanyards everyone wears. He clearly has a silver ring attached to match my lanyard, the same way mine has a red band at the bottom.

He was usually alone until I came into the picture. Less and less people watch him now, and no one tries approaching me. The bands on my neck at the beginning kept interest down, and now we come as a package deal.

David's fingers skim my hip as the silence lingers. "Why are you overthinking?"

I don't think I'll ever get past it. I can't. I always think of every scenario to the point of obsession. Maybe it's Liam's fault. I started second guessing myself with him thinking each action through before I responded.

We're window shopping, nothing more. I turn to him with a smile, making sure to rub every part of him I can. My fingers rest on his suit jacket, and I wish he hadn't worn one. It's too close to his work attire. "It's fun to look. But isn't it rushing?"

David shrugs, that self assured look still in his eyes. "Some people only buy the collars, not the rings, depending on their dynamic. Some only want the commitment here, not the knowledge that the rest of the world knows what's between them."

Is that better or worse? I think I want David. At the very least I'm not ready for this time to end.

When he's finished training me, he'll find someone who isn't so much work. The idea stings and I smooth back the hurt before he notices.

He's done enough. I'm not going to obsess over the inevitable now.

"Nobody knows what's between us," I say, regretting the sigh that slips through. "You said I've been doing better."

"You have," he agrees, brow furrowing. "I'm impressed with your desire to learn. You're more capable than you give yourself credit for. This role is natural for you, but you aren't getting lost in it. Submission doesn't need to be your whole identity."

I like that he sees progress. It's even better that he knows I can't make this my entire life. I need my own independence.

I want to be devoured in the bedroom. And stand firmly on my own outside it. So I don't have to depend on anyone to take care of me and leave me high and dry.

With David, I like relying on him. He makes me feel safe where I haven't before, and doesn't restrict my wants. He's fully open to me being my own person he gets to play with. It works for us.

If I can think up a way to keep this from ending,

I will. But deep proclamations of love don't seem to be David's thing and I won't bullshit him.

Who wants epic claims of love anymore anyway? It's always extreme. And otherworldly. And usually heaped with challenges to deal with some other day.

He runs his fingers up the column of my throat, and I can tell I've been obsessing. His lips quirk up in a grin. "I need to give you something else to focus on."

My skin heats. He denied me all day for this. Promised we could play anywhere I wanted in the club. His fingers flex on my neck, the hand necklace better than any he could purchase.

Removable at any time, but stronger than the chain here. I feel oddly complete like this, with David's hands on me, his crystal blue eyes focused on absolutely nothing else. When his lips descend down on me, my toes curl in anticipation.

He nips at my lip, pulling back to grasp my hand and lead me out of what is essentially a gift shop. I bat my lashes, the smirk pulling at his lips. "I'm ready to play, Sir."

~~~

There's something up, but I haven't figured out what. Laci appears Tuesday after work, sporting a collection of nail polishes and hair accessories.

Her vise-like grip on her Dyson hairdryer is unreal, and David backs off when she glares at him for trying to help move it. Laci will beat you with the hairdryer before she lets anyone walk off with it.

One of her exes took the last one. High quality products are expensive, and now she'll fight you over it. Once way too many things sit in David's once clean hall bath, she grins at us. "We're doing a makeover!"
~~~

"On a Tuesday?"

She waves a hand. "You have court tomorrow, remember? Anita promised to video chat for a while and check out the process. You've gotta take care of those split ends."

I scowl, fiddling with my hair. I don't like going to the hairdresser on my days off. Before I feared giving up time for Liam. Now I don't want to lose out on it with David.

He holds up his hands before the process even starts. "Nope. I don't want any part in that. You two have fun."

Frowning, I tilt my head. He was distracted at work today, possibly because Liam called a half dozen times demanding to speak to Melissa about the inaccuracy of having his case thrown out. Every receptionist told him it's the judges decision, not the attorneys.

Laci got one of the calls and told him to not drink before court. I got the pleasure of overhearing it, since we were on our way out for coffee. I worried at first about seeing Liam. But he can't just take me on a crowded city street with my best friend right there.

Plus, I've learned if you make a scene downtown the media eats it up. At worst I'll accuse him. It's not like I have to stretch far from the truth before he'll shut up.

"Are you going out?"

"For a few," he muses, kissing the faded gash at my hairline. It's gone now but he still gets the right spot each time, like he's fixed on the memory. "Don't fog up the hall with all those products."

"It's a trim!" Laci huffs, tugging out her tools. She wanted to go to trade school for this but she's always held off. I absolutely think she should go for it. Tugging out a bottle of detangler, she spritzes it in the air. "We'll be done before you get back from wherever."

I want to ask what he's up to, but all David does is wink. He bends to give me a real kiss, and Laci is swooning in the background.

Every time I convince myself the feelings between us aren't real, he leaves me second guessing myself. He kisses with passion and possession, and I fall into it each time.

"I'm getting some air before my house is contaminated," he jokes, stepping back. "I'll pick up something to eat too. Text me what you want."

"Okay," I say, shrugging it off. He only leaves when I'm here with Laci, and I think she's his failsafe. Even if Liam pops up, Laci hates him enough to report first and ask questions later.

I don't know if he's aware, but Laci has an arsenal of self defense at her disposal too. I didn't want her to fight Liam in the office because it's her secret to keep. She shares that information with almost no one for a reason.

But maybe she brought David into the loop. They've bonded over a mutual, all-consuming hate for my ex.

I let Laci tug me into the bathroom, ignoring Liam's messages once more. He keeps texting pictures of the girls he's apparently dating. It's entirely too much, and the block button on my phone has never looked better.

Gasping, I drop my phone when Laci shoots me with water from the detachable shower head. I didn't realize there's one in both his upstairs bathrooms. She laughs at my now damp face, my phone falling to the counter.

"Is this what made you stay over?" She asks, wiggling her eyebrows. "A little preview before you saw

David's head?"

I groan at her bad joke. She's always like this when she wants to drag me out of my head. I wink at her, deciding to get the gears in her head going. "It's not even an opener. The shower setup in David's bedroom is better. That's the only one worthy of being a showstarter before the main event."

Her peels of laughter fill the upstairs, and I realize David is already gone.

20 DAVID

Getting to Liam's is easy. The route is already planned out in my head and I've monitored the camera enough to know his routine. The device hasn't picked up anyone coming in the last few days, nor does he have anyone staying over recently.

A camera inside would be better, but I'm not looking to hang around when the job is finished. He'll be in agony, and I'm looking to split before he can raise suspicion.

The drug-induced haze will be incriminating enough if someone catches him too soon. Better to play it safe. I don't want Myla having a stroke when I get home later.

Power is everything to him, directly proven by his overwhelming need to belittle and abuse Myla. The habit won't stop just because they broke up. It'll carry on to the next girlfriend who falls prey.

It always does. I've read more than enough reports about repeat offenders. No one else needs to deal with his delusional methods of control.

She can be pissed at me later for dealing with him. He's had it coming; showing up at the office to intimidate her was the last straw. I never cared that he had no idea who I was. He was so insignificant in her life once she left the apartment that it didn't matter.

It worked out to my advantage as is.

And it was fun as hell punching him in the street. He was so dazed for a moment afterwards I thought he might pass out from the hit alone.

The haircut at my place is a two-toned distraction; keep Myla off her phone for a bit, and make her feel as beautiful as she already is. The marks have all but faded. It's time for her fears to stay in the past. Laci doesn't know my plans, and I hope to keep her in the dark too

The key I swiped off Myla's key ring slides easily into the lock, and I've timed this according to his past habits. A gamer tag is easy to create and cross platform integration is a thing of beauty. I don't own a gaming console aside from my laptop; there's no point when I don't have the time or patience to deal with kids acting like they are better than they are. My fake profile tells me he spends about six minutes from the time he gets home to the time he hops online. He hasn't deviated yet.

I'll have just enough time to catch him before he hops online. Can't have his gang of online buddies catching on.

The eviction notice glares at me from the door as I enter and swipe off the sensor I placed on the doorframe. The camera from outside is already turned off in my pocket. Colorado law gives him thirty days from the date of the notice, and I hope he gets the picture and books it out of here long before then.

As expected, Liam jumps up when I let the door fall closed. He's on his feet, wearing a loose pair of flannel pants and a plain tee. He's barefoot and ready to waste away an evening at home.

And I've ever so rudely interrupted his plans. I slip my hands into the hoodie pockets, perfectly at ease as I watch his eyes narrow.

"*You*," he growls, and he's definitely caught on to who I am now. There's no more confusion when he sees me after our little showdown on the street. He thinks he's better prepared now because he knows who I am, which really doesn't matter.

Liam bares his teeth at me, and I offer a lazy smirk at his aggrevation. It'll be easy to catch him off guard. He's pissed that anyone is challenging him, let alone in his own home. He stalks towards me, the headset completely abandoned on the couch.

I watch him approach, giving him no sign that I'm going to strike. He swings wildly at me and I sidestep him, hands still in my pockets. His anger outweighs his logic and he stumbles past harmlessly.

He's not competent; beating someone smaller than you who doesn't have a skillset isn't a show of strength. It just proves the only people you can best are the ones who don't have a chance.

Myla isn't the type of girl who fights with her fists. She's harsh words, logic and undercuts. She'll sneak up on you and surprise you, but she isn't going to beat you within an inch of your life. It's not in her disposition.

But it is mine. And he crossed into my line of fire the moment I discovered his abuse of power. He beat Myla because it was easy and offered a fake sense of dominance.

I let him try again, taking into account that I don't want to waste valuable time. Myla is nosy by nature, and she'll ask me too many questions if I'm not careful. When he swings a third time I uppercut to his chin, socking him where it hurts and listening to the pleasant sound of his jaw crunching together.

It'll be easy to get what I want. He needs to

remember submission is given, not taken.

I'll show him exactly what it means.

He stumbles back from the impact, and all I've done is piss him off. It's important that I don't give him an opportunity to get a strike in. Explaining my bruised knuckles is a hell of a lot easier than talking my way out of a split lip.

Myla's going to notice something. It's inevitable. I'd rather she calm down enough to listen to my explanation before she tries to rip me a new one.

When Liam tries to straighten I grasp his shoulders, kneeing him in the stomach and he doubles over again. It's not my favorite form of dropping someone, but it's effective. As much as I want to drag things out I have a schedule to keep.

And I haven't even started yet.

The papers pressed to my side itch to come out, but I'm not there yet. He coughs on the ground, glaring up at me. His lip is bleeding, but not enough. Not nearly enough for splitting her head open.

"Here to gloat?" he taunts, glaring up at me from the floor. Ballsy move when he hasn't managed to push back up off his hands. "Enjoying my leftovers?"

I laugh, flexing my hands. Winking, I let his rage simmer. "Myla's doing great, thanks for asking. After the first few inches it's almost like no one's ever touched her."

He lunges at my knees, and I kick him square in the chest. His gasps are pleasant, but enough of this. I have an agenda to keep and his bruised ego is already stretching this out.

The less time I spend with Liam, the less likely it is he'll end up dead.

I pull the envelope out of my pocket, mindful to aim

it in his direction. The drug is toxic; it'll settle over both of us.

The trick is to know it's there. Know what you're fighting. This is a heavily mental drug, and the influence is severely lessened when you know what's going on.

I triple checked. It was a bitch and a half to get a hold of, but worthwhile. And it cost a damn pretty penny. I'm using the whole damn thing.

Staying in touch with a couple of my dad's old friends really paid off. I spoke to an old client too, and all the pieces fell deliciously into place to put this plan into action.

Liam spits up blood, and I can't have kicked him that hard. He likely bit his tongue and is suffering the consequences. I walk around him, tilting the envelope down as the smell settles over the room. It's a hallucinogen, but a lot more powerful than your backstreet acid trip.

He glares up at me, managing to get to his feet. It's impressive given the state he's currently in mixed with the drug I'm letting pollute him. It takes a minute, and I can see in his eyes he thinks I'm batshit crazy.

Righting himself, I see the moment the drugs hit him. The focused angry look in his eyes wavers, a confused expression settling over him. He's still full of rage, but it's misplaced now. He can't focus enough to aim it at me.

I smirk at him, crossing my arms. I don't give a damn if the pages wrinkle a little. I drink in the confused look a moment before pointing at the couch. "Sit down."

Liam glares at me, fighting it, but he ultimately gives up. He sits, stiffly, looking around angrily. He doesn't want to obey, but the power of suggestion is heavy in the air.

Laughing, I look around the room. He's really let things go to shit since Myla moved on and stopped cleaning up after him. "It's a horrible feeling when someone takes away your free will, isn't it?"

His jaw tenses, not following my meaning. He's not quite dazed, but he can't stop listening either. The drug removes clarity and weakens the defenses of the mind. It'll last for a while, long enough to get what I want. Whatever the hell he does afterwards is entirely on him.

If he so much as looks in her direction after tonight, I'll end him.

The bottle is out of my pocket before he can focus, and I tap my finger against the sharpied-on letters. "Familiar?"

His instinct is to deny, but he's already nodding his head. "Yes."

"I know it is. I swiped it off your dresser when Myla got the fuck out of here. She's still in denial over your shorthand, but I know a date-rape drug when I see one." Shaking the bottle, his glossed over eyes stare at me. "How many were in the bottle when you got it?"

The words fight to leave his lips, but it happens regardless. "Eighteen."

I eye the bottle. There's maybe half that inside. "Where did the rest go?" He's shaking his head, and I let out a sigh. "This will go so much more smoothly if you give me the answers I want quickly, Liam. You'll confess your sins to me either way. But maybe I won't have to break every finger."

I know exactly what I'm doing. Dad never did play fair, and Emilio's father got a kick out of teaching us to fight at a young age. The best way to break a nose, hold your arms to block a hit, the pressure and placement needed to snap someone's hand The most painful points needed to break fingers. Liam is disoriented, but not immune to pain. I can't stay here all night, but history proves the neighborhood isn't keen on calling the cops when someone screams. The marks on Myla are a testament to that.

Even if she didn't scream, there's bound to be noise. Noise draws attention, and this requires privacy.

He doesn't struggle like before when I grip his hand, pressing hard on the center of his palm. His fingers curl in on instinct, and I grasp the pinky.

The pinky is always a fun place to start. It makes a satisfying snap as it breaks at the first knuckle, and Liam lets out a scream.

It's a pissy little scream. This is the guy that somehow busted her head open, and he can't take a little pain.

I make a clicking noise with my tongue when I let go, his eyes wide as he stares in disbelief at the digit that sticks out sideways. "Better keep it down Liam, or I'll have to keep you quiet."

He's hyperventilating over a pinky, and I'm ready to punch him in the face for the dramatics. I tug the tablet out of my interior pocket, setting it on the table with the cable from Callie already connected. He's panting, but focused just enough to follow instruction. "Transfer all of your media files onto here. *All* of them. Even your private folders. You're not going to call anyone or do anything aside from transfer the folders to the tablet."

There's hesitation again, but the pull of the drug is too strong. I can feel it too, ever so slightly. It's giving me a boost of empathy I don't want as Liam fights off a tear, typing like mad to transfer over the pictures from his phone to the burner tablet I brought. The thing is old but it'll do its job. The wire connecting his phone to it is frayed, and it'll probably only last through this one job but it was the best one Callie had on hand.

That's all I need. I don't like making a habit of interrogating and torturing people. But I've reserved a special, cold place inside myself to deal with Liam.

She's not going to relax until she knows his access to the files is gone. She's too damn curious to let things be and it'll eat at her not knowing. She can't remove the last thread of his control so long as he's in the background taunting her.

Another thing to deal with. The excessive messages are going to stop. Myla checks her phone too much throughout the day, dreading messages from a guy that's made her bleed.

It isn't a fast process. I watch him work in boredom. The process isn't long, but he's going to do the work. There's nothing on the tablet aside from what he's transferring, and I watch him carefully. So long as the drug is in his system he won't be able to fight it off enough to delete the incriminating evidence.

I didn't ask if there's really a video. Liam gets off on exerting control over others. There's absolutely a video. I know it in my bones. I'm going to watch it when he's finished and he's busy signing the paperwork. I want to know how badly he deserves to be punished.

In his house, a place that offers fake security. Supposedly apartments are less dangerous because people are more likely to hear you scream. It doesn't mean shit though if the neighbors don't give a fuck.

He transfers his entire gallery. Most of it I'll

probably never sift through, but I want it downloaded anyway. I have no plans of speaking to Liam again after today.

"See?" I mock, watching the last file transfer. "That wasn't so bad. Now delete all the videos you took of Myla off the phone."

His eyes tighten. Now he really wants to fight. He wants to hold onto whatever he's got on her, which is exactly why it has to go. I chuckle at him. "Pictures too."

It takes time. Enough so that I draw the papers out of my pocket, setting them on the table. I snatch a pen out of a cup in the kitchen and set it beside him. He has to finish his task before coming for me. The drug makes him want to listen. I lazily sit on the opposite couch, turning the tablet to me as he finishes the task.

"Scopolamine is a tricky thing to get," I say to him as he goes through his phone. "It's expensive, and controversial. Given the right amount in a powdered form, it induces a suggestive state. Like right now. Your mind is so open to suggestions so you can't fight me on the orders."

His glare is volatile as he continues working. I open the file on the laptop, click on the first video I see, and watch. This is definitely a shot of their bedroom. She's wearing what looks like the shredded lingerie I spotted on the floor when we grabbed her things. It's whole, at least for a moment, before he's ripping it off of her.

"This is your fault baby," he growls into the recording. His phone must be set up on the dresser from the angle and height of the video. *"You're not listening. You don't appreciate everything I can give you. You make me hurt you baby. I don't like hurting you more than you deserve."*

I'm debating breaking the tablet as he draws his

hand back on screen, striking her hard enough she falls back on the bed. I don't remember a handprint, it mustn't have been hard enough to bruise. He's dragging her around now, telling her more lies, and she's moving sluggishly.

The bottle I stole rolls into view of the screen, the very end of the sharpied shorthand *rohypnol* shining in the corner of the screen.

He couldn't have set a better scene if he tried. Nobody would question what this is if he's ballsy enough to post it. It makes my stomach roll. She's entirely unresponsive, the drug working its magic. But he's totally in the zone, and I'm going to break the tablet if I'm not careful.

"See? You just need to learn to relax. I hate having to give it to you Myla, but you're too uptight. Too needy. You should enjoy what I give you already. Not ask for more. What have I done to earn your disrespect?"

He strikes her again, whipping her head back into the headboard. There's a muffled sound, and he's cursing.

He hit her into the frame. That's where the gash on her head came from. When she turns a red mark is already forming, blood dripping down her face.

And he's laughing at it. *"That's better. I like a little red on you."*

I'm up off the couch before I think about what I'm doing, forgetting to check his progress. I grab his hand before he can retract, the one he used to strike her, and break the first finger I grab.

He yowls, and I tug the blanket over the back of the couch and stuff it in his mouth. "You're going to be quiet. If you think striking someone you've drugged is okay, then you can take every knuckle breaking." I break another, glaring into his eyes. I don't need to see every video to know I absolutely hate this guy.

He's struggling, and I command him to sit still. It's harder to keep him in place when pain fights logic. His fingers snap with quick efficiency. I break from his middle to pinky in two places each, watching with detachment when his broken fingers stick out in different directions.

Not the thumb and forefinger though. Not yet.

I pull the paperwork I brought up to the edge of the table, and he's shaking so hard I think he's going to piss himself. I indicate to the table, tapping the pen. "Sign your name. Both pages. Right next to the 'x'."

Liam is a mess. I know he doesn't read what's in front of him or he'd be fighting the drug again. I doubt he followed my scopolamine explanation. A lot of people don't know much about its uses outside of being a pain anesthetic. There's a better purpose for its powdered form in my opinion, even if the cost is sky high.

His signature will be off with the snapped fingers but it doesn't change the fact that it's his penmanship. I know getting the paperwork a little damp will explain away a smudge. No one's going to think about a handwriting test over something minimal unless there's a need to go to court. By the time Liam speaks with anyone, traces of the drug will be long gone. The envelope I used is already in my pocket to toss out with the jacket. It'll look like he signed the paperwork on his own and he can't recant something he signed.

I know what lets cases slip through the system and steps to take to avoid evidence getting thrown out. Myla wants to avoid court, wants to avoid airing her business out for the world to see. I'll humor her, but Liam is a problem. He could slip up again someday, and if that time comes, I'll have it in writing.

It's a DV statement. The alleged abuser can sign a waiver stating what happened. It clears the air of misunderstanding, with the expectations that sentencing is lessened. Most offenders would never sign because they can't be wrong. I rarely see one pass through the system. It's usually a father who slipped up and is trying to right a wrong, whether or not it's deserved.

Rarely are they sincere. Hardly ever do they make a difference. But having one on file would be interesting to say the least.

Liam never retained council when I punched him, likely assuming he would win outright because he didn't fight back. Not that he could, but that's besides the point. He rambled to the judge about everything under the sun.

He complained I stole his girlfriend, that his girlfriend left him high and dry and he's waiting for her to come back. He claimed to not know where she is or why she would leave. He couldn't think of any reason why she'd be avoiding him.

The judge was unimpressed. Coupled with his clearly intoxicated state, I'm surprised he made it into the courthouse. He was a blithering idiot, and it's a wonder he didn't let something slip then. I almost wish we went instead of opting for a teleconference.

"You wanted to sign the paperwork. You don't know where Myla is and you aren't interested in locating her again." My tone is firm, willing him to believe the words. I tug on his pointer finger as he finishes and he whimpers. The rest is yet to come.

I lean back on the couch, at ease now. The imagery is burned in my head from the video, but I'm not through with Liam just yet. He's still gagged, and looks too terrified to remove it.

Smirking, I shake my head. "You probably started beating her down because you know she's too good for you. Instead of admitting your shortcomings you raised a hand. You don't understand dominance, you are not an alpha. You're simply a trickster in sheeps clothing. Myla never submitted to you because she knew you weren't worthy."

He drops the blanket gag to bare his teeth at me, and I enjoy the little act of defiance. He'll be back to crying in a moment. Leaning forward on the couch, I rest my elbows on my knees. "You're not going to tell anyone about this, are you? You're going to come up with a clever excuse to explain all your broken fingers. Because if you so much as utter a word, I'm going to take all these videos you just gave me to the police and tell them you shared them with me during a moment of guilt."

Liam growls, and I sense the challenge. He wants to challenge me, and I'm prepared. "You can fight all you want with the courts, but I have your signed statement. You can try and say I drugged you. A guy dating your ex, who you abused and manipulated for a year. She's got stitches in her head from you." My hands clench together. "She didn't even like sleeping in the room with me because of you. You forced yourself on her when she didn't want you and destroyed her trust." I sneer at the half surprised, half drugged-over look on his face. The scopolamine is still hard at work. "Your little threat, the video you wanted to post online? I'm sure no one would call you a rapist with a rohypnol bottle rolling into the camera screen."

Scoffing, I stand up. He makes me unreasonably angry. People who feel threatened and want to assert dominance always go about it in the most abusive way possible. Even if he wants to file *another* case against me, there's a ton of obstacles to dodge to even get his point across.

He won't look like a lover scorned if he releases the video. I doubt anything he ever recorded of her is PG enough to earn sympathy. He looks like the abuser, and from the hate burning in his eyes he knows it too.

Taking my time folding the paperwork, locking the tablet and pocketing the cord, setting everything in order, I enjoy the way he fidgets. He's anticipating my next move, the threats hanging in the air as I exude a casualness I don't feel. There's a sheen of sweat across his skin from his fingers breaking, but he's too enamored by the drug to defy me. My fingers burn to wrap around his throat and squeeze until there's a ring there to match the built-in necklace Myla bore for weeks.

But if I wrap my hand around his throat, I'll squeeze until there's no life left. I know my limits, and giving myself the option to remove him completely from this world is all too tempting, especially with the last of the scopolamine floating in the air.

Standing, I collect what I need before approaching him again. He's wary, sweating from the pain as I grab his thumb. His whole body tenses as he waits for what's next.

I lean down, enjoying the way that, drug or not, he pulls back from me. "This is for raising your voice to my girl. If you're smart, you won't speak to her again."

His thumb is a little stronger, but it still snaps easily with enough pressure and his screams pick up all over again. I shove the makeshift gag back in his mouth once more without missing a beat and resume torturing him. "This is my warning to never say another word to her."

Leaving his thumb pointing the wrong way I grab the last finger I haven't mangled. "This is for pointing at her like she's something you own. Myla is her own person, and she doesn't belong to you."

The snap that follows is satisfying, and I'm disappointed our time together is ending. His lip is still split, the uninjured arm clutching at his stomach.

I wink at him, snapping the last joint in his hand. "This is for pretending to be an alpha, when you'll only ever be an omega."

21 MYLA

David looks like shit when he gets home, sans dinner. Laci left an hour ago, and he messaged me claiming he got sidetracked and we'd DoorDash something.

My eyes can't decide what to focus on when he steps in. His knuckles are cracked and bloody on one hand, and he's wearing a basic tee instead of the jacket I thought I saw him leave in. There's a tablet tucked beneath his arm, and he looks tired as hell.

It's the blood on his hand and the stain on the collar of his shirt that sends me leaping up off the couch to meet him. My fingers fly over his chest, but it doesn't look like he's injured. "What happened? Where were you?"

His smile is tight, forced, and a long sigh follows it. His arms wrap around my lower back, holding me to him. His fingers tense, and I feel his jaw clench above me.

Frowning, I try to rub soothing circles along his collarbone and still the tremor in my hands. David's seen blood on me before, at work even, and he managed to not have a meltdown. I don't need to be so unsettled over this, but all the worst scenarios flicker through my head. He got mugged, Liam attacked him, something happened with the club -

My thoughts don't run away from me like I expect. None of that makes sense. *Maybe* he got mugged, but he was supposed to be out on a drive. I'd blame a cut for the spot on his collar but there aren't any marks. Liam attacking him seems just as unlikely. David punched him in the head last time. He wasn't afraid then and unless Liam formed a group to attack him I don't think he'd look like this after a real fight. He never really fought with his friends, Chad included.

Liam would fight until he's knocked out. He is not focused when he punches, he just kind of goes for it. And I can't think of a reason David would be getting into a fight with the club. We already signed the paperwork.

I can't think of a reason he would fight at all.

David chuckles. "You're overthinking again. Come, shower with me. Let's order something." His fingers stroke my back before speaking again. "I have something I need to show you."

"Is this about Liam?" I ask, a bubble of stress popping up. "I don't want you to feel like you have to do anything. You've done so much David. You already got in trouble for that scene in front of the office-"

"Myla," he sighs, and I can hear the exhaustion in his voice. He really is tired. "Shower first. Now."

It's not a demand, more like a plea, and I give in. He tells me to order whatever I want, and I place it while he sets the temp for the water, slipping out of my clothes.

My hair looks beautiful after Laci clipped off the dead ends and blended my grown out bangs in with the long layers, and I'm regretful to wash it away. David eyes me as he strips, and my worries slip away when I notice there isn't a scratch on him aside from the split in his knuckles.

Eyes shifting up to his, I see the truth in his gaze. This is absolutely about Liam. The lack of blood on him is just as concerning as it is relieving, and I bite my lip as we stare each other down.

His eyes drift over me from head to toe, and the familiar pull at my core calls to him. David plays my body like a fiddle, and I shouldn't be begging for a touch when I don't know what he's done. I don't know if I should be angry, relieved or a mixture of both.

Violence isn't my favorite thing. But Liam was violent towards me. Where is the line drawn?

"Talk to me," he says, eyes just drinking me in. "Just chat with me, Myla."

I frown, wanting to dig at him. There's a heaviness in his eyes that I've rarely seen. Difficult cases don't drag it out, and when we speak of Liam he's usually either pissed or sarcastic. Not burdened by something dark.

Titling my head, I tell him all the petty office drama Laci filled my head with while he showers. The room fills with steam, and goosebumps prick over my skin from the AC. I know before I start moving that I want to join him. He's always taking care of me and my fears. I can't get a read on him and I'm worried that he won't open up to me when I've bared my soul to him.

The water is burning when it splashes my legs and I step back from the spray. He's scrubbing his face, the blood gone from his hand. There's no other spots on his skin, droplets of water dripping down his chest. I run my fingers over his shoulders, feeling the heat on his skin, and he stops cleaning his face.

The skin around his eyes is red as he opens them, like he's exclusively rubbed there. A breath escapes as he eyes me, letting his blue orbs roll from my shoulders down to my toes and back again.

His hands press to either side of my face, heat bleeding into my skin. His kisses are feverish, uncontrolled, and usually I'm the one throwing myself at him. He's always calculated, taking pleasure as much as he receives, but these kisses are needy and desperate. Selfish almost.

He drags me into the sting of the water to press me back into the wall, his hands already trailing over my skin. I gasp into his mouth, running my fingers through his soaked hair.

There's no lesson here. This is something different altogether. He isn't smirking at me, asking for his favorite terms, nothing at all. He's too busy picking me up to press me into the wall, my legs finding their place around his waist. He's already hard for me, his hands pressing me close to his chest instead of hard into the wall.

It's more intimate than normal. I don't have the focus to stop him and question, moaning when he rubs along my slit, his attention zeroing in.

He's kissing along my neck, and I reach between us to grasp his length. His moan is breathy, and I manage to lift my hips up enough to slide down his length, impaling myself before he dares to change the position as a moan escapes me.

I don't want to drag this out. My desire for answers is high, but I want David more than anything else right now. His eyes are desperate when he finds my gaze again.

There's no build up. I hold on for dear life as he fucks me into the wall, nails scratching down his shoulders. My breath can barely keep up with the speed of his hips, and I think he's saying something I can't catch between the force of his thrusts.

"David," I moan, and he doesn't correct me. He's dragging me to the edge faster than I expect, not controlling any aspect of me. I'm completely free to claw at his skin and moan as he fills me with each thrust.

My orgasm is fast and unexpected, arriving at the same time Davids does. I'm just tumbling over the edge when he pulls out of me, hitting my thigh with his release.

It's the fastest fuck I think we've had. My breaths can't catch up with everything, and the temperature of the water is still warm as he sets me down. His lips find mine, kissing me all over again.

When he pulls back to rest his forehead against mine, his eyes are closed. I glance up at him through our mix of wet hair and the spray of the shower. "What's wrong?"

He's shaking his head again, turning to look away from the water. His cheek rests on my head. "You're too nice, Myla. Darkness shouldn't have found you."

He doesn't explain, and I fix him with a glare as he washes me off. I catch the sponge, cleaning skin he's already washed once, and repeat the favor across his body. I never wash him, he always washes me. But the troubled look in his eyes calls to me, and I want to do my own little bit of aftercare.

David doesn't argue, closing his eyes at the feel. That's how I know something is wrong.

By the time he's willing to talk, I'm sitting on his bed with the tablet I saw him bring home and folded papers resting on top of the keys. He pulled the pages out of his jeans, although I don't recall seeing him take anything when he left. Our cold delivery is sitting by the television, and I've slipped into my favorite sleepwear; one of his shirts and lounge pants.

"I believe you deserve the right to choose what you know," he says, and it sounds like a giant contradiction.

"Liam lied to you under the guise of a D/s relationship to make you obey him, your mother shuts you out of her new life because having a wayward child doesn't fit into the picture perfect family she wants."

My back stiffens at the jab at my mom. I don't understand how that has any place in a conversation about Liam. "What did you do?"

He knows I'm digging. He nods to the papers, and the tablet. "Read them. Then pick a video. I'm sure they all have about the same message."

I frown, opening up the papers. Maybe he found something else incriminating on Liam, or he wants to revise our contract and I'm not -

My thoughts stop jumping around as I read the paper in front of me. *Admission of Domestic Violence.*

I don't read it, looking up to stare open mouthed at him. "What did you *do*?"

"Just read."

It doesn't make sense. It's a legal form I never see actually used, admitting to DV. *My* DV, because Liam signed the form. I stare at his signature, trying to understand. I know he didn't sign it freely, I don't even have to ask.

My eyes narrow on David and I toss the forms between us. "You're avoiding answering."

His sigh is heavy, and when he meets my eyes there's no guilt. I don't know what I expect since I don't know what he's done. "Watch the video, Myla. You can be mad and hate me if you want, but I won't apologize."

My ears burn at his words, and I open a file. The images before me cause my fingers to still. It's mainly pictures of me, but I see videos too. I remember some of these. They are Liam's. There's no way David just happened to find all of these.

David's eyes meet mine, and I find myself clicking the first video I see without hesitation.

"This is your fault baby." The rage in his voice registers in my head, dredging up things I try to ignore, and I feel like I'm choking on air. I shove the laptop away violently, and it almost tumbles off the bed. David catches it, sending me a calculated look as I glare at the device.

I don't need to watch the video. I recognize the words. Liam always said that exact phrase when he believed I'd done something worth punishment. I touch the faded mark on my forehead and David's eyes follow my movements.

"You remember that?"

Shaking my head, I hold his gaze. "No. I just remember those words." My tongue is too thick in my mouth when I speak again. He did something, he had to if he's got all of Liam's videos and pictures on a tablet. "Did you watch the video?"

"Enough."

Dread pools in my stomach. I don't like thinking about what Liam did. I don't know if this is the video that depicts the gash in my head or something else. Shame picks at me, imagining what David sees now that he's witnessed me at my lowest. Even if I don't recall one occurrence I know each of our more violent escapades looks like a bulletin for abuse.

I lean forward, tapping the spacebar to continue the video. I only get through another minute or so before I'm pausing it again, uncertain I want to finish the whole thing.

"I didn't watch all of it," he muses, his fingers running across my cheek. I lean into his touch, avoiding his gaze. I don't like watching something that feels like an out of body experience. I'm clearly the woman in the video, and the sickening thud of my head hitting the headboard until I bled echoes in my mind.

He turns the device away from me, locking the screen as he flips it over. "I don't expect you to watch it all either. I just wanted you to know I have it, and he no longer does."

My mind bounces around, warring between impressed, terrified, and grateful. It's surreal looking at something that happened to you without relating to it.

Watching the video doesn't bring back memories. It makes me jump at his wording, but I just don't remember that specific point in time. If it was audio instead of visual, I may still be in denial that it really happened to me.

Sight is a powerful force. Words reap our soul and touch at hidden spots inside of us. Sight dredges up memories that we'd rather forget and forces us to face the truth.

Words bubble up in my head, and I force them away. I don't say what's on my mind. I can't. It feels wrong, and even if it's real in my mind I won't say it out loud. I don't want him to run off because my emotions are running away from me.

Not right now. Not at this moment. I look up into David's eyes as he strokes the pad of his finger along my cheek. Instead of asking about the videos, I wet my lips and ask a different question? "You're knuckles?"

He shrugs. "Liam got what was coming to him. Some problems can't be fixed by courtrooms and paperwork. Sometimes you have to take matters into your own hands."

A thread of worry weaves through my stomach. Liam is a leech. Catching his hand, I start to shake my head. "I don't know what you did, but Liam is going to report it."

"He won't." David nods to the paperwork I've nearly forgotten about. "That'll slide into his file at work. It'll get discreetly scanned sometime when the file is closed. There's two original copies in case something happens to the one at work. It's on file that way, without having to be brought up. The other one will stay with you, if ever you need to use it."

"But Liam-"

"Has to fix his broken hand before he tries anything," David says with a shrug, and I still.

The blood on his knuckles makes sense. "You broke his hand?"

His lip twitches, fingers gentling against my cheek again, like he's thinking of something. "Only the hand he struck you with."

My heart flutters despite the morbidity of the situation. I lean into him, trying to figure out what to do now. He broke Liam's hand. He somehow got his signature on the DV paperwork. And he doesn't look afraid like the cops are going to show up at any moment.

"Why isn't Liam going to report it?"

"Liam is the hero of his own story. He doesn't allow himself to believe he's the villain. Victim perhaps, but never the villain. He's likely already passed out in a daze and when he wakes up he'll sound a little insane. The memories might be jumbled."

I frown. "Why is he gonna pass out?"

This time David smirks, a little of his sarcastic nature bleeding through. "Because he's lost control."

I stare at the collection of things on his bed. Liam values control above all else. That's why he wanted to jump on my D/s relationship suggestion. I wanted to spice up our sex life.

He wanted to control me. Entirely.

Leaving the items in place, I sink back into the pillows with David. There's more to tell, I see it in his eyes. But above all else, I'm glad he's here with me now.

Not delivering whatever justice he thinks Liam deserves. And not suffering at his hand. I doubt he'd sit here so calmly if he thought the cops were about to knock on the door. It doesn't make sense, but David has a way about him. He'll explain, I'm certain of that. But the events of tonight weigh on him, and he's fighting to carry the burden alone.

I need answers, but I need David's comfort above all else. I lean into him, and his arms slip into their place around me.

For a moment, it's like nothing has changed at all.

22 DAVID

Myla, as expected, doesn't know what to do with the knowledge she gains over the coming days. Liam mysteriously stops messaging her, and I don't tell her where the DV Admission goes. One slips into my safe if it's ever needed for her, the other is lost in the blur of office work.

The case from last week is nothing but a memory. Liam doesn't press charges. Myla doesn't ask about it.

I don't lie to her when she asks me questions. She Googled the hell out of scopolamine and I hope if he does decide to report, the cops don't start digging through our search history. Her searches are bound to come up if something else goes to court between us.

Myla deserves the truth, so I don't sugarcoat the facts. There's an air of uncertainty around her when I tell her exactly what happened with Liam, but her eyes flutter back to the videos kept on the otherwise blank tablet, ammunition if Liam ever wants to fight over this. I doubt his transgressions towards her would have any weight on the fact that I strolled into his apartment and broke all the fingers on his right hand with the use of a powerful drug, but that's not the point. I can handle Liam just fine, and given some new perspective, I believe Myla could too.

Liam is the coward I figured he would be. Pain is something he can dish out but can't handle. Myla's elusive friend Anita sends a novel-length message to her about his mysterious appearance at the hospital to reset his fingers.

I have yet to meet the doctor prodigy that stitched her head closed and didn't report Liam. I think I would like her.

The rohypnol is gone. I took the bottle, crushed the contents, and washed it down the drain. Then I cleaned my bathroom, because you can never be too careful.

Laci isn't as in the know as she thinks, and Myla keeps her out of the gritty details. She doesn't hesitate to ask for what she wants when we're home alone, and our sex life continues in jaded bliss even after she digs the truth out of me.

I want her to know the truth, because she's dealt with the lies and rebelled. Truth is the foundation of a healthy relationship.

I'm laughing in my head at the irony, since our partnership is built on mutual kinks. She's getting dressed now to go to the club, and there's a pull in my chest.

She knows how to balance her Submissive quirks and her real life position with finesse. This isn't a hard-stance relationship between us. I'm not that controlling of a Dom. If she wants to learn more than what I've given, I'm not the right teacher.

I won't limit her more. I like picking her outfits when we go out, because then she wears my favorites. She doesn't pick an underwear set, because there's no point. Our tastes work together.

But our contract has limits, and I won't hold her back from everything she deserves in a true D/s commitment. But I'm also not sending her off without telling her the truth. So I'm taking her back to the club, where she learned her kinks aren't out of the box at all, and realized how few people really deserve your submission.

She's subdued as we walk, and by the time we make it to her favorite spot on the roof she's simmering with anger.

This is why relationships are hard. There's more talking about emotions, different expectations and levels of communication. I suck at it. Learning the map to someone's body is easier than untangling the secrets of their mind.

Myla spins on me when we get up there, eyes full of contempt. "Why are we up here David?"

Pursing my lips, I guess I give her credit for jumping right to the point. Setting aside the flutes of champagne we picked up at the entrance, I sit down beside her.

"We agreed I would train you until you understood the basis of a D/s partnership," I say, watching her brows knit together. "You've more than surpassed my expectations. Training was obsolete when you were no longer being repressed. You didn't need training Myla, you needed someone who understood what you wanted without tacking on abuse to make up for his shortcomings. Liam couldn't handle you so he made you believe his faults were your own. He treated you like the failures in your sex life were your fault and not his." Her eyes harden the longer we stare at each other. "There's nothing wrong with your abilities. There never was. Everything was a misplaced notion from a seed Liam planted."

"Then why did you agree to teach me if you didn't

think I really needed it?" she all but growls at me. She won't sit down, having a staring contest with me.

"Because you needed to experience it firsthand. You believed that your ineptitude stemmed from not making Liam happy, not because he mistreated you. The abuse you explained away as training, and you wanted to learn from me because being treated correctly made my reactions feel like praise." I pull her towards, staring up into the gray orbs I've come to admire from my seat. "You were new. You still are. There's no mastering a lifestyle. You simply adapt it to your needs and wants. The rules of play are guidelines for what your partner deserves. You love being praised, worshiped, then turned and taken however I please. You enjoy being a good girl because gratitude is something you yearn for."

She subtly arches towards me as I speak. I'm not trying to seduce her, but the words tumble out of my lips unbidden. She needs truth to balm the pain that's to come, not sweet nothings.

Myla stares at me for many moments. Her hair is piled high on her head tonight, a look she rarely goes for. Now that the skin on her neck is smooth as it should be, she's wearing a strapless dress that's sat forgotten until today, showcasing the perfect slope of her neck and the rise of her breasts. I love seeing her so comfortable in her own skin. The peach color jumps off the few locks of her hair that tumble down to brush at the neckline.

She's beautiful, back to the person she should've been before Liam's heavy-handed influence. I don't regret taking the measures that I did. The threat is enough for now. He's afraid of his own comeuppance too much to just go file something with the court.

The scopolamine influence is long gone from his

system. There's no way to backtrack it now that it's gone, and he's going to sound like a delusional lunatic trying to piece together the evening. It's not going to erase his memory by any means, though he might be a little confused on the details. The drug only ever opens your mind to manipulation. I manipulated him like he manipulated her, although the scars I left behind are a lot more physical than his on her.

I don't know what story he fed to the hospital. He didn't report me or we'd be going through the incriminating videos on my tablet. I plan to pass it along to Emilio to back up the system. I'm not tech-savvy, but I know how to be impressionable enough to get someone to hand over their sins. And Liam gave his up at the first sign of violence.

Looking up into the eyes of the woman beside, I hope I never regret walking away while he was still breathing.

"Are you saying goodbye?" she whispers, the sound nearly carried away in the breeze. After a beat she sits down beside me, leaning towards me as she always does. Touch is our language, and we've learned too much from the way each other moves. The fear of rejection hangs heavily around her.

I blow out a breath. "We've come full circle. You don't need training Myla. You need a partner you can grow with and love. A Dominant to your Submissive side, a Sir to hone in your brattiness when you're in a mood." I let my breath tickle her lips, gaging every reaction from her. "You deserve more than a temporary trainer."

Myla pulls back from me, and for a moment I think she's going to kick me with the high heeled shoes she chose. Standing in a rush her hands move to her hips, glaring down at me. "If this situation taught me anything, it's that I need to use my voice and speak what I'm feeling."

A smirk slides across my lips at that. The brattiness I enjoy is back in place, even if I'm unsure what that means for me. I cross my arms, studying her. "I do prefer you to use your words."

She lifts her chin. "I don't want to learn how to do all of this again with another person. It was stressful for me to open up in the beginning and even allow you to see this side of me, let alone trust you to take care of me when I'm vulnerable." She swallows, the nerves kicking in. "I didn't expect things to go this way. When I asked you to train me I expected you to be cold and calculated like you are at work. But your partners are entirely different from coworkers. You treated me better than my boyfriend did."

"Ex," I toss in. She hasn't kicked me yet, which is a good sign. I half expected her to blow up at me for doing this here, but I didn't want her to feel trapped at my house either.

"Whatever," she huffs, fighting the smile that tries to lift her lips. "I don't want to work on doing this again. I don't wish to parade around the club and wait for someone to approach me and see if we're compatible for a D/s relationship." She shudders. "I don't want other people touching me, even the club members who like the same things I do. And my dating life is forever more complicated the second I explain to someone that I want to be the Submissive, but I don't serve them."

I scoff. Yeah, that wouldn't work at all, for anyone. I try to speak but she's letting those nerves of hers run rampant, rambling on. "I don't want to get comfortable with someone else when you already know every spot on my body better than I do myself." Her eyes flicker to my suit of the night, pulling into a grin. "And I don't want to learn about anyone else having their hands on you."

My interest kicks up a notch. I thought she might duck out, excited to escape this entangled web of problems that surrounds us. Finding another Dominant to pair to her Submissive side would be work, and she has to want it. She'd be free of the Liam situation, but there would be other issues to handle. I raise a brow as she sits down on my lap, the short flowy skirt sliding up her thighs.

Her forehead presses against mine, and I breathe her in. "I don't want to put my trust anywhere else."

I run my fingers down her back, letting her words linger in the air. "You want to stay with me, in my house?" I slide my hands down, pressing to her lower back instead of traveling to cup her ass. Her eyes roll as I avoid giving her anything she wants. "In my bed?"

She nods as her eyes flutter, and I grab her hips instead of helping. "Words, Myla. You were doing so well."

Her chuckle is music I didn't know I needed to hear. The tension around us the last few days slowly fades away. Dealing with Liam was a necessary evil, and somewhere deep inside Myla knows he deserved to suffer. She's eyed the videos a couple times, but she never watches them, just looks at the proof of his mistreatment. He isn't a saint, but neither am I. Waiting to come out here until Saturday was killer, but we needed to give each other time to work through everything that happened.

We've been dodging the problem of discussing this, fighting to stave off an end neither of us is looking for. I hoped she would decide to stay with me and continue to grow the relationship bubbling between us, but ultimately I don't control her.

Myla controls herself. She understands that now fully, embracing the side of her that likes to submit to me. On her terms. And she gets more back than she ever has to give.

I capture her lips and she moans into my mouth. I'm not letting her go. Pressing my hands lower into her ass, I pull her against me. Hearing her admittance is all I need.

My lips pull back from hers, nipping at her neck. She arches like she always does, and I let my hands travel across her torso. She looks lovely like this, ready and willing to let me take care of her.

I kiss along the tops of her breasts as her fingers find my belt, pulling it loose. "When you're ready Myla, you can pick out your favorite collar. Perhaps one with a matching ring."

She doesn't say a word, but her eyes are heavy with lust when I capture her gaze again. She fits perfectly around me as she adjusts and slides down my length, stretching her out like I always do. Her moans are loud, and this time I don't care if they echo off the rooftop.

Everyone is inside anyway watching the weekly show, but we're putting on a performance of our own.

Grasping her wrists, I tug them behind my head. She locks them firmly in place while I lift up the dress, gripping her ass with one hand and sliding my fingers around to her clit with the other. She's rocking on my hips, gasping as I refuse to move.

The moment I lock my fingers over her clit, she gasps. "Ride me, doll. Show me what a good girl you'll be. You're all mine."

Myla is skilled, and I should've spent more time

letting her ride my cock as she finds the perfect pace. Her skin slicks with sweat as her nails dig into the back of my neck. I groan as she slams her hips down into me, and I can only hold out for a few moments before I'm slamming up to meet hers.

I think about the collars I'd love to decorate her with, the ties I'll enjoy knotting around her wrists and ankles when she's being bratty. The discreet little vibrator I never had an opportunity to use on her that's going to come out of its box as soon as we hit home. The fun little clit stimulator I'm going to buy from the store downstairs and position over her clit so she stays a mess the rest of the night.

Her hair comes down in my hands, keeping her in place so I can buck up into her. She cries out at the difference in force and I smirk up at her.

"Take it, doll."

"Yes, Sir." Her words are loud cries into the starless night, and I know she's going to leave my neck a mess when I release her. She wants to change her position, squirming around on my lap, but I keep her there.

"You're going to cum for me just like this," I tell her, breathing into her ear. "You're all mine. And I'm going to fuck you again when we get home."

She's nodding, bouncing on top of me, and I know she's close. There's a look in her eyes just before release, and I capture her mouth with mine to keep the words from tumbling out.

I love her too, but we aren't going to say it for the first time in a night overshadowed by choice. When I tell Myla I love her, she'll know it's true in every corner of her heart.

EPILOGUE

"This is it," Myla squeals, looking at herself from every angle in the mirror. I handed her the box not long ago. She's asked several times for one, hinting not so discreetly whenever we're out at the club at the ones she likes.

I made her wait a month. She's only been mine properly for that long. The office knows that we're officially a couple, and her friends have come to terms with it. Laci and the unknown Anita may not know the depths of our relationship, but no one seems unhappy that I've taken Liam's place. The club knew first because I signed an addendum with her the night we agreed this is more than training.

It was never just about training. Not from the moment I looked into her eyes and wanted to learn more. I was curious because she wore a collar she feared. I was tempted because she responded so willingly to me.

I was consumed because she dug her nails in and stayed with me even when it would be easier to start fresh.

She turns in the mirror again, hair high on her head. She wants it up tonight to show off her newest addition to the closet.

A collar.

Specifically, the one she practically salivated over at the club. The chocolate diamond shines radiantly against her pale skin at the center of the heart pendant, and it's not too tight against her throat to restrict her airway.

That was her request when she mentioned it a week ago. If she ever wore a collar she doesn't want to feel choked. She didn't even need to bring it up to me. I know her reservations since Liam. I have no intention of reminding her of him.

Liam isn't saying a word. We heard through the grapevine that he left the apartment he was evicted from. I know from asking Emilio to keep an ear out that he's decided to leave town. His hand is still an issue he's struggling with.

Hard to get a job with your dominant hand broken eleven times. I didn't divulge the details, and Myla never asked. I told her Liam would think twice before hurting someone again.

Her only comment was she's glad he isn't dead. I assumed correctly she's the type of person that hesitates at capital punishment, even if she isn't the hand delivering it. The lingering worry remains within her, but Liam won't soon forget what happened.

Drugged or not, shit sticks with you when you need surgery to reset your fingers. Breaking one knuckle is easy. Breaking and twisting both knuckles in each finger takes a bit more work.

I'm more than happy knowing he's long gone. One less problem to look at daily.

She twirls again in the navy dress she bought earlier this week. It's elegant and makes the rose gold in her collar pop. She fingers the delicate band, eyeing the box.

There's no ring. It's hiding in the pocket of my jacket. I don't think I'll use it tonight. I have no intention of giving it to her just yet.

But when the time comes, she'll have the matching set. I don't think of one being more important than the other, but Myla is more comfortable wearing the band than discussing a ring. The ring signifies a union to everyone outside our inner circle that we're fully committed. She isn't ready to deal with that in everyday life yet. And I'm in no rush.

It's perfectly fine with me. Months ago she wasn't even on my radar. I want to keep exploring every inch of her before I place a ring on her finger and her friends flock like vultures.

Laci might pick up on what the collar really is. She overheard me speaking with Emilio, who seems to be around her more and more. She did a double take when she noticed the box, but it's slender enough to hide in my jacket. I'm not hopping down the rabbit hole to discover what kind of kinks Myla's BFF is hiding so I didn't hang around to keep chatting.

I smile as Myla inspects the design once more. There's no key, she can freely remove it whenever she wants. The heart pendant at the front is part of the design, crafted from the same chain as well. There's a Chocolate diamond set into the band itself along with the hanging pendant design.

Discreet, pretty, intricate. Just like I always pictured Myla. But there's a siren hiding behind her sweet smiles, one only I get to please.

"You look beautiful," I whisper, wrapping my arms around her from behind. My hand slides up her torso, caressing every curve along the way. She leans back into me as I wrap my fingers around the collar, easily holding on through the ring circling the lightweight pendant.

This is how I grabbed her the first time I found Liam's collar and started finding out all her secrets. I kiss her ear, watching the heat of her gaze.

"Whose is this?"

Her joy in the mirror is genuine. "Yours, Sir."

Smiling against her skin, I kiss her again. She hums at the contact, and my hand slides from her waist down to drag up the skirt of her dress.

The little vibrator from earlier is in place, the remote in my pocket. Her breathing picks up as she stares at herself in the mirror, her eyes traveling up and down our frames.

I pull her against me, letting her feel my dick pressing into her back. She chuckles, wiggling her ass against it as I watch the mischief in her eyes through the mirror. When she goes to turn I tighten my grip on the ring, keeping her there.

The button in my pocket clicks on, and she arches into me as the toy spasms inside her. The front hugs her clit, and her fingers scratch along my sleeves.

Chuckling, I keep her facing the mirror. "I love watching you come undone for me, doll. You'll be desperate when I fuck your greedy little cunt later."

Myla moans, rubbing furiously against me. I need to switch it off or we'll miss the show entirely. My hand doesn't make it to the button again before she spins around, smirking up at me.

"I love you, David." Her voice is sultry, smooth, as she wraps her arms around my neck and tries to find my zipper. I press her tight to me, clicking my tongue.

"I love you too, Myla, but you're still going to have to wait," I warn her with a wink.

We discussed this recently. Love is something we

say to each other, not to the names we use during play. There's more meaning with purpose behind it.

She pouts, but it's quickly replaced with a frown when I click off the toy and kiss her nose. "You wanted to see the show."

"I'm having second thoughts," she jokes, smoothing her hands over my shirt again. "I'm sure Julio will be back next month to demonstrate."

Smirking, I grasp her hand. "This is the Halloween showcase. You don't want to miss it."

Her eyes sparkle with interest. "I've never had sex in a car with one of these. I think it will feel amazing to try it on the way, Sir."

She'll be the death of me. Still, a growl escapes when I drag her back into me again, the show tonight forgotten as our lips connect again. There will be others.

But for me, there's only one girl who's ever graduated from a partner to a relationship. And as I drag her down to the sheets with me, I plan on keeping it that way.

BOOKS BY THIS AUTHOR

Rules Of Play

Sins and Secrets Club Book 1

Myla & David's Story

Christmas Side Hustle

Holidays & Hijinks Book 1

Lucas & Lucy's Story

Made in the USA
Middletown, DE
20 March 2024